UNEARTHING

Kyo Maclear

ALFRED A. KNOPF CANADA

PUBLISHED BY ALFRED A. KNOPF CANADA

www.penguinrandomhouse.ca

Knopf Canada and colophon are registered trademarks.

Library and Archives Canada Cataloguing in Publication

Title: Unearthing : a story of tangled love and family secrets / Kyo Maclear.
Names: Maclear, Kyo, 1970- author.
Identifiers: Canadiana (print) 20220272964 | Canadiana (ebook) 20220273006 |
    ISBN 9781039006706 (hardcover) | ISBN 9781039006713 (EPUB)
Subjects: LCSH: Maclear, Kyo, 1970- | LCSH: Maclear, Kyo, 1970-—Family. |
    LCSH: Family secrets. | LCSH: Parent and adult child. | CSH: Women authors,
    Canadian (English)—21st century—Biography. | CSH: Authors, Canadian
    (English)—21st century—Biography. | LCGFT: Autobiographies. |
    LCGFT: Biographies.
Classification: LCC PS8625.L435 Z46 2023 | DDC C818/.603—dc23

Text design: Jennifer Griffiths
Jacket design: Jennifer Griffiths
Interior images: courtesy of the author

Printed in Canada

10 9 8 7 6 5 4 3 2

Penguin
Random House
KNOPF CANADA

For you. Haha ni aiwo komete.

I can't stop
putting plants in the ground. There's a hunger in me . . .
ADA LIMÓN

But what is the point of writing if not to unearth things . . .
ANNIE ERNAUX

CONTENTS

prologue 1

COLOPHON NOTE

THE JAPANESE TRADITIONALLY RECORD THE SEASONS IN twenty-four *sekki*, or "small seasons." I have borrowed the names of *sekki* (節気) as section titles to offer a different way of thinking about the ever-changing ground of our stories.

PROLOGUE

MA WAS A GARDENER. WHERE SHE SAW GRADIENTS OF celadon, emerald, sage, olive, I saw only a thin green blur. When given a plant by someone who thought I looked capable, I would start out full of hope. I admired the buds for opening with confidence and the buoyant way the leaves unrolled. But before too long, the sprightly leaves would wilt or crisp. The Madagascar jasmine, enfeebled by too little sun or not enough water, would sigh toward the ground. The peace lily, overflooded with daily attention, would sag and expire. All the sad plants . . . I could not, in spite of my mother's effortless example, and my effortful efforts, keep them alive.

Then things took an unexpected turn and what I had dismissed as *not for me but for my mother* suddenly moved to the fore. In early spring, 2019, it was determined through DNA testing that I was unrelated to the man I had always thought was my father. Well into the journey of my life, the imagined map of my family, with its secure placement of names and borders, was suddenly very wrong. All at once, my silver-haired mother became unknown to me. She had a big story to tell, a story of a secret buried for half a century. A story that she struggled to express—or had no wish to express—in her adoptive language, English.

I wanted my mother's story. I wanted a tale that could put my world back together. But each time I pressed, my mother shook her head.

My mother had never really liked stories. She looked at them with suspicion. All my life she questioned both the ones I read and the ones I wrote. All my life, she asked: *What are you doing?* And nine times out of ten, I replied: *I am writing* or *I am reading*. Both answers brought forth *the look*. The look rightly asked, *What purpose is there to your efforts?* The look accurately said, *No one can eat a story, no one can dine on a book*. On the rare occasion someone commended my writing in her company, she bore a weary smile. A smile that pitied the speaker for not realizing there were better, more reputable products out there; better, less soft ways to spend a life. But the look also said: *Don't squander it. Write something worthy and practical . . . write a plant book*.

In 2019, what did and did not work between us was now irrelevant. All the ways we had been at odds in life no longer mattered. I needed to understand my mother better, and the only way to do so was in the language she knew best. Given the state of my forgotten first language, Japanese, I chose her second fluently-spoken language, the one she never pushed on me: the wild and green one.

This is a plant book made of soil, seed, leaf and mulch. In 2019, I turned to the small yard outside our house and the plants my mother had woven into my life, to bridge a gap between us. The yard was scruffy and overgrown. It belonged to the city, to the bank and, most truly, for thousands of years, and still, to the Michi Saagiig Nishnaabeg. With my sleeves rolled and my fingers mingling with the rose-gray earthworms, I set to work.

It did not go well. Not at first. The garden quickly informed me: I did not know plants. I knew only my *idea* of them, and you cannot grow an idea. The garden said: *This will not work if you are only here for the metaphor.* The garden asked me to remember the child I was, a child who loved getting dirty, and to remember that first lesson: *Nothing grows if you keep yourself clean, smooth, undisturbed.*

When I stopped attributing every little plant event to my own doing and realized I did not have control (the opposite of a storyteller's mindset), the plants began to grow. When I remembered that plots are often driven and overturned by underestimated agents, I stopped underestimating.

A mother enters a story. But how does she enter? How does she walk across the pages of a book? Does she enter wearing her regret, rage, sadness or humor? Does she enter boxing away clichés and pushing against containment? Does she enter demanding payment? Does she enter as a gardener?

I learned more about my mother's plant passions, to feel the events and landscape that passed through her heart, to take stock of what I had failed sufficiently to notice and love—the unseen greens, the hazy "scenery" of life.

I am the sole keeper of my family's stories.

"What stories? Why stories?" she says.

ONE:

DAIKAN

(greater cold)

THE BEGINNING

WHEN MY FATHER DIED AND I WAS STILL HIS DAUGHTER IN all ways and without question, I began making weekly visits to a public greenhouse. For seven Mondays, I rode the streetcar across town to warm myself in a glass building full of plants. No one had warned me that hard-hitting losses sometimes take the form of ordinary problems such as temperature-related discomfort. I had not seen this play out in stories, so I was not prepared for the cold current that entered my body and spread like ice through my veins. I did not know ski gloves and wool fleece would be my mourning vestments.

For seven Mondays, I sat with leaves the size of airplane wings under a glistening dome. I basked in winter sunshine, buried myself among the dripping fronds of palms and cycads. The busy trees put on a good show as I folded inward, as the vines tunneled through me, binding the grief. *Slow, slow,* the leaves and petals moved at a pace I understood.

For seven Mondays after my father died, I came to this glass church to sit with the plants and feel their deep sweat. It now occurs to me with some curiosity and a little sadness that people, particularly the "faithless" and those without reliable rituals, grieve in unusual places and that these places are not always so obvious. We all have ideas about what happens after a loved one dies but these ideas are often wrong or, at least, incomplete—because everyone has a different grief and, therefore, a different bereaved state of being.

WHEN MY FATHER DIED, when I was still his daughter in all stories, those he told and those I told, I was tasked with funeral arrangements. A week after his death on Christmas Day, he was returned to me in a purple velvet pouch. The funeral home sent the ashes directly to the cemetery and they were waiting for us at the reception desk, in a sack so reminiscent of a Crown Royal bag I would not have been surprised to hear D&D dice rattling inside. "Please check this," said Maria, our host, inviting me to confirm the name on the box inside the bag. I nodded, *Yes, this is my father*, as tears pooled quickly in my eyes and the room with its solemn chairs and my seated sons became a swimmy blur.

"I lost everything this week," I overheard my mother say to a man offering her coffee in the corner. "I lost my husband and I lost my Air Miles card."

In keeping with his wish to be buried with simplicity and privacy, we were the only people present at the service. At the end of our short, improvised ceremony, my husband sang a song. When we first married, he was studying to be a professional cantor, but ended his training when he was told he could not continue unless his non-Jewish wife converted. Now, as we stood close in a huddle, the bended beauty of his voice twisted and twirled in the cold air, ribboning the sky like a bluesy liturgy. "You chose a good one," my younger son whispered to me with a nudge and nod in his father's direction.

Shoveling dirt into a grave is hard work. The ice-frosted mound would only budge with great exertion on our part. *Don't worry*, said Maria, *we can do that for you.* But the physical labor was soothing, so we kept chiseling and shifting clods of soil. The air filled with slow, percussive thuds as we took turns spearing the spade into the ground, jumping on it a few times so it would cut sharply downwards. Maria told us again not to worry. She nodded toward a groundskeeper a few meters away, a man I noticed for the first time seated in a small backhoe, wearing a fur flap hat and mirrored sunglasses, who now slowly raised a hand in greeting. *Thud, thud, thud.* A frozen wedge toppled. My sons' digging and grunting movements were determined but somehow upbeat: they would tuck their grandpa into the earth and bury their mama's grief.

Walking from the gravesite across the frozen ground, I made out the blunt tapping of my mother's cane behind me. "I was hit by a car a few years ago and injured my foot," I heard her say to Maria. "I could have been killed! But I am a survivor!" A village of human dust lay beneath our feet. "I am a survivor," she repeated, this time waving her arm around as if to say, *Clearly, I am not of their number.* Then, after the briefest of pauses, Maria replied: "Well done."

A SIMPLE ONE, my father said, when asked by his lawyer what sort of funeral he wanted. He wished *to be cremated at a modest funeral site, that the attendance be that of my family* ONLY, *that the exception might be my half brothers . . .* He wished *for the ashes for a moment to blaze over the home of those I love.*

MY FATHER WAS a dramatic storyteller and now there was no story. The car on the way home felt quiet and empty, even though it was full of us.

When one person leaves, the old order collapses. That's why we were speaking to each other carefully. We were a shapeshifting family, in the midst of recomposing ourselves. What is grief, if not the act of persisting and reconstituting oneself? What is its difficulty, if not the pressure to appear, once more, fully formed?

❧

DURING THOSE WINTER weeks and months when I began visiting the greenhouse every Monday, I craved rooted, growing, ongoing things. Rolling moss, misty leaf, moist vine. I wanted more *leaf* of all kinds: wispy fronds, bubbly strings, wide strips, loopy lines, huge paddles, serpentine ivy splaying like my heart in all directions.

I missed my father's charm and his sly humor. As far back as I could remember, my favorite activity was to sit with him and have long conversations about politics and life. If someone had asked why I was hiding under glass, I might have answered: I am waiting.

My father's last months had been very hard and after the medical chaos of his final weeks, when his body hurried deathward, it was a relief to have him sheltered inside my heart where it was safe, but I still wondered when we could chat again. A part of me did not accept the situation's irreversibility; could not believe that nothing new or unplanned would ever happen again. I'll see him on my birthday, I thought, holding out for another moment. I was still only at the beginning.

In the Cactus House, one morning, imagining I was in the driest desert on earth, drier than Death Valley with its prickly pear and prowling coyote, I studied the arms of one spiny pillar in particular, thinking about the genius of adaptation. A cactus's entire life is about protection against insects, predators, the elements, and that's why they are scarred and wrinkled. They have been through some things.

A man in a blue chore jacket emerged from the potting shed with a drip tray full of plants with fingery leaves, upraised like birthday candles.
Blue chalksticks, he said.
Where do you belong, blue chalksticks? I wondered.
They're from South Africa, he said, reading my thoughts.

WHAT IMMENSE JOURNEYS had these plants endured, across oceans and seas, occupied lands, through dramatic shifts of weather and landscape, parted from parents and community, to arrive in this living museum, this plant zoo, brimming with pampered "exotic specimens"? What had they lost?

One night, I began reading Jamaica Kincaid's old gardening columns. Openly enchanted by the deep history of plants, Kincaid described how the world of the garden changed in 1492 when Columbus set sail from Spain. She traced snared histories of violent transplantation and radically transformed landscapes, the grand dreams of landed gentry enthusing about native flora, the looting in the name of inventory and order.

But she also insisted the colonial encounter was not a finished or unidirectional story. And maybe this was why I came across visitors from all over the world at the greenhouse, each with a different history of migration. The plants might have been a strange mix, opening and closing at the wrong time; the clusters of orange clivia and hibiscus clearly out of season. But, still, people sat with the floral riot, to breathe familiar smells and for a moment be among others far from their homescapes. The well of a "back-home" flower was not just a fraught vortex of loss but also a deep, fortifying pleasure.

Much to my surprise, I was falling in love with greenhouses in general, and this one in particular. I was falling in love with the plants and people that gathered in this magical, fragile, neglected corner of my city.

THERE WERE MONDAYS, when at certain moments, I felt my father, the person I most wanted to be earthbound, everywhere. He was there in the ferocity of my missing him, in the bright smell of green. At certain moments, I felt light. I felt buoyant.

MY FAVORITE ROOM at the conservatory, after the Cactus House, was the Palm House with its cathedral ceiling. This is where I came to eavesdrop on conversations and this is how I knew that others, quiet as orbits, were lugging phantoms too, carting them to this place where they could be freely acknowledged. The windows were fogged with trickling ghost breath. The inverted glass jar, which we knew as a conservatory, held us in a bubble of soft dewiness. This is what it must feel like to live inside a terrarium, I thought.

One Monday I saw a long-haired woman alone on a bench, a guitar case at her side. She had a French-chanteuse energy. She was wearing a shaggy calamine-pink coat and looked up at the domed glass above her head while quietly weeping. She seemed to have lost someone and I assumed it was to death, because there were many deaths around the time my father died. As my Uncle R. put it, the portal between the living and dead was very open. *The gates were free for coming and going.*

The portal took Jonas Mekas, Diana Athill, my dad's friend Joe, Tomi Ungerer, Ann's mum, Kathy's dad, Deborah Bird Rose, John Burningham, Brenda's dad, Andrea Levy, Mary Oliver. I imagined a convocation. In life, they may have been of differing stature, but in death, to their loved ones, the members of this sad cohort were all on the same plane of loss.

In the Palm House, I watched the no-longer-weeping woman press her cheek and nose against the cool foggy glass, leaving a wet silhouette, before continuing on her way.

A conservatory worker, an Asian woman who looked to be in her sixties, sang to herself in an atonal hum as she placed small shoots under a twisting screw pine and watered the dark beds with a hose. In that moment, I had a memory of my mother, not long after my parents separated, hiding in the final garden she created. I saw her kneeling in the soil, surrounded by shaggy fern and stiff-postured horsetail, and I saw her hands in action. Hands bright but calloused from the work of raking and shoveling. I saw her hauling manure, burying, unearthing, patiently planting. Dirty hands and unalloyed happiness.

Most Mondays it was snowing. The light kept shifting in the small green world. The sun that reached through the conservatory windows glowed weakly like drugstore neon. But somehow that weak sun filled me.

Sometimes, while I sat in the conservatory, my mother would text me voluminous paragraphs in Japanese. "Why don't you speak your mother language?" she wrote when I replied with a question mark.

❦

BACK AT HOME, my sons greeted me with a hug and a "Hey Mama" before rolling off to forage for food or games or a couch to flop on. Occasionally, I heard them whispering, worried they might have to wait a little longer for their mother to stop leaking tears into the salad bowl.

My older son gifted me a pack of bubble gum with a look of sacred seriousness. My younger son lit incense at our Buddhist altar, dinged the singing bowl three times with noisy solemnity, and offered up long and focused prayers. One Monday on my way out to the greenhouse, I stared at his back as he knelt to pray, I stared at the inwardness of his prayer, the way he sat in his own solitary dimension, and the heat kicked back on in my body.

That was my last Monday visit. I had spent seven weeks at the conservatory to mark my father's passage between worlds. I had gazed at the sky through all the different windows.

In many Buddhist traditions, seven weeks, or forty-nine days, is the traditional mourning period. On the forty-ninth day, the spirit arrives at its destination and attention is returned to the living. It was time to break the glass case and leave the small green world for the wilds. I would show my sons it was okay to let others hold you and unsequester the sadness as it worked its way through you.

The father I had trapped in my mind needed to be free, his spirit needed to ascend.

CURSES

WHEN MY FATHER LEFT THE PLANET AND I WAS HIS EARTH-bound daughter, his much younger brother arrived for a visit from England. He had news to share. My uncle R. told me there was a love curse on our family. The curse was six generations old, he explained. A Swiss psychic named Anita had told him so. According to Anita, six generations ago, an ancestor of ours had thrown his mistress off a cliff. Because of this we, his descendants, were in spiritual trouble. Burdened by his crime, we were destined to be adulterous, to be married but unhappily, to nurse unhealthy addictions and endure frosty emotional connections. We would forever have difficulty expressing ourselves and form nervous, ambivalent attachments. Thus, we would be able to love others or be loved only in passing or from a suspicious distance. We would, in all likelihood, die alone. The curse, which had afflicted my Casanova grandfather and my restlessly single, often cruising Uncle R., apparently, had also lodged in the Catholic priest to whom the murderer confessed but, in that case, there were no descendants.

My uncle had flown to Toronto to attend my father's memorial. A few days before he landed, our furnace broke during a record-breaking cold spell, causing our water pipes to burst—so we were huddled by a portable space heater in a kitchen that smelled like river while a contractor opened walls. The arctic weather in our house was a mild difficulty in the scheme of life-and-death, but it was likely the reason I felt so cold all the time. I knew my uncle to be the sort of person who believes there are spirits in the basement of his office, tampering with his business. So while we shivered, I waited for him to outline the steps necessary to exorcise the curse. I had entered the "burying years," to use Marlon James's sad and powerful phrase, and it seemed a good idea to properly bury all the unnecessary things lodged inside my family and me, all the patterns and configurations repeated, the injuries and inheritances that preceded my arrival, which now included this genealogical shadow I might have been dragging around unwittingly. But my uncle, adjusting the wool blanket on my shoulders, had switched to a new conversational topic.

The curse was never mentioned again. My mystic-minded uncle returned a few days later to Sussex, where the first swallows had reached Britain's south coast a month earlier than usual, where the air was unusually perfumed with early-blooming flowers, surprising those who still believed in the predictability of seasons. I was left to consider it all.

The truth is, the question of what made the artists and writers in my family so fiercely self-reliant and lonely had bothered me more with each passing year. I did not like the family tradition of dying alone. Where were the examples of lovers who grew old together, the life companions who gentled into a comfortable twilight?

The possibility of an unresolved trauma being passed down from one generation to the next was as credible as the lineal transmission of ways of walking, talking, speaking. But this love curse my uncle described did not sound like mine. It sounded rather like the curse of white manhood, to which some members of my British family owed their cool detachment. My blockage, my own tendency to hold others at a remove and become frozen and folded. inward at times of crisis rested elsewhere, I suspected. I didn't know where. Or what karma across lifetimes had made me, at key moments, so scared to unguard myself. I only sensed my spiritual trouble had little to do with the horror of a woman being pushed off a cliff in Victorian England.

LOVE

WHEN MY FATHER DIED, AND I WAS HIS DAUGHTER IN ALL blessed and cursed circumstances, I thought about love.

The story of love labors under many curses. The curse of soppiness. The curse of romantic dogma. The curse of insecurity. The curses of capitalism and hearts replaced by gold and gemstones. The curse of possessive communion and domestic captivity. The curse of planetary human-centeredness. The curse of private property cloaked as "loving one's own." The curses of mistrust, timidity, generational trauma, an overactive amygdala and hazardous addictions. The curse of squashed ardor and no infinite mystery. The curse of mixed feelings and little deceits.

I had spent far too much time pondering a deviously simple question, one that would be obvious to anyone who was not born apprehensive: *What's the difference between love and fear?* (There is no difference, was the answer I divined from a psychology book titled *A General Theory of Love*. "Many of our ultralow-anxiety ancestors were bitten by snakes, gored by tusks, and fell out of trees." In love as in life, one must learn to creep "from beneath the protection of a fern.")

The truth was I knew very few people who relaxed easily into love, operating without an ounce of doubt. Inexpert as I was at love, I wanted to do better for my sons and put forth a new repertory of habits and options. I did not want to be shut down and withdrawn. I had been trying since they were born to create a better operating manual. Could we crack the curse or pattern and proceed like eager puppies, holding nothing back? Could I be anything but a wobbly love guide?

GRANDMOTHER

WHEN MY FATHER DIED AND I WAS HIS DAUGHTER ASKING
questions about love, I became a sleuth. Under protection of a fern,
my aim was to get to the bottom of the curse of fearful attachment, which I sensed was connected somehow to the mystery
of my Irish paternal grandmother, Carlynne Mary Gallagher, a
woman who did not reach old age and about whose life there were
very few details. My father, raised in foster care, hardly ever spoke
of her. "Let's talk about something else," he said, whenever I asked
for a childhood memory. All I had was her name, a photo the size
of a chocolate square, and some offhand remarks made by my
uncle and my father's now-deceased stepmother. One comment,
in particular, had stayed with me, words repeated by my uncle
during his recent visit. *She was depressive. Troubled. Not quite well.*

Not knowing my grandmother had made her feel eerily close
to me, closer than almost anyone. She had come to represent all
the unknown things; all the tangled feelings that needed to be
unwound to the source if I was to understand more about our
family and the genealogy of our phantoms.

I set off to do ancestor repair work, to give my ghost matriarch
a shape and shake her free from the silence that had erased so
many women from our family history. In the old days, I would
have pored over microfilm, scoured through ancient cardboard
boxes, scraped the dirt off proverbial gravestones. Being a detective
is so easy, almost instant, nowadays. Within a few hours I had

tracked down her marriage and death certificates and discovered she was not always a ghost with a fitful relationship to happiness. She was a baby once (Chelmsford, 1904), a baby who had two younger siblings, only one of whom survived childhood; a baby who became a girl who became a woman; a woman who fell in love, got pregnant (1929), shotgun married (Paddington, 1929), had a son/my father (1929), changed nappies and nursed her son through a severe case of the mumps, was left by a womanizing husband who would try to hide the fact of his marriage and child entirely, gave her son over to foster care (1933), never remarried or had further children, and died at age fifty-five (St. Pancras, 1959).

The barest biographical facts. Maybe she loved jazz, Branston pickle, steep impractical shoes and whodunit novels. In the meagerness of detail, my new mission was to find someone, maybe a Gallagher, who might have known her. One anecdote, one memory, one more photo, was what I wanted, but also an answer to the question: Was there any truth to my uncle's offhand remark about her mental health? And could this history reveal anything about the vapor of depression-anxiety that had carried forward to my father, myself and my younger son, possibly pressing its way into our genes?

In a 1997 performance titled *Sometimes making something leads to nothing*, the artist Francis Alÿs pushes a large block of ice through the streets of Mexico City until it completely melts. After nine hours the block is reduced to no more than an ice cube, so small that he can casually kick it along the street. I imagined somewhere back in time a large and obdurate block of sadness that was being pushed through generations, awaiting a hot sun. But this was mythical thinking and what I wanted was to return this shadow history to the material world and proceed with all the data in hand. I wanted to build a story around the tiny photo of my paternal grandmother that sat on our family altar and maybe undo some of the lingering stigma surrounding mental illness. To find someone to speak to and remember her, to trace the origins of our epigenetic sadness but also our epigenetic joy and strength, that was the idea. Let all our demons and angels into the light. Let us face the clout of ancestry. Building a true story, I thought, might protect us from becoming heirs to hearsay.

My father, the person who knew the most, had just exited the room—leaving clothes, books, papers and the flotsam of care scattered in his wake. The answer couldn't be found in what he had left behind. While he had maintained some contact with those connected to his father, he grew up and away from the relatives on his mother's side. I needed another path to those who might have knowledge of the challenges and hardships she faced that were hers but maybe also, constitutionally and historically, *ours*.

A DNA test, my friend suggested.

MYSTERY

WHEN MY FATHER DIED AND I WAS HIS GRIEVING AND WON-dering daughter, I thought of a word. The word, *yugen*, or what the Japanese call a state of "dim" or "deep" mystery, evokes the unsettled feeling I had at various points growing up as an only child. Our family was a tiny unit with strange ways. My parents acted like criminals on the lam—loading up moving vans, changing house every few years. I was four years old when we left England, shedding backstory and friends overnight. What made a family behave this way, like people drawn to erasure? Why were we always leaving like this, so unceremoniously? I did not know. Growing up, I assumed that everyone was shaped and suffused by what they could not perceive clearly, the invisible and voiceless things imparted atmospherically within families.

The first time I introduced my husband—who was then my boyfriend—to my mother, she greeted us at the door in a bra and underwear.

"We don't really talk about things," I said when my mother went to fill the kettle for tea. "In our family everything is kind of tamped down." I watched my sweet, naïve boyfriend forming opinions in his head and I wanted him to know you can be the kind of person who openly greets a stranger in undergarments but is closed in other ways.

TEST

WHEN MY FATHER DIED AND I WAS HIS DOUBTLESS DAUGH-
ter, I stared at a small white cardboard box. The DNA kit came with
Terms and Conditions, which included information about data
privacy and a statement that read, "You may discover unantici-
pated facts about yourself or your family when using our services
that you may not have the ability to change." In late January 2019,
I spat in the plastic tube and put it back in the box.

I did not see myself as expressing fetishistic wonder about
my ethnic roots and genetic predecessors. I did not wish to
"[track] down the exact ingredients" of my "European genetic
cocktail" (Joshua Whitehead) or feel "wistful for aristocratic origins" (Saidiya Hartman). Coming from a mixed-race family, I had
no patience for chauvinistic kinship narratives or the treacherous
idea of purity. From a young age, I noticed that Japanese people
did not regard me as recognizably or legitimately Japanese, did not
view me as one of their own kind. I noticed that white people saw
me as *very Asian*. I was used to inconsistent reactions. They were
commonplace. If we hybrids have a superpower, it is the ability to
side-see, to scour the periphery of stories and a heritage industry
that view the world too narrowly. We know the world is a con-
tinuum of polar things, and the words "my people" and "my roots"
can be a carnival of confusion.

I took my muddy urge and mailed off the box. The kit was
prepaid. I did not expect anything remotely surprising. Not for

a moment did I consider that some of the things I'd assumed basic to the story of *who-I-am* and *where-I-come-from* would be revised.

CIRCLE

WHEN MY FATHER DIED AND I WAS HIS DAUGHTER AT WORK and at rest, I traveled alone to a residency in the mountains. What was to be revised appeared in my inbox as I sat alone in a room, 4,500 feet above sea level. What I saw was a circle bisected into two halves. I had inherited half of each parent's DNA—but the paternal half bore no resemblance to my father's genetic history, at least as it had been told to me.

An error, I thought. A glitch. I casually refreshed the page several times, tapping my cursor as though it were the "spin" button of a slot machine and the reels of cherries, bars and lemons might, through repeat attempts, align in a different pattern. The page did not realign.

I texted a screenshot to my husband.

"A mistake?" he replied.

A minute passed.

"You don't even like herring," he added.

A few minutes later, he texted again.

"*Mazel Tov*, now you know what that means!"

ALONGSIDE MY DNA RESULTS, the company provided migratory maps of my ancestors, which showed my paternal family originating from Lithuania, Latvia and Belarus. I had never heard my family speak of any of these countries.

For a fleeting moment, I wondered if my dad's assumed ethnicity was 100 percent wrong—if he wasn't who he thought he was—but then I remembered the records of my Irish grandmother and the names on my father's birth certificate and the documents tracing the Maclear lineage back multiple generations. From those details and the endless scroll of strangers appearing as my closest relative matches, it became clear: the test revealed something else. I closed my computer. I didn't know what to do with this news except to start walking.

Alone in the mountains; the sun flamed. No half-obscured low light. Just brilliant, blazing warmth that felt like relief. Inside the chamber of my heart, I carried a list of facts and a list of feelings. I tried to get them to speak to one another as I walked by the river, where great slabs of ice were loosening. The sun shimmering plates shifted and collided in a ballet of solidity and solubility.

Among the feelings I carried was my own raw shock, I realized, but also shock I felt—or assumed—on my father's behalf. I imagined having to one day explain to him, the man I had always known as my father, what I had done, how I had stirred up trouble yet again with my curiosity and capers. Surely an awkward and heartbreaking conversation at the best of times and towards the end, when my father's memory faded, one that would have been greeted with a baffled half smile. Still, his death was not far away enough for this imagined dialogue to feel implausible.

The two griefs I now felt shifted and collided. The grief of his dying followed by the grief of having our story break down and crack up as a result of my impulsive action.

When I returned to my room, I lay down. A couple of hours passed and during that time I lay very still and made my mind blank. At some point, I fell asleep and woke up to a glowing blue window.

❧

NEAR THE END of my father's life, I befriended a neuroscientist who told me a story of his nephews traveling on a plane for the first time. My friend was seated a few rows ahead of them. Shortly after takeoff, the plane was hit by severe turbulence, which rocked the cabin and sent belongings flying everywhere. Passengers were screaming. Worried for his nephews, who were surely experiencing the same stomach-plummeting terror, my friend looked back to find them with arms raised, cheerfully shrieking: ROLLER COASTER!

I was struck by this story, by his nephews' joyful bubble and their ability to experience upheaval as adventure. Was it the joy of young children tossed into the air, knowing there would be waiting arms and rescue? Was it the effervescence of those who do not possess crash data?

In the early spring of 2019, I found myself thrown clean from the seat of my old story. There was a feeling of falling.

Forty-nine years after my birth, when my father died, I lost all feeling for certainty as the ice floes were breaking up.

TWO:

SHUNBUN

(spring equinox)

LITTLE PEACH

MY MOTHER LIKED TO TELL ME SHE FOUND ME AS A BABY floating on a river. I arrived inside a large peach blushed with rose and when I emerged, I was so bewildered, sticky and small, she had no choice but to bring me home and rinse me off.

She told me this story a dozen, two dozen times, before I realized she was telling me the story of Momotaro, one of the most famous of all Japanese *mukashi banashi*, or folk tales. In the legend, Momotaro appears on earth to become the son of a poor, "barren" couple *who every day and every night lamented they had no child.* Now elderly, the couple find their youth and happiness rejuvenated by Momotaro's arrival. *So lost with joy were they that they did not know where to put their hands or their feet.*

The story, the only one my mother ever told of my birth, spoke to me and said a family could occur by happenstance and strange handiwork. A gathering of currents could carry a baby toward a random port of arrival. Some origin stories have human fingerprints all over them but this one, I thought, must have been written by an orchard. Only once did I wonder out loud what the experience of miraculous birth must have felt like from Momotaro's perspective: *Was it scary inside that dark pit of a peach, Mama, rolling along that quick water to who knows where?*

In mid-April 2019, the results of a second DNA test confirmed the first one. My ancestry composition: 50 percent Japanese and 50 percent Ashkenazi Jewish.

I worked up the nerve to call my mother, preparing myself. How difficult could it be to get the truth? *How was I conceived?* There was nothing to do but ask.

When she finally understood what I was asking, she fell uncharacteristically silent. I listened to her breath, the sound of rustling paper. *Wait a minute*, she said, and put down the phone. I heard her walking across the floor, the sound of a kettle being filled at her kitchen sink. *I am making tea*, she said from a distance.

Then, as if we weren't in the middle of a conversation, she picked up the phone and asked if I was cold. She told me she had received a letter from the cemetery and read the heading aloud: "Customer Satisfaction Questionnaire."

I asked again.

It was difficult, she said finally. *We tried for so long . . . for seven years, so long, I wanted to have a baby.*

She told me my father arranged for her to go to a clinic on London's Harley Street to see a doctor. It was the obstetrician-gynecologist who would later deliver Princess Diana's babies. *A very special specialist!* The doctor placed her under a general anesthetic and later, when she awoke and asked what happened, my father said: "Everything will be fine."

Everything will be fine? I repeated. My voice had thickened. What did he mean?

He was the one who made the appointment, she continued. *You should ask him.*

She repeated it three times. *Talk to your dad.* As if his death had been a hoax; her voice no longer blurry but brisk with fear.

HEAD GARDENER

"YES, LET ME TALK TO HIM," I THOUGHT, AS I SAT ON A bench listening to the discourse of two house sparrows trapped in the Palm House. I had returned to the greenhouse for a private tour that had been arranged months before. As my story land-slided and uprooted, it felt good to be domed to the earth.

I craned my neck to look at the glass ceiling and imagined fire licking through the original dome, as it had in 1902. For several minutes, "the cracking of the flames was relieved by the curious tinkling sounds of thousands of falling panes" fracturing from the ceiling, the *Ottawa Journal* reported at the time. Many of the plants were scorched to a crisp, and the structure itself was reduced to "a heap of ruins." A new crop slowly took root when the Palm House dome reopened in 1910.

The head gardener, a muscular man with close-cropped hair and a studious smile, had arrived and was now using his well-built arms to explain how branching greenhouses had been tacked onto the sides of the Palm House. I followed him to the Tropical Landscape house, where he showed me a rare cycad tree. Then to the arid room where he acquainted me with a barrel cactus and jade plant that had been companions for fifty years. I tried to con-centrate on what he was saying but it was bright, too bright to focus on any one spot, with the light bouncing from the white sky to the dirt-fringed windows. *You might notice the aloe is browned . . . we leave the scruff. Under everything is old-growth and yellow leaf . . .*

the imperfect . . . His measured words floated above my wavering thoughts, until they rose high up near the glinting ceiling.

"I believe plants have feelings, so I will never tell," the head gardener whispered when I asked him if he had a favorite plant in the gardens.

SOMETHING

IT WAS ALL BEING PULLED FROM SOME SHADOWY ROOM.
The details she remembered. The broken chain of events. What
she spoke arrived in fragments. But there was something else, a
hitch and hesitance, that made me alert.

I did not yet understand the need to hold on to an invented story,
even a falsified past, at all costs. I did not recognize her dissem-
bling. Usually impervious, I thought she seemed out of sorts.
Maybe a little distraught.

She does not want to tell me something, I thought.

FACEBOOK

NPE IS SHORT FOR "NON-PATERNITY EVENT"—OR, MORE colloquially, "Not the Parent Expected." NPE is one way a life story can swerve, and here I joined others who had come upon accidental discoveries, who found themselves stumbling for footing on terrain that was no longer dependable.

DNA NPE Friends, self-described as "the best club you never wanted to join," involved an online intake questionnaire, beginning with: *What test did you take and how are you doing?* The woman vetting requests was a former member of the NYPD and had recently retired from a global security firm specializing in protecting "enterprise-level facilities from high consequence threats."

There were many steps in the admittance process to this secret Facebook community, the last of which involved a promise that I would not publicly share any of the posted stories or names in the 8K–member group. "Let me give you some abbreviations and guidelines," said the moderator. "BF is Bio Father, BCF is Birth Certificate Father, HS and HB are Half Sister and Brother. DC is Donor Conceived . . . There are no F bombs and only thoughtful and compassionate posts. We don't tell anyone 'to get over it.'" Then finally, the gateway opened. A welcome post appeared with my name, festooned with pink hearts.

Everyone new to the group was saying a variation of the same thing. *Genetic Bombshell. Not in a thousand years. Brain never shuts down. Slipping off the edge of the earth. Reassure me it's like this for you too . . .*

I quickly lost myself in the bounce and echo of emotions, feeling sparks of solidarity and synchronicity. Our stories were starlight, blinking and flashing for connection. Our stories were all the same. We were here because we had the same issue, the same condition. Affirmations were instant and insistent.

Some of the people in the group had come out the other side by solving the puzzle of their misattributed paternity. A woman named S. was having the most monumental day of her life, meeting her IIB for the first time. A man named T. was hugging the IIS he never knew he had. In the photo they wore matching T-shirts, underlying the recurring theme of family "likeness" as tether.

But the question remained: What about those still in limbo? Many people were still searching years later, wandering genealogical hallways. Some had made peace with the perpetual search, as though it were a game or riddle that did not need an end. Others found the endlessness to be a nightmare. "I don't think I can accept 'not knowing' as my biological paternal parentage," said one woman with a sobbing emoji for punctuation. With a missing first chapter, she worried her story would always be a deficient narrative. And then there were a mysterious few who seemed to cling to limbo by choice, resisting leads, unable to summon the psychic strength to take the next step.

I lasted only a few hours. I have never been a comfortable congregant. In quantity and in volume, the sharing of stories felt dubious and overwhelming. I returned only occasionally to see if the searches were thinning out.

HARLEY STREET

OF COURSE, MY MOTHER DID NOT KNOW THE AGREED-UPON abbreviations or updated terms, which might have made the storytelling easier or at least less messy. The right terminology could have offered a banister. As it was, her story was a blur of waiting rooms and wards and curtained-off beds. It contained doctors and invasive procedures. It contained a possible verdict of severe childhood mumps leading to paternal sterility and the end of so-called "natural options." It contained a scared woman and a husband who whispered reassurances.

Seeking more information, I wrote to my father's two half brothers. I was reluctant to share my news. It wasn't the possibility of rejection that preoccupied me. It was a quieter fear—that they would view me a little differently. That the shift would be much too subtle for anyone else to notice, but I would feel it. Dispelling my worries, they both responded with immediate, effortless assurances. "It changes nothing of our feelings and love for one another," wrote Uncle A., my father's youngest brother. Uncle R. similarly replied: "Slightly in shock but this really changes nothing." (Did he feel relief I was now free of the family curse—the biologically determined "fate"—that had ostensibly coursed through the generations? He never said.)

When asked if they remembered anything unusual from that time, anything about Harley Street, they had no immediate recollection but, then, a few days later, Uncle A. wrote again. "Extraordinary what the memory retains. This morning a small sliver of information came to the surface. This is not much but now I do remember your father saying to me, around this time, 1969: 'we have to go to a clinic to find out why we're not having children.' That is precisely what he said. I remember it very clearly. I do not recall the conversation evolving further than that, or further references being made after that."

I imagined the transactions that must have occurred on Harley Street in the days when male infertility was a deep source of shame and often denied or under-investigated. It now seemed obvious: they went to diagnose the "wife's problem" and the tests determined there was nothing actually wrong with my mother. Hence: *Everything will be fine.*

I was now beginning to suspect I was "DC"—the result of donor conception.

Outside my window, the magnolia and cherry trees flowered and then released a confetti of petals that papered the road and parked cars. I tried to picture my unmet father's face, both drawn to and repelled by this figure who now shadowed my thoughts. He must have been a medical intern, I thought, as I read about London clinics in the late 1960s and how, on most days, donors would visit offices with "samples" in hand, eager for cash and assured of their anonymity.

Thousands of people were conceived through sperm donation on London's Harley Street, from the 1950s onwards. I came to know two of them. One, a Toronto-based filmmaker named B., had uncovered the identity of his prolific donor. The other, a UK scholar named J., had a hunch about her donor's identity but was still searching. We had all experienced the moment when the story of self that had been invented for us was shattered. Knowing they had carried this experience and its residue for years, I turned to them for help. They had logged the grief and search miles. They radiated safety.

B., who lived nearby, sat with me when I was overwhelmed by facts, percentages and new DNA matches. We combed over relatives together—T. Lerman (2nd Cousin, 2.23% DNA shared), K. Rubenstein (2nd Cousin, 2.41%), N. Rosenberg (2nd Cousin, 2.30%) . . . *All the numbers! Was this how family arrived these days?* His serene humor steadied me. His sturdiness became a promise that I would not always feel a ghost to the present, hovering over a break in the past.

J. was less optimistic. *You have to be dogged but prepared, even when they claim records were destroyed,* she said, leaving me voice memos full of fire. *Once you start digging, people will tell you to be grateful that you were conceived at all. They will be all "god's plan" and "everything happens for a reason." As if it's not enough they lied and hid things from you, now you must be grateful and say, "Thank you! Aren't I lucky, lucky!" They will tell you to stay quiet because "all that matters is love." If that was all that mattered then why not swap babies at the hospital! If it didn't matter, it wouldn't matter.*

They both questioned my mother's story about being placed under general anesthetic. From their doubt, my own grew. One morning, I posted a question with DNA Detectives about the use of general anesthetic during insemination procedures. *Much remains unknown,* I confessed to the group of strangers. *It's difficult to explain.*

To my surprise, the post was met with confusion and then alarm. The comments made it clear that light sedation was not uncommon in early insemination procedures but a heavy surgical general anesthetic would *never* have been used. The suggestion that my mother was not informed of her insemination seemed implausible, even in the context of the male-dominated medical establishment of the time. The implication of non-consent was *highly disturbing; a sign that something barbaric must have happened.*

I closed my browser. I was shaking. I reached for a cup and knocked it over with my hand. Within a few hours my post and all related comments had been deemed triggering and removed. Even before this happened, part of me understood that something was off.

GENERAL

I THOUGHT OF MY MOTHER THAT SPRING WHEN I MET MY
own anesthesiologist, a man in his fifties with extravagant eyebrows and a blue paper cap. He squinted at an open binder in his
hands and asked questions about my medical history. Genetic
vulnerabilities? Adverse reactions? Any history of heart problems?
The question marks proliferated. I explained that half my family
was a genetic mystery. I knew I was ancestrally Jewish but, beyond
that, I possessed no forewarnings or information. The absence of
backstory was now a health hurdle rather than a mere puzzle of
personhood. He squeezed my hand.

Think of this as research, I thought, as the anesthesiologist
walked me through the thick double doors of the OR and told me
to lie down. Doctors and nurses in masks stood over the operating
bed, peering down at me until I stopped hearing words and felt
only the rhythm of voices.

For the first time in my life, I was put under general anesthe-
sia and—*tilt, spin, oblivion*—woke up shivering under a pile of
blankets. The part of me that had housed my two sons but which
had subsequently caused great stabbing pain, chronic blood loss
and anemia was now gone.

The nurse covered me in warm blankets as I stared upward at
a hanging IV bag trying to establish what had happened during
my medical adventure, imagining my mother doing the same. I
could smell salt water, lemon and mint. I could hear the healthy

ovaries they had left, pumping out estrogen, as the nurse continued her rounds. I was shaking so intensely my teeth chattered. At any moment the nurse was going to bring me a baby and say *it turned out you had one of these inside* and I would try to hide my joy and excitement and appear nonchalant. I would tell her I had an urge to push out another one. But I knew she would just shake her head and say, *No, I don't think so.* And I would nod agreeably, *Yes, you're probably right.*

I thought of my mother when I was transferred, incongruously, to a high-risk pregnancy ward to recover, fuzzy with painkillers, flimsy curtain tugged around my bed; when I felt the hush of a hundred women holding their not-yet-babies, where an open window said the world was green and lush as a fever.

PEACHES

MOST LIKELY I HAD MISUNDERSTOOD WHAT MY MOTHER had tried to tell me, was what I thought as I opened a tin of halved peaches, my father's favorite, the last tin left from the provisions I kept in our cupboard when he was alive. I heated them gently in a saucepan, swirling the dark-orange fruit in the pool of syrup. The smell used to lure him to the kitchen, calling him from his deep afternoon naps. I placed the warm peaches with ice cream in a small blue-and-white bowl and placed the bowl on our altar, calling him back.

1969

A SENSE OF MYSTERY HUNG OVER THE SUMMER OF 1969, the months of my conception. There were some things, the mystery said, that might never be fully understood.

In summer 1969, as my mother sang a song about a peach boy, a man stepped on the moon for the first time while 650 million people around the world watched. It was the season of the Stonewall riots and the Manson murders. In summer 1969, 400,000 people showed up at a farm in Bethel, New York, for a music festival. A similar number of people attended the Harlem Cultural Festival, where a reporter for a television network hoping to gather celebratory soundbites about the moon landing discovered a crowd with little time for space-men—"*Never mind the moon, let's get some of that cash in Harlem.*" Sexual freedom gusted through the air. The number one song in the UK was "Honky Tonk Women." It was a fertility fiesta. London was "the Permissive Society," according to my father, who filmed a documentary with that title, interviewing teenagers on Carnaby Street and his friend Yoko Ono about her *Bottoms* film, which proceeded with a one-line script: "String bottoms together in place of signatures for petition for peace."

The breaking down of bureaucratic society, the breaking down of old moral rules—the only hope of a movement, was the way my father wrote. Snappy. Sonic. Punchy beatnik oratory. Sometimes he used "cable-ese," the language adopted by early reporters who practiced verbal thrift to save on telegram bills. That summer the number of American military personnel in Vietnam peaked at 543,000. My father was in the thick of it, traveling in-country from 1969 to 1970. As a war correspondent, he wanted to capture the unreported North Vietnamese perspective.

"'I guess we all like to be recognized not for one piece of fireworks but for the ledger of our daily work,'" he once wrote to me, quoting Neil Armstrong. My father thought a lot about his legacy, about what and whom he would leave behind. Possibly more than Armstrong.

Of his footprints remaining on the moon, Armstrong apparently said: "I kind of hope that somebody goes up there one of these days and cleans them up."

My father also interviewed the returning moonwalkers.

1969 was the year of *anything goes*, according to my mother.

ANGEL

A SENSE OF MYSTERY HUNG OVER THE SUMMER OF 1969. The man at its center, my secret father, filled my thoughts, accompanying me everywhere. His presence kept me in a state of permanent agitation that felt at times like romantic obsession. When would he appear? I needed, at the very least, to know his name, his whereabouts. But I was an inept sleuth, hopeless at solving this mystery sitting inside me. So in late May 2019, on B.'s suggestion, I posted to DNA Detectives hoping to find a volunteer who might help me in my search. What I needed was a good old-fashioned father-scavenger. Almost immediately, I received a message from a woman in San Francisco who had experience sorting filial threads and bloodlines and chasing down hunches. A "search angel." *We will build a family tree*, the angel said, warning me that there would be phases to our quest.

The tree grew bigger. And bigger. As if fed on Miracle-Gro. But it was the angel and her countless hours of detectival research that were behind this growth, this biographical restoration. Every morning I awoke and hopped in my chair, experiencing a feeling of tense anticipation as I opened my messages. What motivated this angel's dedication I did not know. I had never experienced such limitless commitment and fidelity from a stranger, known to me only through a screen. Was she an adoptee herself? Whenever I tried to get closer and find out more about her, she deflected my questions or answered them politely but perfunctorily, as if her problem-solving mind needed at all times to remain singularly focused on sorting my missing genetic pieces, penciling in the names of the dead.

"Angels apparently have no individual personalities or qualities; none have ever been noted," writes Eliot Weinberger. My angel's impenetrability and the ethereal nature of our relationship only made her seem more holy. I imagined her parachuting through the sky in her flowing robe, assisting others in her celestial way.

As the tree grew, through late spring and early summer, 2019, I became addicted to her updates, witnessing with joy when a new branch would appear.

The tree entangled me with names I had never heard, unfamiliar dates, geographies, histories. It included a famous romance novelist whose books had sold more than 500 million copies, a lifelong stammerer and philanthropist who founded a specialist center for stammering children, a doctor with long Buddha-like earlobes. *I am absolutely sure those are my earlobes*, I said impulsively, as my search angel talked me down from the cliff of possible fathers, as she sorted bones of my lineage with the painstaking care of a zoologist piecing together a whale skeleton.

The process, she explained, would have been different if this were not a search into Jewish diasporic ancestry. A long history of endogamy meant dozens of genetic cousin matches, not a single one of whom could be connected to a proven lineage. Name changes added to the difficulty. As we sifted through passenger and naturalization records, my search angel worked to divine root surnames. *The Kogans who changed to Kogens to Cohens to . . .*

We were in a holding pattern. The data had exhausted itself. *We aren't giving up. We are entering a new phase.* What was needed in this new phase was something like intuition and imagination.

I waited. I stared in the mirror at my long earlobes.

"Do you remember anything or anyone unusual from your childhood?" asked my angel.

THREE:

SEIMEI
(clear and bright)

OUTTAKES

IN APRIL WHEN THE WEATHER WAS WARM AND BRIGHT AND everything was undeniably green, I invited my mother to sit in the garden. The days had an expectant feel to them as if we were in a waiting room, only it was possible the person I was waiting for was right beside me. Whenever I tried to broach things directly, there was a strange note in her voice, something steely, protective. As we sat together in the garden, I resolved to keep things light: *Let's just enjoy the afternoon with all its color and all the passersby with all their dogs.* My mother's hands were tucked inside the leopard-spotted LeSportsac resting on her lap.

Shortly after I spoke to my mother about my DNA results, she began carrying plastic sleeves of photos in her nylon handbag. Her dreams were suddenly full of floating moments from her youth— a memory of warm moss on her cheek as she napped by the pond near her mother's house, the sun on her face as she sold ice cream at Tsukiji fish market in Tokyo. She recounted these dreams to me almost daily and I listened carefully, realizing that when I asked about my birth, it was as if the pores of her history opened.

Many of the photos she unearthed were entirely new to me or were ones I had only ever glanced at quickly. Stored for years in boxes of outtakes, in no particular order, they documented my mother's life before I was born. Now they began to sprout from the recesses of her apartment, representing the seven childless years of my parents' marriage. Were these salad days, I wondered, or long days of waiting?

The photographs showed her modeling in a bikini, sleekly draped on the hood of a car; eating a plate of pasta on a crowded patio; posing barefoot on a pile of rocks near a Greek temple with Doric columns and caryatids reflected in a silty puddle of water below.

Sometimes she would pause over a photo and click her tongue like a Geiger counter and I would know we'd hit something hot. What was she recalling when she saw herself in that flouncy pose, that outfit of yellow shorts and sleeveless lace, against that over-grown bed of canna lilies?

"Why are you holding the photo so tightly?"

"I don't know," she said.

I asked my mother if she could tell me, her mind a card shuf-fle of landscapes, when she'd felt the most beautiful. She looked at me to see if I was serious and then pointed to a photo of herself in a red floral minidress, seated on a balcony overlooking the Eiffel Tower. Her hair cut in a tidy bob, her face turned away from the camera.

FLOWER CARDS

I HAVE A PHOTOGRAPH OF MY PARENTS IN TOKYO, TAKEN IN the early 1960s. My dad was a pale, long-legged Brit working as the "Far East correspondent" for the Canadian Broadcasting Corporation. My mother was a twenty-three-year-old art student with a flair for parties, fashion and rule avoidance. She spoke almost no English but liked mingling with foreigners. As the youngest of her family, raised by a widowed mother, she was protected by six older siblings who found her roving, collide-with-the-sun energy a mystery. The oldest of her brothers warned her not to be the "nail that sticks out." With her habit of questioning and her low tolerance for respectability and "group unity," no one really thought she would last in the conservative and xenophobic village of Japan. Twenty years later, I would notice how she never stood with her feet close together, in quiet practical shoes, the way her sisters did.

My mother was playing Hanafuda when my father noticed her. Hanafuda is the Japanese equivalent of poker, with each suit represented by a different type of flower or plant. My mother played all night long, piling up cash to pay her rent. My father, a lifelong gambler, watched her tuck her winnings into her coat pockets. *There are days when you meet someone who just seems to come from the same place*, was more or less the way they both put it.

She introduced herself as "Mariko." This was the artist name she had chosen; this was how she was addressed among friends and intimates more often than by her given name, "Yoko." Between her sparse English and his feeble Japanese, they barely shared fifty words. But, somehow, they found their own struggling language, a stop-and-start conversational manner, unencumbered by nuance or words to dig up the past. Mixed-race couples were still a rare sight in Tokyo. People stared when they passed by on the street. On one occasion, students with Zengakuren, the anti–military base movement, followed them yelling *Yankee go home*.

When they married and moved to London, my mother became an expert at improvisation. When Japanese food supplies were hard to find, she made do with local ingredients. When work opportunities were scarce, she reinvented herself as a guide—leading, or misleading, Japanese visitors on tours of city landmarks, one time circling the Tower of London for hours in the fog. She dubbed herself an "interrupter" instead of an "interpreter." What she lacked in knowledge, she compensated for with charm. She set out "fast thing" every morning. She showed tourists "beats and peaces" of her adoptive city. She befriended other Japanese expat artists and ventured further into the impure creative wilderness of her new home.

My parents were together for seven years before I came along. Four years after my birth, we left England and came to Canada, where my mother improvised again. She missed her friends and the busy cosmopolitan life she had left behind in London and Tokyo. Her English was still sketchy, the future undisclosed.

I thought we would be a good match, my father often said.

A PHOTOGRAPH

"IT MIGHT HAVE EXISTED," WRITES MARGUERITE DURAS, "a photograph might have been taken, just like any other, somewhere else, in other circumstances. But it wasn't. The subject was too slight. Who would have thought of such a thing?"

SCENERY

IN APRIL WHEN THE WEATHER WAS WARM AND BRIGHT AND everything was undeniably green, when I invited my mother to sit in the garden and she showed me photos she had brought in her nylon purse, I realized that of all the photos, the ones that interested me most were those of my mother standing in gardens.

I have always loved snapshots of women in public and private gardens, gardens that look like voluptuous Edenic clichés. Emerald haze. A frenzy of bougainvillea. Camellia branches and bands of hills in the distance. There is an obvious twinning of plant life with femininity, but a ravenousness overcomes me when I look at these old photos caught on supersaturated film—particularly the ones showing women in floral dresses who, engulfed by leafy exuberance, look as if they are blurring into the scenery, daring you to pick them out. The dreamlike blur is a reminder: it is not easy to bring a mother into the world, to form and figure her on the page. Every time I have tried, I have done it wrong.

BECAUSE IT IS the 1960s, the beauty in the photographs seems more consciously composed. I never learned the art of displaying my body, the ornamental shapes, the tantalizing geometries, but my mother has clearly read the book on being seductive. The way she angles her legs, turns and points her foot alluringly, lifts her arms up, or places a hand on her hip. She knows what a camera is for. I remember one of her closest friends, Yasuko, was a "Bond girl," another master of pinup girl poses.

One day, in my twenties, my mother and I settled in the dark to watch Yasuko in *You Only Live Twice*. She appears in the bath scene, where James Bond is pampered by four silent Asian female attendants dressed in pink satin bras and high-waist panties.

"Place yourself entirely in their hands, my dear Bond-san," says the host, as Bond is about to be soaped and scrubbed. "Rule number one is: 'Never do anything for yourself when someone else can do it for you' . . . Rule number two: 'In Japan, men always come first. Women come second.'"

In the IMDb credits, Yasuko is Bath Girl #4.

Fifty-two years after the film was released, Yasuko attended a film conference and said, "Some people remember me from the James Bond movie, but in James Bond I did nothing . . . The parts I was offered, me being Japanese—either hospital nurse or housemaid or prostitute. I was just so limited in my offers."

When I watch Yasuko, sharp and confident, being interviewed, I think: How does the story change when the scenery becomes the subject? When landscape becomes the protagonist?

My mother never said, "Yes, Mister Bond," but when I look at the photos of those seven years before my birth, I see her acting a part.

Yasuko and my mother were wise to the pull and power of attraction. They knew the monoliths of identity assigned to Asian women and the demands of a transactional society in which youth and prettiness operate as capital. They often assumed the roles assigned to them—posing like sublime figurines, acting coquett-ish—to be comprehended. Self-presentation is a form of stagecraft. The trick is not to let the meanings placed on your body squash your living. Never enter a story that takes you in and won't let you go.

THE SUN DROPPED as we sat in the garden. The houses and trees were now dusky blue. There is a French phrase for the darkest part of dusk: *l'heure entre chien et loup*. Literally: when it is too dark to distinguish between a dog and wolf slipping through the shadows. Or, put another way: when one cannot separate the known and the unknown, the tame and the wild.

AT SOME POINT in the mid-1970s, my mother stopped posing as fervently. As she grew older, she found it increasingly difficult to gaze directly in the lens. She had reached the age when actresses disappear for want of roles, cast on the periphery of storylines. There are many photos where she is looking away. If she can't see the camera, perhaps it won't see her. There are many months, years, when she doesn't pose at all, when she gains the power of invisibility. When her picture is taken, she no longer bothers to compose her face. No longer in hot demand, it is hers now. Not to be given away.

The garden photos are about how women smudge prettily into the background or age quietly into the margins, amounting to nothing more than a wash of unvarying "thereness." But that only makes sense if we see plants as mere "setting" rather than as active world-builders creating conditions for life to exist. It only holds if we insist on an ego that demands to be differentiated from a shrub.

What if a woman in a garden is not posing but simply widening and gentling her boundaries? What if she is embracing the sensory experience of being alive and entwined? To live with things growing all around, to be in the center of all this life, is to dream inside the Endless.

＜

MY MOTHER GAZED off at a squirrel jittering across the telephone line. I took her photo in the darkening garden. I asked if she could tell me when she was happiest. I asked her to show me the photo when she was most at peace. She chose a photo taken by a tree in Gibraltar, a Barbary macaque seated on a branch before her. Her body skimmed by a semi-sheer knit vest, the mood relaxed and off-duty. Solitary.

JAPANESE ARTIST

A FEW DAYS AFTER MY MOTHER SITS WITH ME IN THE garden, I am driving like a cabbie with my pizza-fed sons across town, listening to a well-known Japanese artist on an episode of BBC's *Desert Island Discs* and finding hidden routes through the city. My sons want me to explain to them why we can't speak about this Japanese artist in my mother's presence. My sons consider their Obaachan a true original—unconventional and dramatic, a *real character* who does not like to be upstaged. They love her but she also makes them nervous.

"There was a feud, or maybe it was more of a grudge," I say.

"What was it about?" they want to know.

The format of *Desert Island Discs* is soothing in its predictability. A life reduced to eight favorite recordings over the course of forty minutes. The theme song, accompanied by the sound of gulls, hasn't changed since the show began in 1942. Yet the structure allows for surprising detours. "Guests usually accustomed to delivering the same old talking points drift off as a stray tune reminds them of the lean times of their youth," writes Hua Hsu in *The New Yorker*. The Japanese artist's first castaway choice is Édith Piaf's "Non, Je Ne Regrette Rien."

"Maybe they were too similar," I tell my sons.

My mother befriended the Japanese artist, Y., in 1966 London. Y. had published a conceptual art book, full of creative instructions, poems and drawings, and was performing an art piece in which she sat motionless on stage and invited audience members to cut away small pieces of her clothing with a pair of scissors that lay in front of her.

The Japanese community in London was minuscule in the 1960s and my mother and Y. felt a kind of instant recognition. They had both lived through the Tokyo bombings as young children, devoted themselves to art, set out on a path of cultural dislocation, married white men with working-class roots, emigrated to new countries.

"It's probably just jealousy," say my sons. "Competition."

For a time, my mother was making some money with her interpreter work, so she would prepare meals for the Japanese artist, who was still struggling to make a living. When Y. and her husband barely had enough to pay for rent and utilities, my mother also began caring for their young daughter, ensuring she had "good food, clean clothes and a warm bed." Some nights, without any notice, the little girl would arrive in a cab at the door and my mother would pay the fare. When the little girl became sick with pneumonia, my mother nursed her back to health.

"So maybe she didn't like being treated like a babysitter?" my older son says.

After two years of caring for the little girl several times a week, my mother asked the Japanese artist if she could adopt the daughter, whom she had come to see as her own. According to my mother, Y. replied: "Ask my husband and if he says yes, I will think about it."

I don't think she wanted to give her daughter away entirely, but rather wanted to let my mother share the role of parenting. When my mother and father asked the little girl's father, he apparently said no. At this point, the little girl was four, as old as my mother and father's childless marriage.

My sons and I are still in the car, intermittently listening to *Desert Island Discs*. Intermittently speculating. The castaway tune is now "Lili Marlene," sung by Lale Andersen.

Not long after my mother spoke to the little girl's father, the Japanese artist met an English musician, and after their respective marriages ended, they became inseparable. My mother and Y. slowly drifted apart. "We are not seeing so many people from the past," said the Japanese artist. "The English musician and I are very much in love." My mother did not understand this explanation.

On Christmas Eve, 1971, when my parents' marriage was no longer childless, the little girl disappeared with her father in violation of a custody order. Their disappearance prompted a massive, but unsuccessful, search. The little girl and her father spent the next seven years hiding in a Christian cult led by a man known as "Apostle Stevens." It was twenty-seven years before the Japanese artist and her daughter were reunited.

"Maybe Obaachan felt rejected by Y.," my sons suggest.
    "Maybe she couldn't accept that her friend became a star with a big, famous life."

RECORDS

APRIL PASSED QUICKLY. WE CELEBRATED PASSOVER WITH MY husband's family, where my nephew sang the four questions and my sons found the afikomen someone had hidden in a rain boot.

The warm weather came and we put away the winter tires and shovels and tidied the yard.

A couple of weeks after my search angel paused work on the family tree, she messaged me suggesting I contact the National Health Service (NHS) about obtaining my mother's medical records and possible information about her donor insemination.

I RECEIVED SEVERAL replies shortly thereafter:

> Because the Trust is moving towards digitizing our paper records & because you may receive a complete record, even if you have only requested specific data & because we cannot locate any data relating to the specific episode requested & because the notes would have been destroyed & because we only hold on to records for eight years & because I have checked our information in storage to be sure & because unfortunately there were no records held

at the hospital any more, we are sorry to inform you that Imperial College Healthcare NHS Trust has found no trace of your mother's case.

FOUR:

KOKUU

(harvest rain)

TWO HANDS

I WAS SITTING ON A TRAIN WATCHING AN OLDER MAN WITH big hands. He gestured with them from side to side in the air as if to say: Once I slipped on an icy road. Or: This is how I dance when I am happy and free. Or: Sometimes I feel like a man caught in a giant wave.

I was sitting on a train reading a message from my search angel, who was telling me about a chromosome-mapping tool called "DNA Painter" that might allow us to advance our search. She felt we were *getting closer, we could be on the edge of something.*

I had no idea who the old man was talking to, so I craned my neck and spotted a younger man with long brown hair across the aisle, likely his son. The son was laughing and saying the words, *Sim, sim, surfando.*

My search angel's message made me nervous. Her thoughtful way of leading the hunt when information remained murky had pushed aside the hesitation in my heart, but now, with the word *closer,* the doubts came rushing up the vents.

I am being carried along in a direction I cannot control, I thought. I was traveling toward an imagined genetic community, which included people I might meet or never meet, but who DNA technologies had revealed were "just like me." There was only one course for this storyline, this narrative path that would drag me through to the end, toward a possible "reunion."

On the one hand: wariness.

On the other: the reflex to put myself in a line, a lineage. To see what had trickled down.

I watched the old man as he stood and made his slow, wavering way up the aisle.

"We live in a death-drive culture," said the graduate student behind me to her seatmate over the tapping of laptop keys. "You can call it capitalism or efficiency but it's basically a death-drive economy that's destroying the whole planet."

I had been proceeding with the idea that a name might return me to firmer ground. It was on the train I first considered the possibility that the endpoint might not be a source of great comfort or vindication to me.

WOODS

THE TRAIN WAS TAKING ME INTO THE WOODS OF LATE spring. As my phantom father drifted through the air, still a faceless shadow, not yet named, I set out walking. I had traveled a distance from my home to meet up with a group of eight strangers, all international artists, for a week-long botanical expedition.

The project was to "germinate." To ask whether plant life could also help us rethink our relationship with the world, shift our art to the planetary. We had come to meet with arborists, herbalists, "just food" farmers, foragers and archivists; to see wild plants—not precious cultivars—in their own homes, borderlands, meadows, wood grove.

Our residency host was an artist and mycologist who kept, throughout her crammed house, jars of salvaged butterfly wings and boxes of animal remains, including the skull of a bear and a deer and the bones and skin of a fox. Each morning, we moved like a small herd into the misty air, hiking a path through the Gatineau Hills, traveling in spirals and circles through a cloud of coolness, along verges and across ground that squelched with moisture, into bogs full of whispering reeds and bobbing cattails.

Often the slowest, I trailed behind my companions, who were patient with my epic ignorance. They hypnotized me with their knowledge, showed me the bristling ground, the tiny insects nibbling on leaves with their tiny mouths, seedlings bravely emerging from the frosty mulch, the earth beginning to make fertile what had rotted during winter. I followed where their eyes led me, listened as each plant was named, feeling the beneficent indifference of the forest.

Germination is a feat of time, warmth and light, and a reminder of the earth's quiet and constant stir. What gets worked at patiently all winter unfurls. One morning, while crouched on the spongy forest floor to better see the blush and swell of a magenta lady's slipper, I sank into softness that felt unending. A wet green embrace. A continent's ancestry. In the spring woods, surrounded by tiny temporal explosions and buds lifting their heads almost unnoticeably, what had been folded densely inside opened.

FLAT PLANTS

THE SKY WAS TINTED A LILAC GRAY ON THE DAY WE VISITED
the National Herbarium, a windowless refrigerated room filled
with over six hundred metal cabinets and more than a million pre-
served specimens. Outside, looming storm clouds grew billowy
and full. Inside, we gathered in the climate-controlled vault, looking like mimes with white-gloved hands. Before us on a carefully
arranged long table were "pre-chosen specimens"—plants that
looked as though they had been comically steamrolled by the
Acme Corporation. Whorly leaves, gathered, dried and pressed to
page. Flowers flattened in mid-bloom.

Our guide explained that herbarium sheets were a way of pre-
serving "the morphology of life" and encouraged us to take a close
look at the artifacts she had selected. The order was appealing but
eerie. The paper seemed too immense for a tiny, centered piece of
seaweed, too flimsy for the bulky dandelion straining against thin
strips of cloth tape. I noticed how the tentacled leaves of an alpine
flower had been wrapped decoratively to fit on the page, a small
human decision that broke the illusion of cool matter-of-factness,
revealing the tension of an archivist trying to mute intrusions of
art and affection.

As we prowled through the specimens, I felt the limits of the
archive. Plant identification began with the brutal abstraction of
plant life from local and Indigenous ecologies. Stripped of context
and habitat (or what Emily Dickinson once called "circumference"),

the plants appeared stranded. Everything dirty and gritty had been brushed away.

Standing beside me, I watched one of our group, a Māori artist, resist the urge to run a gloved hand over a pale, dry plant that came from her homeplace in Whangara, Aotearoa. A delicate fumitory flower, splintered from the great spirit of the world. She looked fascinated but also disoriented and I felt that way too. Where was the insect buzz, the birds in wavering flight, the warm damp mist, the upward-drifting earth smell?

We were waiting for the plants to step out of the conservative poses into which they had been forced. We were waiting, in this strange garden, for the plants to shoot into action. To be released.

An archive is built on the idea of separability—namely, a belief that the life of one is separable from the life of another. To turn a big entangled world into a museum of flat plants is the epitome of archival logic.

Our guide removed her glasses and cleaned them on the edge of her blossomy blouse.

"If we continue on our present course," she said, "the herbarium will play a different role." She took a bushy clump of paper-mounted lichen and held it aloft on the plinth of her palm.

The lichen, she explained, came from a high alpine environment that had experienced increased air pollution and warming over the past thirty years. It had grown inch by inch over millennia. Whereas the archive was once a place of dry taxonomy, the species identification records were now being used to table crucial shifts, in this case the disruption to a mountain ecosystem, that might otherwise be ignored or go unseen. The seasons and plants were slowly drifting out of place.

She invited us to look at recent pressings from citizen scientists, telling us it was impossible to predict what information would be important eventually, that all we could do was monitor what was happening at ground-level with fastidious sensitivity to shifts in the landscape. Change at the level of seed, grain, vein, bud, pore. I could tell she felt mixed, and mostly aghast, about the archive gaining this degree of testimonial power.

Small and precise. Tender and restorative. I thought of what it meant to be pinned to paper, tethered, so as not to float away. I looked over at the heavy metal doors of the herbarium and felt my thoughts about the archive change hues. My immediate reaction had been one of dismay at its almost violent, individualizing nature. But it began to look more like a way of seeing nature as an ensemble; grasping the qualities and depth of every indispensable character in the landscape. The archive as a theatrical cast board.

⇌

MY MOTHER SAID the pressed plants looked "very stiff and thirsty" when I sent her photos from the herbarium later that afternoon, thinking she might enjoy the little details. Then, as though I had become a parched plant myself, she suggested I find a nice bath, or even better, "go for a good long swim."

On cue, as if maternally orchestrated, it rained that night. A heavy, hydrating rain. Everything was black and shiny.

LIGHT

I WOKE EARLY TO FIND OUR TWENTY-SEVEN-YEAR-OLD expedition leader happily watching the soft rain from a covered deck. She was wearing a T-shirt that said: "introverted but willing to discuss plants." A few days earlier, I'd noticed a sun rash bloom on her arms while we walked through a wildflower garden. She now explained, lightly scratching the flush on her neck, that the rain eased her environmental sensitivities. Her favorite place to sit as a very young child was by a window overlooking her family garden, a sheltered but scenic spot, where she grew like a potted plant. As a performance artist in Alberta, her home studio now housed over seven hundred rescued and rehabilitated houseplants, some given to her after the deaths or illnesses of people who could no longer tend to them, some stolen from inhospitable corporate offices. Her "collaborators," she called them.

A few hours later, we arrived in the Laurentian forest for our final trip. We were there to meet a French Swiss–born artist who was known for photographing trees that grew in the ash of Auschwitz-Birkenau. In German, the word for birches is *Birken*. The name *Birkenau* was taken from the silver birch trees that ringed the camp. Shortly after the end of communism in Poland, the artist began walking through the camps. What did it mean for the trees to continue the work of life in such a desolate place, and how could one begin to translate the resonance of the site, and the vibrations that many visitors "feel acutely," when representational photography proved inadequate?

She now lived with her partner in the mountains of southern Quebec in a simple but beautiful wooden house built among a large stand of red oak and white pine. Below the canopy of trees were delicate plants spread in dense carpets, staked and circled with string to protect them from foot traffic. Red trillium, clintonia, trout lily and bellwort—the artist explained that these fragile groupings, some upwards of one hundred years old, had a greater capacity for reproduction and survival than single specimens.

Fragile groupings. Perhaps this is what we are, I thought, looking around at my fellow artists standing in the woods, artists who had come from nearby and far away, who ranged in age from twenty to seventy, artists with children and artists without, "just" criminals who saw the theft of seed heads and cuttings from private gardens as communal service, who appreciated plants as a pharmacopoeia informed by the wisdom of ancient and Indigenous apothecaries. Guided by the forest's collaboration, we had spent a week circled by invisible thread, falling back on each other. Eight unrelated organisms briefly entwined, positing "tiny plant joys" as proof of a wakeful, turning earth against the global roar of fascism; apocalyptic news of floods and storms and imminent ecological collapse.

The longer we spent in the forest, the more I felt myself melting into arboreal time, losing track of hours and days. I closed my eyes and stood still, listening to the creak of bending tree branches, trying to imagine the secret communication of the rhizomes and mycelia sprawling like a galaxy beneath the earth. I wanted to understand the invisible forces beneath the surface, the distress signals and kinship overtures transmitted by fungal threads and flaring roots deep in the soil.

The artist led us into her home and offered us a pot of twig tea. The little cups tinkled on the tray she carried and placed before us. She invited us to sit on floor cushions beside a projector.

For some time, she said, she had been working on imprints of plants using electromagnetic photography and techniques of Kirlian photography. What this looked like was luminous images of leaves, each one burning and glowing along the edges, like radiantly charged suns.

The idea was to visualize how plants connect and relate, through proximity. "We obsessively probe the inside of things with sophisticated imaging technologies," she explained. "But the real revolution will occur when we begin to see *relationships* in action and what truly emanates from all living entities."

Her project was to think about the edges of matter. Where does matter start and where does it stop? When she said this, I became suddenly aware of the scant distance between my skin and my neighbors'. Our knees almost touching. Fine hairs rising. I imagined being haloed by a shivering fringe of light. I thought of our auras splashing outward and colliding, disproving the farce of self-containment.

The electromagnetic waves were very powerful and, as a result, the artist explained, she had developed cancer. I now realized she was wearing a wig. When someone asked if she planned to stop working with light fields, she said no. There were ways of reducing the risk but she suggested, with the resignation of a radiation-dosed Marie Curie, there was a price to be paid for her investigation. Her mission was to undo frozen ways of seeing, shaped by Cartesian logic. It was only through dangerous frequencies, currents and waves that she could dissolve the frames of an old story, proving that matter was not bounded and sealed but, actually, dynamic and porous.

She was creating what she called an "energy herbarium," to capture what was inaccessible to human perception; evidence of *the universal life force running through everything.* Her wish was to one day have her photographs deposited in the Muséum national d'Histoire naturelle in Paris.

As the artist spoke, I moved restlessly on my cushion, like a child, preoccupied with not sitting. I was deeply interested in what she was saying but I could not stop moving, as if my body was squirming to understand something. It had something to do with this proof of our fizzy edges and those overused words "interdependency" and "symbiosis."

I thought of the buzz when you accidentally touch someone you like, how the air feels electrified. But I was also starting to understand how difficult portraiture or memoir become when we cannot trace the area around "me" and "you," how ludicrous the tidy mechanics of narrative and display when there are no solitary individuals, no privatized selves, separate from the wonder and wreckage of the world; what is "I" if we are all just light and energy, going to pieces?

Whereas the archive invited us to see in isolated units, the artist returned us to life as a seething and electrifying panorama. "Much remains unknown and difficult to explain," she confessed as she ended her talk.

It was time to say goodbye and head out of the woods, the woods in which the artist, perhaps ironically, had chosen to lead her isolated life. Or was she not isolated at all, but rather unbound-aried—enmeshed with the trees and mosses and other lively constituents of the Laurentians? As our group piled into the van, I thought of the energy rising out of the silos of our bodies and climbing toward the sky, ignoring the limits of our limbs and selves.

RELATIVE STRANGERS

WE DROVE HOME THROUGH A FLOOD ZONE AREA IN Gatineau, where sandbags encircled houses and swimming pools owned by wealthy residents had disappeared, submerged in the river which had overflowed its banks. The river inundated houses, lapped at basement ceilings. People moved their possessions off the ground, emptied bottom drawers, piled food on the highest shelves.

BACK IN TORONTO, I received a message from my search angel letting me know that after importing information from my family tree and DNA matches into the "DNA Painter," she had narrowed the possibilities down to five. Five hypothetical fathers. Five suspects in the room. They were named on an abbreviated family tree, a version I had never seen before. Each name had a hypothetical score ranging from 1 to 124, with the highest score indicating the most probable person.

I reported these findings to my sons, who were seated on our living room couch, legs sprawled, the bony knees I loved pointing in every direction. "This is getting stranger and stranger," they said, folding their long limbs away, "but it will be okay."

The plan was for me to begin contacting the possibilities. I neglected this plan for several days in favor of painting the bathroom and binge-watching *Russian Doll*.

There were literally hundreds of cousins—but only three cousins who lived in England with whom I was closely matched. I contacted my closest known relative via the testing company's message system, the daughter of a well-known writer, and received no reply.

That left two cousins.

Hello, I said to N....
    Hello, I said to K....

The words I wrote were overly formal, garbled by fear and nervousness. *I have been researching my family history with a view to establishing an account of some kind.* Outside in the breezy night, the branches tapped the window like impatient fingers. B. had advised me that my DNA relatives might be initially circumspect, even those who had chosen to make their information public. "We live in a paranoid world." He encouraged me to make it clear I had no financial interest in connecting with family, to emphasize I was not a threatening force.

I am writing to you now with the hope you might possess information relating to my biological father ... I was likely conceived by donor insemination. The insemination may have taken place at St. Mary's Hospital. Do you know of anyone in your family who may have been a practicing physician or medical intern in London in the late 1960s ... I don't wish to intrude or upset anyone's life ... I just hope to view photographs and maybe learn about my family's medical history.

Cousin N., with whom I shared the second-closest DNA, replied straightaway that he did not recognize my name and dismissed further conversation, a classic "computer says No" message. When I pressed a little more, *what I need is so small*, trying to use charm and humor to spackle over the awkwardness, he wrote: "Sorry, I work in IT security so I'm very cautious."

What was the nature of this caution? He had opted to make his DNA matches visible, inviting others to share their family history. He knew how closely we were linked. When I gently asked if I might be put in touch with anyone else in the family, assuring him again that I had no designs on any fortune or family business, explaining I was in the unusual process of looking for a context, a history, and just hoping for a tiny lead, he said: "Sorry, we're all very wary."

In those months, in that post-Brexit moment, it was hard not to imagine an anxious man drinking a cuppa Typhoo, chiseling a stone wall around his tight-knit family, zealous about enclosure. Zealous about protecting his market economy and the small scared territory of his "self."

I wasn't asking to be admitted to the family. Or was I? I wasn't kin and he didn't owe me anything. Or did he? The questions were not just about myself but about all people who are, to a greater or lesser extent, shaky arrivals, showing up unannounced, trying to migrate into a kind of safety or homecoming. Some of us stood outside the door campaigning for admittance, and some of us were thinking *It's a minuscule country, for God's sake, how many more can we fit?* And every one of us was related.

"Well, I suppose from his point of view, you might be a threat," said my husband, gently, seeing that I was starting to cave in on myself. "You might, after all, represent a family secret."

From this perspective, I had arrived from a shadow land to point to a hidden story, the great silences in the family record.

I didn't care if I was the return of the repressed. His nasty suspicion was hurtful. I wasn't looking for love or a festive welcome, but it was disquieting to see myself through the eyes and mood of a stranger making an appraisal. And it only made me more stubborn.

❧

IN THE END it was Cousin K. who allowed me to get closer to what I wanted to find. As soon as I wrote to her, she replied with a mobile number, inviting me to call, right away. *(There's plenty of space.)*

I reached her just as she was about to leave for her painting studio. Her paintings, I later discovered, were full of deep-blue pools, tall palm trees and mid-century architecture, carrying the calm and lonely glamour of David Hockney's California work. On the phone she listened and right away offered to help me.

One way to look at family is to see it as the perimeter we draw against all those we don't know; something to be fortified and patrolled through the logic of protection. Another way is to see family as forever fluid, regularly and gladly made strange. K. welcomed me with an artist's spongy spirit, curious and pervious, open to mixing freely. I was overcome, listening as she speculated aloud, conjured, swatted away possibilities. *A family playboy . . . a Japanese wife . . . three sons . . . five marriages . . .* Fingertips anxious, phone clutched, I noted every word.

On a hunch, K. suggested that we approach a particular cousin about doing a DNA test. Soon after, she sent me a photo of a smiling, bearded man named S., a veterinarian in his late thirties, cheerfully holding a collection kit.

Did I feel a sense of ceremony or anticipation? No. I just felt the bewildering, tender pull of someone holding out their hand. I felt relief, while readying myself to wait and wait for news.

When I think back to our earliest conversations, I imagine K. sitting at home when the phone rings. It is a crowded and happy family, with all the good she needs. Or maybe it is a family that goes through seasons of expansion and contraction, periods of rift and reconciliation. Either way, I have often thought of sending K. a story as a way of thanking her. There is a passage I have in mind from Samantha Hunt's "A Love Story." It comes at the very end.

> What's the difference between living and imagining? What's the difference between love and security?
>
> "Unlock the door," he says again.
>
> This family is the biggest experiment I've ever been part of, an experiment called: How do you let someone in?
>
> "Unlock the door," he says again. "Please."
>
> I turn the knob. I open the door. That's the best definition of love I can imagine.

WATERPARK

WE WERE ON THE BEACH AT WESTLAKE WILLY WATERPARK, filling up on fried clams and salted fish, fingers slick with oil, when my phone rang. My phone had been ringing all afternoon as we bicycled in the bright sun, a caravan of seven, along a country trail. At one point, I squinted at the screen: long distance from Portugal. Likely a wrong number, I decided, and kept riding.

Finally, standing on a beach, preparing to step into a lake filled with bobbing inflatable play structures, I stopped and answered.

Hello, hello, Kyo, is this Kyo?

In came the sound of a man's voice. Open and warm. The bearded man named S., the veterinarian.

The man you are looking for—he was my father. I mean, he was our . . .

A giant waterslide teemed with children who slid one at a time into the water. On the dock, three girls practiced graceful dives and front flips. Grilled corn and lake water, a faint stench of exhaust. An older man sold grilled sausages. "Could You Be Loved" was blaring on tinny speakers. It was hard to hear. I walked to the parking lot.

. . . hear me now? . . . Kyo, listen, I'm very pleased to tell you that you are my sister.

I listened, slow, incredulous, wondering if this was some

lead-up to a prank. *Are you sure?* I held myself steady as heat rose up my neck to my cheeks and my small bathing suit tightened around my ribs.

⤛

AND THEN, just like that, I had brothers. Four of them. Two: available to meet. Two: for reasons I could not follow, unavailable, their relationship to the family irrecoverable. We spanned generations. Born from 1963 to 1981; living in Faro, London, Shanghai ... S.: the only child of his father's fifth and final marriage. Our father.

He died in 2002. But I know he would have wanted to know you, S. repeated gently at the end of our long phone call.

⤛

I WALKED THE entire length of the parking lot twice. I picked up a few beach balls that had rolled away and put them in a cage. I put my hands on my head and walked in several small circles. Then I walked back to my friends and family and told them what had happened, trying to absorb S.'s words as I repeated them aloud. My husband stepped forward and put his hands on my shoulders and then on the sides of my face. *Google him! Google him!* my sons said.

My friends hugged me tightly and then left me to sit alone on the dock, circling in the distance like small and kind coastguards as I scoured my phone for information. I could tell S. had a hard time believing his father might have agreed at age fifty-five to be an anonymous donor in a child's conception. I had trouble believing that such a thing had happened. After a moment of silent mulling, he had mentioned a young girl his father had fostered and helped raise after they moved to Portugal. "It's possible he helped your mother in the Jewish spirit of repair," he said, explaining his father's charitable tendencies.

Only three photos of my father appeared online. I held my breath as I studied them. Dark hair, mustache. Sunglasses. Tie. The images appeared feathery and approximate, as if the camera that took the snapshots had been out of focus or in motion. A fuzzy likeness, he was old enough to be my grandfather and didn't look anything like the fantastical fog of a man still shapeshifting inside my head. Who was this person and how were we connected? I was scared I would never know. I was scared knowing would destroy everything.

A seagull landed on the dock, turning its head every few seconds to get a proper look at me. I watched my sons do a little dance along the far edge of the dock with their six-year-old "godbrother."

Brother. It sounded strange to my ears.

The footholds were slippery on the giant "Jungle Joe" and I watched my godson standing at the bottom, assessing the peril of the climb. "Old Marcus Garvey" drifted from the speakers. The gulls were flying in all directions across the blue sky, as though someone had told them, FOCUS. Two preteen girls draped themselves on a giant inner tube, looping slowly in the gentle current. "This summer hasn't exactly been a bed of roses for you," the smaller of the two said. "You've got that right," the other replied.

WHAT WAS HE LIKE?

He was the son of Jewish refugees.
He changed his name.
He had five (known) wives.
Of the five marriages, the third and fourth were to
    Japanese women.
He had at least four (known) children.
He was a British racing driver (Formula One, Italian
    Grand Prix).
He had "a way with the ladies."
He published a book about race cars; wrote another one
    about time travel but publishers rejected the latter.
    ("Ahead of its time," he joked.)
He taught himself to play piano.
He sold jewelry, opened a restaurant or two.
He moved to the Algarve in his later years, pounded out
    songs, fostered a daughter.
Some called him "a playboy."
He loved piri piri chicken.
He used "NPW" to describe pretentious "nose-picking
    wankers" or pompous men and women.
He was a "Thousand Island" kind of guy as opposed to
    an "Olive Oil and Balsamico" fellow.
He liked horseradish.

He developed diabetes, kept a secret stash of biscuits in a
     drawer, stole sachets of saccharin (Sweet'N Low)
     from Garfunkel's.
He loved dogs.
He behaved charitably and believed in *tikkun olam*, the
     repair of the world.
And perhaps in helping others through donor
     conception.
He hated having his photo taken and didn't like to talk
     about the past. Not at all.

PRIVACY

"SO, YOU'RE NOT GOING TO WRITE ABOUT ALL OF THIS, ARE you?" S. had asked toward the end of our phone conversation.

His question took me by surprise and left a prickle of shame. Did he see me as the kind of sneaky person who was always writing things down, who saw life as cheap material? Was writing gauche and unnecessary? Was I being gently forbidden? What would my answer, which I had still not formed for myself, determine?

"Of course not," I replied.

"Good. Our father was a very private man."

SECOND BROTHER

IN EARLY JULY, ANOTHER OF THE BROTHERS EMAILED ME after being notified by S. of my existence. He was a teacher in Shanghai with a young wife and seven-year-old daughter. He had long Buddha-like earlobes. Black hair. Skin like my skin. I found an echo, particularly in our teen photos, the ones taken by water. Japanese mothers, white fathers, uncannily parallel childhoods. Our passion for the same music (genetic instinct or zeitgeist?), shared comfort foods. Only three years separated us. What I saw in his life was my life staring back at me.

I was teaching a summer writing workshop and rushed home every evening to find long, lathery emails awaiting me. We were not just siblings. We were delirious collaborators, encountering each other in self-chosen bits, rearranging the framework of our lives.

In mid-July, we spoke on the phone for the first time. The annual Indy car race was taking place in Toronto not far from my house and cars roared in the background. I felt it in my body, the men shifting from gear to gear, driving so fast I half listened for a crash, swearing they would die. Racing drivers like *our father.*

There was no stammering shyness. We were both speaking over each other, over the low roar, there was so much to say. I didn't know what to do with the feeling his voice brought; his voice that was a jokey squeeze and loneliness-eraser, a shoulder nudged against mine, a conjuring and conspiring whisper in my ear, the ear that resembled his own.

"Finding you is a miracle in my life and I couldn't be happier," he wrote that night. "I know now it is possible to instantly love someone by just discovering they are a close relative. I didn't think it possible."

My stomach lifted as if I had just accelerated over an elevation in the road. It surprised me to realize that I loved him too, however suddenly or inappropriately. All my life, without realizing it, I must have wanted a cool older brother to shore me up. All those years that my only-ness ran through me like a foundational spark, an engine—I had been waiting.

There was nothing to pull us away from each other, but as the days passed and our emails grew more sporadic, I realized there was also nothing to bring us any closer. We spoke casually of meeting at a halfway point, maybe in the Algarve, where our father was buried. Was it possible? Could we include S. and braid the three strands of our lives together for a moment?

I pressed both my brothers to decide on a date and then, sensing hesitation, an internal voice said: "Let it go." I did not want genetic duty to be the binder. I told myself they were simply too busy. S. with his London veterinary practice. D. with his duties as a Shanghai schoolteacher.

Separated by oceans, I swallowed my neediness and allowed my brothers to remain airy and abstract, swinging between the belief that this family mattered and that it didn't matter at all.

At night I imagined my home in Toronto connected to a home in Shanghai and another in Portugal and another in London. I thought of the two brothers with whom I had no contact, one evidently "estranged" by addiction and the other living in a long-term care facility for those recovering from mental illness, and I worried about their banishment. Minds are not always hospitable or habitable but a family can be sheltering in times of distress. Was there something about this family that made secrets of its misfit or struggling children?

It was in those days of keeping track of invisible kin that I dreamt of typing my brothers' addresses into Google Street View and zooming in to their four homes. Even if there was no possibility of going inside, I could roam their gardens.

A few days after having this thought, I planted yarrow outside our house. Not the prim white plant resembling Queen Anne's lace, but a rambunctious pink mound with the disposition of a cheerleader's pom-pom. The frothy bounce of it was a semaphore. I was crafting signals; sending a sign to anyone sitting with a tingling sense of a family they were still trying to bring into focus.

SUPPOSE

SUPPOSE EVERY FAMILY HAS A SECRET KIOSK OF SURPRISE kin, ready to rush out at any moment. Imagine that this moment of "reveal" is a life stage or a rite of passage, pulling the plug on any fixed view of self, eradicating any pretense of ironclad family arrangements. Suppose what makes us more permeable to the suffering and joys of others is having this kiosk of unknown clowns ready to say: *"Surprise! For better or worse, we are here to aid you in becoming undone."*

Suppose, therefore, we should greet each person we meet as if they have just exited the kiosk.

NOMENCLATURE

WHEN WE WERE DIGGING FOR ANSWERS, FOR A NAME, ALL I wanted was to speed forward and rid myself of the feeling of restlessness that came with being in the middle of an uncertain story.

Digging was my way out. An impulse born of stubbornness and bred in me by a culture that loves stories of people discovering the truth of their paternity; that champions the idea that concealment is destructive and truth is freeing.

I did not consider, in any deep way, what we might uncover. I did not anticipate this man, this suddenly emerged father who burst forth, opening up strange new questions.

Almost immediately, any notion of resolution that had motored my search, any thought that an answer would provide serenity, proved to be misguided.

❧

NOW, IN MY mouth were all the names of close kin I had learned but not yet fully absorbed. Names I laid out in my head like place cards around a dinner table.

"I think I might need a bigger table," I told my husband.

"I don't think there will be any more," he said.

"Okay. But if there are," I said, starting to cry. The pressure of not knowing what was coming had formed a painful knot in my chest.

"Do you think we're done?" I messaged my search angel the next day. I was not sure I could cope with any more surprises. "Have we reached the end?"

A few days later, she replied: "Actually . . ."

I had a sister named S., born in 1940, who died in 1996. I connected with her son, who sent me photos of her. The cause of death was hazy. Breast cancer was mentioned at one point, a fact that would later become relevant to my doctor. In the photos, my sister had the beauty and mod style of Anna Karina. She looked like a woman who could deliver a joke, deadpan, with a killer twinkle in her eyes.

I had no idea if she had a happy life or if it was full of let-downs, but I recognized the way she held her two young sons, her grip loose but avid. When I stared at her face, traced the ridgeline of her collarbones and the dramatic swoop of her black eyeliner, I felt an ache. I'd found my sister. A sister who preceded me by thirty years, who had moved through spaces that defined how women lived, created, mothered, struggled, flourished. I stared at my computer screen, hypnotized by the dark wave of her hair and the glittering stampede of her smile as she glowed and glowed in the backseat of a car.

I told my brothers about our sister, S., and they said they knew nothing of her existence. "Our father was a very private man," they repeated, conjuring a shadowy paternal figure who liked nothing more than to not be noticed. *A private man?* I thought. *Or a cagey, furtive, squirrelly one? A man who did not want to be discovered, who believed every disclosure had an agenda against him?* My nephew confirmed there had been a father-daughter falling-out shortly after S. married and no further contact after 1965. Another crack in his carefully bottled story. Another child omitted from his narrative or deemed unnecessary baggage. Now that I knew how easy it was to disappear from this family, I felt protective of my sister, wondered who had shown her gentleness. *Tell me what shaped you, what you went through*, I whispered to the photo, to no one at all.

The original mystery, compacted into the question *Who is my father?*, did not dissolve when I learned his name. The mystery only spread, moving around, giant and hot. Learning his name widened me into a large, broken, beautiful family that possessed further confusions, estrangements, secrets, shames.

If you have uncovered a family secret, this may not be at all surprising: the way one secret spawns another, like a spider laying a hundred eggs; the way one name multiplies.

My sons checked in for regular updates, to see if I was still gathering siblings.

❧

THE MORE CHAOTIC my thoughts and feelings became, the more I walked, as if my footfalls might fix everything, tamp everyone into a firm and fastened order. I carried around my new companions, my kin, feigning an ease that was missing in my body. One Saturday, I joined a group hike along an urban park trail. Before we set off, our "nature interpreter," who smelled like the French fries she cooked at her part-time job, pointed to two trees a few meters apart and said: "Those of you who are more interested in learning the names of things stand by the black oak and those who are more interested in general stories stand by this sweet-smelling tree right here." A hawk soared above our heads. I could hear crows somewhere out of sight.

I watched the group of hikers divide into two equal-sized groups.

In my mouth were all the names I had learned, stirring and shifting and never still. Names were important and needed to be gotten right but I stood between the two trees for a moment, looked up at the moon's faint foreshadow, then walked to the sweet-smelling tree.

"Sassafras," said the man beside me.

FIXING SOMETHING

A PART OF ME NEVER EXPECTED MY SEARCH ANGEL TO SOLVE
the mystery of my paternity, and once it was solved, I missed her.

"Why did you help me?" I asked her many months later. Her
detective work would normally have cost me thousands of dollars
I could not afford.

There was no personal motivation, she replied. She had never
been in a similar situation. She was not adopted and her biological
family was not a mystery. She was simply interested in using DNA
to solve unknown parentage cases and break down brick walls in
genealogy. For years she had worked for a nonprofit organization
supporting homeless individuals. In 2016, she started helping adoptees and people who had taken DNA tests with surprise results.

"Your story spoke to me . . . I have volunteered for many things
in life and it always comes from a sense of wanting to improve or
fix something, if someone does not have the means or time to do
it themselves."

By the time we connected, she had worked on twenty-five cases,
helping seekers, many with recent British ancestry, in unknown
parentage searches.

❧

"ARE YOU A tree expert?" a woman asked the Sassafras man.

"Arborist, I think you mean," he replied.

FIVE:

TAISHO

(greater heat)

FALLING

MA WAS FALLING. SWEATY AND UNSTEADY, SHE WAS downward-moving. Ma who had always been durable, stone-strong, now seemed to buckle with the slightest draft or tug of gravity. It was the fiftieth anniversary of the moon landing and my mother watched the television—archival footage of Armstrong and Aldrin bouncing around like happy children—with a sense of being untethered. The next day, following another fall from bed, we found a lump on her left breast the size of a baby onion.

The falling was an illness.

Three weeks after I learned my biological father's name, it all seemed inconsequential as my mother began treatment for a newly diagnosed cancer. There was surgery and eventually radiation treatment and many hours spent seated together in vinyl chairs. I tried to be with her as nurses swayed around us like the kelp at the bottom of the waiting room fish tank. In the uncertainty of the cancer center, my blue-gowned ma gripped my hand while the doctor pushed the needle in for a second biopsy. When the fear-stress traveled from her palm to mine and up my arm, I became afraid too.

I took her to visit the greenhouse after pre-op appointments, thinking it might be comforting to be among hundreds of growing things, while I fortified her with cups of barley tea poured from a thermos. It was very hot in the Palm House, the light at times so green it felt like we were underwater. On the good days, she sat contentedly on a bench, wearing oversized sunglasses and several billowy scarves tied at various angles, breathing in the sweet jammy air. On bad days, she ached and imagined the palms bursting through the dome, spreading through the city. It must be the painkillers, I thought, as she described the tropical plants bounding away like dolphins fleeing SeaWorld, her face openly pleased.

The vision was a reminder: my mother was a *gardener*, not a recreational observer of flowers. And with any luck, she would keep tending the plants she saw as familial, the ones she loved more deeply than she did most people. The alternative—that she would grow sicker, be sentenced to passively watch life continue without her—was unthinkable.

One morning, while my mother rested, I read an interview with the head gardener of the greenhouse. He was discussing the "orphan plants" that arrived regularly at the garden, roughly 90 percent of which he found a way to keep. *One day*, he told the reporter, a woman who was very sick with cancer came in with three prickly pear cacti. "She had a big cry," he recalled. "She had taken care of them for years."

When the head gardener was asked by the reporter what became of the prickly pear plants that had been donated, he said they grew and grew. *About eight inches tall when she dropped them off, they were now three feet tall and flowering.*

Irradicable is a word sometimes used to describe a plant, or a life, that is impossible to uproot or destroy. But what is truly irradicable? I was lying down beside my mother. It was now almost midday and she was trying to blink away a headache. I watched her blink and blink, blinking too much, worry in me rising.

If there was ever hope of mending things between my mother and me, now was the time.

HANDSOME

"I FOUND SOME PHOTOS," I SAID TO MY MOTHER WHEN SHE visited, following her surgery. Complications would arise but for now, she seemed to be recovering well.

"What photos?" she asked, tapping the laptop on the table before us. "Why do you have these photos?"

"What, Ma? Oh. Well," I said, "because my brother sent them to me."

She drew her hand back, became still.

I told her about the phone calls with my half brothers. Even as I spoke, it seemed an impossible idea, that a teaspoon of saliva had led me to a new family almost a half century after my birth.

"So, these are my brothers, S. and D. This is my niece, L. And this, this is my father. His name was A." The black-and-white photograph showed a man in a dapper suit with an elegant, pencil-thin mustache. He looked vaguely like Clark Gable. My mother didn't move. I clicked to another photo of my niece. She asked to see the picture of A. again.

I reopened the photo. My mother leaned closer, placed a hand on my knee to steady herself. "He is good-looking," she said. And then, a few seconds later, quietly: "He was good-looking."

Her eyes were glowing and she had an odd smile on her face. The look wasn't like her at all; it was the face of a soft and moonstruck young woman, a woman whose life was a very deep well.

My husband, who had been sitting across from us, scrolling through messages on his phone, looked up with wide eyes.

"I think I'll check on the boys," he said loudly, pushing back his chair.

A small opening.

"Yes, he is a handsome man," I said, picking up where she had left off.

PROMISE

I GENTLY PATTED HER ARM—ONLY IT WASN'T HER ARM, but rather the table by her arm because she wasn't much of a toucher and I didn't want to annoy her. My fingertips tapped the wood grain. They said: *The coast is clear. Please tell me. I won't judge. I understand.*

I didn't utter a word. I tried to ignore the quiet in the room: the silence that had dominated our life together, shapeshifting like a murmuration of birds. Under layers of chatter, it swirled. A great, vast volume. It was the silence between immigrant Japanese mothers and their half-breed daughters. The silence of a broken maternal language.

My mother's tone dropped an octave. "Don't tell them," she said, gesturing toward the other room where my sons and husband were now watching *2001: A Space Odyssey*. She put her finger to her upper lip, pausing uneasily.

"You promise?" she asked.

I promise, I said.

"He was in love with me. He wanted to marry me."

Oh . . . Were you in love with him?

"Well, he was so helpful. With my passport."

Your passport?

"Yes. I met him in a passport office. Your father was always traveling for work and leaving me behind. My written English was so poor. A. saw me struggling and walked over and began to help me. He was right there, just a yard away."

So, he was a stranger?

"Oh no, not a stranger. We had met before."

Where?

(Silence)

Outside, the sky was getting dark, the trees losing their shape. I was carefully controlling my reactions, saying very little, afraid to move, afraid to break the spell or activate the wrong emotion, afraid she would stop talking.

What came next was more confused. I tried to let her lead the way but the details, beyond a certain point, were scattered. The surgery and medication had taken a toll, dulling her memory with exhaustion; a mental fog that seemed to create a cloudy partition between past and present. When she finished speaking, her account was still incomplete but I didn't press further.

Later that night I told my husband everything she had shared, editing and filling in gaps; and as I spoke, it started to become a story.

PASSPORT

SPRING 1968: MY MOTHER IS A COUPLE OF MONTHS SHY OF her thirty-first birthday. She has recently cut her hair in a precise, Vidal Sassoonish pageboy and made herself a Mary Quantish minidress from fabric remnants she found in a shop on Kensington High Street. Her husband is out of town, yet again, traveling for work. What she wants most of all is to be traveling too. But for that, she needs a passport. With a passport she can visit her mother in Japan, a country that has forced her to renounce her citizenship upon marriage to a *gaijin*, a country she feels she has lost, along with the family, culture and language she has left behind. An airplane can portage her home. But only with a passport. Without one, she is stranded. This is what happens when you legally cease to exist in one nation and have yet to legally materialize in another.

She finds the right line to stand in and quickly explains herself to a white clerk behind the desk, ignoring the way he sighs in advance of her speaking. The clatter of officialdom fills the air. Two other clerks look on. She senses one of them smirking, and her face reddens. She has lived in London long enough to know all the boring and routine ways a "foreigner" can be reduced; knows the rigid ceremonies of class and the tone the clerk is now using.

Please repeat yourself. Slowly. Clearly.

My mother responds to the questions asked by the clerk. Proud, unthwarted, duking it out in 1960s England.

The photo does not frazzle her, once she understands it will require an unsmiling version of herself.

But the application form. The form is a maze of boxes and blanks. There is the family name and then there is the marital name but soon there is the boundary at which the undecipherable begins. Not words. But cold, bureaucratic substance. The form, in this section, appears to be a hundred pages long. It scrolls across the room, out the door and down the street. Its questions are written in faint ink, on tissue-thin paper that dissolves upon touch; the letters turning to runes as she tries to read them.

Those in line behind my mother are growing visibly impatient. One man, glaring, gestures at the clerk: *do something*. My mother feels someone touch her arm. A man, well-dressed and older, nods kindly toward the papers in her hand. He has been standing in line, *just a yard away*, following her exchange with the clerk, watching my mother redden with shame, the slightest stutter appearing as she grows flustered. Perhaps his own Japanese wife has made him notice things more readily.

The man pulls out a blue-ink pen from his pocket and says, "I can help you with that." The man is courteous and familiar. He knows her husband, he explains, leading her to a counter across the room. He names a casino in Mayfair where they all met briefly while playing *chemin de fer*. His fingers smooth the paper, and he begins guiding her through the application. The man is funny and makes a joke about the clerks and their uptight manner.

"Yes. Why do officials always say 'my pleasure' in a depressing voice?" says my mother, imitating the clerk's sour expression and buttoned-up tone. "People like that give me indigestion."

His pen stops moving. He turns and looks directly at my mother, nods.

Something about the way he nods stays with her. "Some people underestimate how erotic it is to be understood," writes Mary Rakow.

I see the scene again and again, trying to grasp the place where it begins. I picture the man's pen continuing on the page. The pigeons flocking at nearby Trafalgar Square, confetti of crumbs, an updraft of birds, drift of clouds. All I can do is imagine.

Something is starting, my mother thinks, holding her breath.

Tell me, he says with a steady gaze. *Which way are you going home today?*

BENEVOLENCE

KNOWING HOW MUCH MY MOTHER HATED BUREAUCRACY, IT
seemed plausible she might be seduced by an attentive older man
who was willing to protect her from obscure paperwork, from
forms written in what Toni Morrison famously called "language
designed for the estrangement of minorities." It seemed plausible she might abandon herself to this "benevolence," even if she
already had a husband who was a more-than-competent signer of
important government documents.

While she was hardly waiting for a knight to take charge, her
tense relationship to English and the written word created a rare
dependency. I was born, in this way, of an immigrant's discomfort with language, a language I now wield for its possibilities of
expression.

These thoughts circled in my head and kept me in the same place.
These thoughts did not get me closer to understanding how the
affair began, what went into the making of it, what she felt.

Not once had it ever occurred to me that I was the product of
infidelity.

HEART

IN 1968, TWO YEARS BEFORE I WAS BORN, MY MOTHER BEGAN an affair. The man she met was the son of Russian-born drapers, old-world Jews. He was a racecar driver. A restaurateur. A dashing playboy with a reputation for taking up with women and then leaving them. My mother was thirty-one. He was fifty-four. They were both married to other people.

In the regular absence of her spouse, my mother was often lonely. She did not always feel properly loved. But how lonely and how unloved? Enough to ripen her to a stranger's advances (assuming he advanced first)? What happened during that initial encounter? Did he take her hand and say, *Come with me*? And, if so, did she believe she was the first person he had ever said this to?

Thinking about these moments made me want to pan away to the curtains. But I was trying to imagine even the embarrassing details, to put myself in her place, in her heart. Even saying "my mother's heart" opened a strange feeling in my chest, a tightness, as though an unfamiliar visitor had arrived.

Stories of maternal secrecy are rare. I wanted to think about my mother's heart away from the troubling moralism that attached to female promiscuity. I wanted to know more about this heart. Not the trapped heart I knew growing up. The heart that found a lover.

FACTS

WHY HIM? I ASKED.

(Silence)

How long? I asked.

"Two years. Maybe less. Maybe more."

They met for a second time at a restaurant, a place he had recently opened. He drove her around London and the countryside in his Cadillac, allowing her to pilot the car every now and then, drifting with the tidal movement of her turns. He took her to the movies. (*Belle de Jour*? *An Affair to Remember*?) They went to Monaco into the heart of a sizzling summer heatwave and stood by a carob and a fan palm. They visited Morocco, where they drove past farm fields. Did she admire the olive trees? Was she bothered by the sound of insects announcing themselves at dusk?

He gave her a secret apartment in Chelsea, which my mother claims she seldom used because she felt guilty about her husband. At some point, he brought my mother to meet his mother, P., "A wonderful, kind, tiny woman." P., who had worked as a seamstress and milliner, welcomed my mother, admiring the dress she had made for herself on an old pedal-operated Singer sewing machine. It was a sleeveless cotton shift. *The seams. The drape. What a good eye you have for folds and fabric.* As my mother twirled on the spot, P. admired the delicacy of the gathered pleats. The turquoise lining. My mother remembered feeling like an artist in P.'s presence, because even though she had been making clothes for many years, this was the first time someone said she was any good.

❧

HIS QUALITIES? I asked.
"Humor. Kindness. Warmth."
His wife?
(Silence)
His sons?
(Change of subject)

❧

SHE REMEMBERED DANCING slowly to "Moonlight Serenade." A regular gift of a bouquet. A hyacinth in a clay pot. Nothing lasting.
He loved you. (I stated more than asked.)
"Yes."
But did you love him?
(Silence)
Complex expressions passed across her face. The more my mother told me, the more I felt there was a stranger inside her, nested like a matryoshka doll inside this person I thought I knew utterly—a being I knew not at all. I was following my eighty-year-old mother through a crack in the wall, into another life, and encountering an inner longing I did not know how to read.

DEAR BROTHER

I WROTE TO MY BROTHER IN SHANGHAI TO TELL HIM WHAT I had discovered. I told him that, as he had already intuited, my mother did know his father. *I don't know how long the relationship lasted. Hard to pin some facts down, will keep trying.*

I told him I was sorry, that I knew it was quite a lot. I told him, for my part, I felt a mix of things but amidst it all *I feel thankful that your father loved my mother for a brief moment. (She hasn't had much love in her life.) And I wouldn't be here if it weren't for him. I wouldn't be writing you now.*

Around the time of writing to him, I began reading about cotyledons, the first little leaves on most plants grown from seed. They were not "true leaves," I read, and generally did not bear any traits specific to their species. Like tiny infant limbs, even on what might become a mammoth and mighty sunflower, starter leaves were a way of testing the atmosphere to see whether the world being entered was clement and supportive enough.

A REPLY

HE WAS SUCH A GENTLEMAN AND OFFERING TO HELP YOUR mother at the passport office just sounds so like him. I confirm he had a Cadillac, he had many Cadillacs. At that time, I think it was a light metallic blue Cadillac with an open top. His mother was indeed a "tiny woman." And I am certain as the moon is round that he loved your mother . . .

I read my brother's reply twice. I tried to imagine what it must be like to have a stranger's truth revise your own past and threaten the core of your story. I was his father's faithlessness made obvious. I represented his father's periodic disappearances. His mother's fury. Arguably, the end of their marriage. It was difficult. But never did my brother let on that my presence was the source of this difficulty. Never when he mentioned my mother did he express a tone of disapproval or discourage me from stitching our story together. Instead of treating me with distrust, he embraced me to disburden me of my worries, taking care of me like an older sibling would.

My brother and I were still in the seedling stage of our relationship. The air was sometimes dicey and uncertain. But when I read his words, I felt us reaching out to the sun, forming our first true leaves.

AUGUST 6

THE PLANTS IN THE GARDEN WERE DONE WITH ANY COM-manding, correcting, steering. Drunken butterflies flew in wobbly patterns. The widow next door was busy with her clippers. I could see her looking at our yard, eyeing the leggy Russian sage that had bolted many feet from its bed, neither tricked nor bullied by fences. My widowed neighbor devoted hours to her tiny plot, a chorus of potted plants that sang her history of moving oceans.

I was in the garden, thinking about the depth of a family secret that had required the intervention of science to unearth. I was thinking about my search angel, who went to great trouble to crack a mystery that could have been solved by a person I saw almost every day.

I was thinking of my mother whooping it up, face aimed at the sun, up to no good. I pictured her swerving through the country-side and diving into silver salty water. Euphoric and loose. If she ever did anything that carefree and at odds with her professed marital "sacrifices," I wanted to know it was on her own terms of wanting and not just to please the needs of a man. This was all on my mind. I wanted a story of agency and choice. I wanted there to be reason to light sparklers at the brink in the story when she might have run away forever, never stopping or looking back.

When it sank in that I would never find a photo of my mother and unmet father together, I panicked: *That means there's no proof.*

I feared the lack of it. I needed evidence. Of what? For whom? My mother did not need me to prove her heart's existence. She knew it was there all along.

My neighbor, the widow, asked me to cut back the Russian sage. Her face was soft and round as the moon. She had a big heart for her perfect garden.

"Of course," I said.

ESCAPER

A PLANT PERSON I MET TOLD ME SOMETIMES A PLANT WILL move to a particular spot of its own choosing—dry or moist, shady or sunny, journeying toward the kind of soil it prefers, beyond the area in which it has been cultivated. Such plants are called *escapes*.

The father I knew was constantly escaping, ceaselessly traveling, leaping into liaisons. The extent of his infidelity was only revealed to me after he died. At his memorial, held at a French bistro, after the men had joked about all the money they had lent him over the years, a woman unknown to me came to offer condolences. I remember her standing with her husband, watching me before approaching. She introduced herself, tenderly clutching my hand with both of hers. Her eyes were moist. Her voice coated me in warmth.

Before long, others I only knew by mention stepped forward to explain the part they had played in his life. These secret people were ghosts until he was gone. Then they were no longer vaporish but real; evidence of my father's affection—the parts of him that had spun outward, promised to others.

ONE DAY, OVER COFFEE, a family friend shared information about an early affair, one preceding my birth. In the summer of 1968, as Bobby Kennedy lay on the floor of the Ambassador Hotel, bullet-ridden and cradled by a hotel busboy, my father lay with a script assistant somewhere in Toronto. When he heard the news of Kennedy's assassination, he apparently jumped from bed and, grabbing his clothes, rushed out the door. Later that same day he was on the streets of Los Angeles filing his report for the CBC. The family friend had heard this story directly from the script assistant.

My father reported on momentous events: assassinations, hostage takings, military escalations, independence struggles, coup d'états, peace accords—the list was endless. His extramarital affairs spanned some of the most bloody and violent decades in human history. He was a firsthand witness. *Those reporters needed human comfort*, the family friend said. *They were on the vanguard.*

IT WAS STRANGE to discover my mother had probably been right, all those times she suspected her husband of cheating on her with "tall, blonde, long-legged" women. But I wonder about the first infidelity. Was she devastated when she found out? Did everything feel ruined and endangered, the latch now open? Or did she have songbird ideas about marriage, expecting monogamy to last no longer than a single season?

She never openly divulged her feelings. But I know there *were* feelings, feelings she transferred for a time to a sweater. An olive sweater knit for my father by his first love, Betty. The kind of soft, bulky sweater you just wanted to crawl inside. Betty, judging from the one photo I've seen of her, was a beautiful Chilean-British woman with a mass of black curls and a wide, fetching grin. They met when they were both seventeen and used to cycle to distant heaths and downs, anywhere they could be alone.

My dad would have the sweater for a few months before it mysteriously vanished again. And then, like magic: it would reappear.

The mood of my parents' marriage could be measured by its presence or absence. I wonder now why my mother never gave it away. Am I misremembering, or did the sweater sometimes resurface when my father was at a low point, approaching sadness? Was it her way of making things seem less bleak? It would be in keeping with their painful tenderness—amidst acrimony and setbacks, the small ways they thought to mend, retrieve, repair each other.

As the affairs continued, did she grow numb and incurious or was she still caught by surprise? At a certain point, there must have been some peace made, or some refusal to imagine her husband finding a new woman in each new city, spending so many days in other women's beds. The storm passed over. My mother learned to share my father's love or they both learned to look away and go blithely about their business.

MEETING

MY FATHER LOVED MANY WOMEN. IN HIS OWN WAY, HE WAS faithful to each of them. After he died and I discovered he was not my biological father but had yet to solve the mystery of my paternity, I asked one of his former mistresses to talk with me about him. She was the person I knew most closely, a talented filmmaker half his age, the great love of his later years and the one whose name I knew to avoid at all costs in my mother's company. To my mother, she was *the concubine, the enemy, the devil.* After their relationship ended, my father fell into a deep depression and for two years, there was no lifting him out of it.

I had imagined this meeting for many years, a meeting that had seemed disloyal to my mother when my father was still alive but now seemed reasonable and even inevitable. When I arrived at the restaurant, she was waiting. The air inside was thick with humidity and coffee steam, like the moisture-saturated air inside a cloud. Soon a light rain will fall, I thought as I slid into the booth and began speaking rapidly. I wanted her help in understanding my family chronology and dynamic. I bulleted her with questions, becoming the world's fastest talker. She answered patiently. Her face was open and delicate. Her brown hair, glossy and straight. Of course, my questions were normal. No, she did not know about my parents' struggle to conceive, although this made sense in hindsight. No, she had never wanted a secret romance, was not interested in the illicit aspects of their affair. She had left a marriage in order to live with my father openly, she said, a look of sorrow coming over her face. It was only much later she realized it could never happen because a part of him would always be tied to my mother. She wanted me to know she was not his first long-term relationship, not a home-wrecker, etcetera. There were at least two great love affairs before her, overlapping with my early childhood. *Women you probably knew.* When she told me this, I mulled, hesitant, and began speaking like a slow robot.

Later that night, I decided to contact another of my father's mistresses. *I hope you don't mind me reaching out to you . . . my parents' respective relationships with people unknown to me . . . no judgment . . . wondering why they both felt they had to keep much of their lives hidden for so long.*

At my most generous, I thought of these women as people rebelling against the enclosure of marriage, "tearing down fences and digging up the hedges that enclosed private land" (Eula Biss). But I could only do this if I placed my mother in a mental antechamber and closed the door.

"I hope this helps you get to the next chapter," my mother's enemy said, kindly, as we parted.

SUNFLOWERS

BOWLS HEAPED WITH CELLOPHANE NOODLES AND PLATES of slippery cool radish. Water hisses as it hits the pan just before the lid is placed on top. I am seven years old and standing in a small kitchen in Toronto where my mother and three other Asian women are rolling *chả giò*. They are all married to white reporters whom they met in Manila, Saigon, Tokyo. Standing by a counter, they lean together, pointy high heels traded for jelly shoes. Four of us watch, four mixed-race Asian daughters who can pass as sisters to those not paying attention. If we are flowers, as our fathers sometimes like to say, we are heliotropic; faces following our mothers' movements like those of the sun.

Our dads are routinely absent and all of us daughters, dressed in terry cloth shorts, sparkly typographic tees and North Star runners, have learned to use grown-up English so we can be translators and protectors. We step forward when our mothers are rudely ignored or denied good service, using our people-pleasing-good-girl vibes. Sometimes we even pretend we are our mothers, as I do on more than one occasion when Ma loses her credit card or has to renew a prescription. What are our English skills for if not to be our mothers' voices when they need them?

Fluency happens elsewhere. It takes the form of a knife cutting scallions in rapid chopping motions, so the pieces come out in thin, even rings. Fluency is burdock root foraged from a nearby park with a small rusted shovel. It is a windowsill crowded with flavor-popping perilla, basil, cilantro; plants that grow in recycled containers with a subway rumbling underneath.

Fluency is a first language spoken faster and livelier to a family member who has newly arrived and who is now feeling the loneliness of transplantation; words streaming like sparkling ribbons from our mothers' mouths, like strings of condensed milk into the filtered cups of coffee they endlessly drink.

In the kitchen, we slurp yellow mango and eat crispy pork skin with pickled carrot. Love and wealth are transmitted body to body not through words or currency, but through ways of eating, grooming, sitting, chatting, laughing. Kin becomes kindred, vigorously plural. For a few brief years, our mothers are entirely the subject and the story, and our white fathers are the shadowy backdrop. They may hold the keys to the kingdom but it is our mothers who are the revolutionaries, banging down walls, refusing the limits of prescribed domesticity and *Good Housekeeping*, playacting obedience and then roaring with laughter. When our fathers aren't listening, and later when they are, our mothers call them "big white chiefs" and laugh until tears stream down their faces.

No one seems very much in love.

I study the Asian mums to see what my options are for future "womanhood." When we, the daughters, are old enough, they will get "outside jobs," maître d'ing, managing a restaurant, selling pottery, fielding questions like: *How do you Ornamentals manage to stay so slim?* and *Is that a natural wave?*

The Asian mums shelter me when my parents' marriage spikes with argument. They convince my mother to give my father *one more try* after she leaves him, running away with me to Niagara Falls, only to return a day later on a Greyhound bus to a husband full of apologies and promises. The Asian mums are languishing in their own unhappy marriages, suffering through their own stories of infidelity, marital spite and shaky reconciliation. I do not know it yet but when their white husbands disappear for weeks and months into wars and far-off work, virtually incommunicado, unencumbered by family, it is not just to field questions like: *What is the human condition, the state of the war, the future of this geopolitical region?* It is often to meet mistresses and lovers, the women they keep *on the side*.

I never hear the arguments in their bedrooms.

The daughters never really talk about it: how when our mothers fly into a rage, they really soar. How our lives are punctuated by explosions. Electric ire. Screaming fights. Eggshell-lined mornings. How we learn predictive watchfulness; in my case, memorizing the tight hold that distorts my mother's mouth right before she explodes, the pent-up look of a firestarter. How we sometimes hide under the kitchen table, gnawing on the wooden legs like beavers felling trees.

Our parents are not merely a protective canopy or a fixed and unchanging stage for our theatrical becoming. They are an evolving drama unto themselves. This discovery is both exciting and terrifying.

Over the years, I spot the trait of watchfulness in others, most notably in a documentary cinematographer who worked for the National Film Board of Canada, tracking subjects such as Igor Stravinsky and Glenn Gould with a camera so closely attuned it seemed to anticipate every flicker of movement, seemed to detect shifts of mood others would have overlooked as neutral. A friend who knows the story of this cinematographer's erratic childhood tells me his creative flinch, or "startle reflex"—which informed the innovative, close-tracking, leaping style of his camerawork—was established early in life when he learned to gain power through minute observation, through a mission of noticing.

NEWSPAPER

IN 1978, A TORONTO NEWSPAPER PUBLISHED A PROFILE OF my parents' marriage. My father and mother were quoted at length.

He said: "I soon found out that women from the Orient aren't as docile as Occidentals think. Mariko doesn't do any bowing or kowtowing. I've yet to find my slippers waiting for me at the door. I've never been known to tug my forelock to a boss, and neither does Mariko. She's her own person, very strong-minded, in some ways more independent than me."

She said: "I'm not one of those giggly Japanese maidens you see in old movies. And I'm not a stereotype Japanese wife, dominated by a husband who runs around with geisha girls. It would drive me up the wall just to be a stay-at-home waiting for Michael to come back from an assignment. I'm a businesswoman. I'm as committed to art as Michael is to journalism. We respect each other's individuality. We're learning to compromise and reconcile our differences."

Reading the article, I don't recognize all of my mother's words as her own (particularly the words "compromise" and "reconcile") but I recognize the general sentiment.

JUDGMENT

IN MY EARLY TWENTIES, AS MY PARENTS' MARRIAGE WAS collapsing, I knew a few married men who were unfaithful. I did not seek them out, consciously, but I had brief relationships with several of these people. I found myself outside the walls of monogamy, inviting chaos into my life. I became a scholar, analyzing appetites for unholy pleasure, observing the stupid things one might do when magnetized by an unavailable stranger's perfect jawline, cantilevered cheekbones or pianist-like fingers. Maybe I was trying to understand my father's adulterous behavior or drain myself of hatred for the women who had driven my mother "crazy." A fleeting investigation. Some actions cannot be easily explained or defended.

Programmed by all the movies I had ever seen and all the books I had ever read, I assumed an affair was about the thrill of transgression. What I came to understand was that sometimes love could be a spur. In one case, a man, who was much older than I was, loved his wife *too much* and suspected she loved someone else, had a grander passion, and his attempt to seduce me was his way of understanding her better. A way of "loss-proofing" his heart. Or maybe this is just a rationalization he devised, a story told by a Lothario about a couple pursuing their separate infidelities as a form of marital devotion. I didn't buy it at the time but a part of me was taking mental notes, building a theory of love *in extremis*.

PEOPLE TOLD ME they did it for the adventure or to let off steam. To renew or maintain a marriage. Because the affair was where they sorted themselves out, gained new insight and resolve. Because everyone did it. For the thrill. For the sex! For the boost! Out of boredom or stupidity. As an insurrection! "To call up a forgotten part of myself." To rebel against the strictures of coupled domesticity. Because they were impelled by a desire that refused to remain an obscure feeling. Because they were good compartmentalizers or had a quiet conscience. Because it was hard to dedicate yourself to love, singularly, for so long. And wasn't it possible to love more than one person at once? And weren't there things that a spouse, even a good one, could never provide?

I CONFESSED TO my father during a faltering period early in my own marriage. Things had become stagnant, and a person I thought I could love better wanted to run away with me. I told my father: I love this other person's beauty. I love their quietness and their attention and the way my life feels more fruitful and independent, less like my life and more like Agnès Varda's, when we're together. We were sitting in a coffee shop overlooking a busy intersection and I was looking for his supportive wisdom. He had recently encouraged me to make a choice in another area of my life that seemed, possibly, flagrantly unwise—forgoing secure employment for the greater security of creative independence. From this, I understood him to be, surely, *on my side*. When he responded to my confession with agitation and judgment, I was taken aback. Visibly distraught, he told me I had a responsibility to sit tight and wait out this bad patch. He told me, "We don't abandon a marriage at the first sign of trouble. *Don't even think about leaving.*"

I couldn't stop the short, unhappy laugh that came from my mouth. *That's rich, coming from you, a man who passed in and out of his marriage.* But for some reason I listened to his advice and things got better and my marriage lifted into a happier phase and we learned to care for each other's solitude and resolve conflict without bolting like gazelles. Restlessness still ran through me, but I was not finished loving my husband—I was just starting.

THE TRUTH IS I was never really asked to run away. It was a fantasy or lunacy the person and I briefly discussed, but we both knew the feelings we had for each other were a dangerous distraction. Even at the time, I knew it was a bad idea that wouldn't end well, but I wanted to see what my father would say. I wanted to connect with him and maybe tell him, *I think I understand you better now.*

MAYBE

ALL THOSE YEARS AGO WHEN I SAID TO MY FATHER, *I THINK I may be like you*, only to be met with his distressed reaction, maybe it wasn't his own "crooked" patterns he saw emerging from my heart.

If he imparted any supportive wisdom that day, it was this: We talk about marriage like it is something winnable, something we can tame into a fixed and faithful orbit, when really it involves a lot of failing and trying again. Marital love is extreme. It's stamina. A marriage with complications or doubt is not a fiasco. It is a marriage.

SEPARATION

MY MOTHER WAS NEVER A WOMAN WHO REMAINED SILENT.
When my father eventually announced he was leaving her, it
wasn't a surprise. But it was also not a surprise that my mother
refused to play the role of the scorned woman or deserted Asian
wife, refused to softly and silently sink into herself or fall apart
like a self-annihilating Cho-Cho San. Their separation was awful
and protracted.

There was Ma in the kitchen pitching plates against the wall,
performing a crashing symphony of crockery and saucepans as she
threw everything to the floor, etching a musical staff on my father's
arm with her nails. Slammed doors, shaking walls. There was Ma
calling everyone my father worked with, everyone who employed
him, shouting his misdeeds into the phone. There was Ma and the
restraining order. "She said she'd come after me with a knife," two
of my father's ex-lovers later told me.

This was not what could be called an appropriate or "right-
sized" reaction. But not everyone believes in reserve or forgiveness,
not everyone sees "avenging past betrayals" as a sign of a bad attitude. In the face of this volcano that was volatile sorrow, I was
unprepared. I felt it would never end.

During this period, my father's white colleagues and friends
said my mother was crazy and pitied my father for staying with
her as long as he had. She had never been viewed as his intellectual match, her "funny accent" proof she had failed to properly

assimilate, the "cultural chasm" proof of their shallow intimacy. But now she had crossed a line and become a "delusional," "belligerent" and "bitter" woman who was not entitled to her confident, energizing rage. I never thought to ask, *What do they know?* Or *What are the criteria for sanity?* Or, as Hanif Abdurraqib would later write: Who gets to decide at what "volume, tone, and tenor" non-white people enter the world "for praise or scolding"? I was eighteen and bottling up the shame of seeing my mother's pain converted into public spectacle and my mother into a monster. If I ever came apart, I vowed I would be a poised and unperturbable armadillo, rolling elegantly inward to hide the strength of my feelings and fears.

Only years later did I discover: we don't get to choose how we will become unmoored. Or "overwrought." That's the horror of it.

My mother was a brave and faulty person who let the wild heat of her temper fly against external and internal embargoes, who allowed hurt feelings to rise, unsuppressed. She had an inner life that white people, at least the more powerful ones she encountered, discounted because they could not really see her. To them, she was simply an "unrelatable" figure who had refused the role expected of her.

At my father's memorial, as I moved around in high hostess mode, talking to different people, a huddle of his old colleagues began discussing my family. *Oh boy, do we remember your mother.* Then there was a silence and it made them laugh. What were they remembering? I felt it, distinctly. I felt the legend of my mother. The myth of her rage. I could see they thought they knew the truth of her, just as they thought they knew the truth of me—a person they complimented for "speaking well" during my eulogy. Their laughter meant it was fun for them to remember. Once again, they reduced her story down to nothing. I remember backing away as a younger man who had been quietly listening threw me a quick embarrassed look. My mother was seated across the room. I felt her eyes on me. I felt her touch my sternum with her eyes and say: *See? We must be strong. It's good I got out, blowing the whole thing up as I left.*

Only later would I wonder how she would have behaved if she wasn't tasked with wifely forbearance, if she didn't have to brace herself for combat in a white world where interracial marriage was trumpeted as a romance of racism overcome, or endure the humiliation of being left by a man she had earlier tried to leave. How would she have related to love and gentleness and other normal things if she were not taught to be in a state of constant defense and secrecy?

During the long nights, through days and weeks, after my father left, my mother floated on an ocean of unhappiness, with no coastlines in sight. This was the flip side of volcanic anger. On weekends when I visited from university, I heard her lying awake, I heard the tiny wet sound of her eyes opening and closing like fish gills. Sometimes I'd find her lying across the double bed as though she had fallen from the sky and I'd pull a blanket up to cover her.

I tried to pour myself into studying, to quell my turbulent brain. But I belonged to her and she was my responsibility so I stayed to keep watch, even if I did so at an emotional distance, unable to fully admit her pain or loneliness.

Her oldest sister, who called from Japan every week, floated in the ocean with her, following the motion of my mother's thoughts and listening to the song of her regrets. Ma had stopped gardening after my father left, in the midst of her heart's gradual and painful descent, but my aunt told her not to be ridiculous. So she started again, making a small clearing in the aftermath, at a moment when beauty and pleasure were fighting to cut through.

Months after he left, my father came to sit in the garden. He was never completely free or happy at having left her. He had a strong sense of duty and was never rid of the guilt. In the end, although they never lived together again, my parents did not divorce or even truly separate.

What is a heart? My mother accuses me of not speaking my mother tongue but I know that in Japanese, there are three words for "heart": *shinzou*, which refers to the physical organ; *ha-to*, which is the anglicized word for a love heart; and *kokoro*, which means your metaphysical heart and soul.

What is a heart but a broken masterwork pieced together from desire, envy, regret, nostalgia, pity, tenderness and hope? What is a heart but a way of muscling your way onward? What is a heart but a fist?

I can still hear the repeated sound of her spade hammering the freshly turned earth. The garden unfolded her at a moment she could have closed in; it allowed her to keep going. It was different than the ones she had made before. This new garden was a place of surrender. It was beautiful, it was a wreck, like anything built on foundations of collapse that seeks to find what isn't collapse.

SOFT

MY MOTHER ALWAYS MADE ME QUESTION THE VALUE OF softness. She did not want me to be a quiet-shoed girl, one that no one could hear when I walked. She bought me big stomping boots so I would be trained for marching and armored for adversity. Impermeable. Untimid. To her, softness was another word for smiling submission, for accommodating others and therefore becoming a stranger to yourself. But I never thought of myself as that kind of soft. I was not the soft of muted good manners or bland taupe pandering.

I wish I could tell her, There is a brand of softness that is lethal and not in the slightest way meek; I have observed the softest people roar ferociously in the face of dubious and destructive ideas. It is a softness filled with pliancy and a desire to protect a space for anger and argument even as we get deeper in with one another. It is the non-docile softness of Louise Bourgeois as a child modeling figurines from warm French bread to house her imagination while escaping the bickering in her house. It is the canny softness of a stoic-faced mother gazing at a freshly made bed and slipping a difficult and worn-down day back under the covers. It is a softness that sees openness and vulnerability as ways of staying human in a hostile environment—because to be soft in an unyielding world is to resist incorporation and the harsh trudge of capital.

And sometimes softness is just a way of recognizing our multiple dependencies, putting the lie to self-sufficiency and showing thought for others; I offer it, a cushioned or shaded space of company, walls that are pillowed, because I need that give and suppleness too, because when we are too hard, we slowly bruise ourselves. From the inside.

When I consider how my mother was denied the relief and choice of softness I think back to her post-separation planting, that freshly turned earth. I can still hear her having courteous, cooing conversations with our cats, feeding them oily sardines one by one with her fingers or lifting her cupped and water-filled palms to their mouths—my mother, almost completely lacking in sentimentality except in the pliant and padded presence of animals who, yawning and stretching in beams of late-afternoon sunlight or watching leaves slowly fall on the stone path, stirred creaturely kindnesses and unspoken feelings from the deep well, a process I thought of as *cat-alyzing*, thereby causing me to think of our feline housemates as *cat-alysts*.

CONTRADICTORY THINGS

1. She remembered attracting other men but refraining from having any more love affairs and staying faithful to her marriage.
2. She remembered continuing to have many affairs. Many suitors. Serial lovers.
3. She remembered he was special. He said he had never met anyone more beautiful. He said he knew she was often alone, maybe lonely. He said if she were his wife, he would never leave her side. They would spend their lives together.

AWAKE

JEHOVAH'S WITNESSES BEGAN VISITING MY MOTHER REGU-
larly after my father left, as if alerted to the lonely wind that now
passed through her house. They arrived as a pair, a well-dressed
young man and woman, and left pamphlets with ombre skies and
paintings of the Kingdom of God. My mother in her gauzy
housecoat stopped pointing in the direction of her altar, explaining that she was Buddhist, and began inviting them in for tea.
She took the pamphlets the church people handed her with their
pictures of people communing with woodland animals and pic-
nicking on the tops of mountains. She fanned them out on the
table, told them she couldn't read them and asked them to show
her how. Believing they were bringing her to the faith, they stayed
and kept returning.

She studied the words about the Creator's promise and life in
Paradise for the anointed, worked through an article titled "Are we
living in the last days?," tracing letters until they assembled into
patterns she could quickly decipher. To them, her eagerness meant
the light of God was beginning to break into her heart. Sometimes she'd ask them to coach her through household paperwork,
improve her poor writing. Eventually, the church people realized
they were being played and stopped coming. She had exhausted
their inexhaustible missionary patience. That was fine with my
mother, who, while clearly not yet saved, now had the ladder to

literacy she needed. A place on the page, in her eyes, was as good as a place in the sky.

She kept gardening. Her older sister arrived from Japan with seeds: mitsuba, shiso, mizuna. My mother and her sister woke early every morning, when dew glistened on everything, and sat on damp camping chairs. They tapped the earth and listened to the seeds, stirring and cracking unseen, which said: Even in the smallest nothing of a moment, there may be a vivacious program.

My mother and her sister speed-talked and laughed in wild bursts without covering their mouths, laughed at how upset my mother had been to have no husband, as if that was something to truly want.

Older by eight years, my aunt had her own difficulties and secrets. She was second mistress to a Tokyo architect. As a child, I was often left with the daughter of the first mistress—a teenager named Miwako, a "love child," who, perhaps sensing a bond I had yet to discover, sent me home with Velvet Underground cassettes and, after I returned to Canada, continued to mail me mixed tapes of "meaningful music." Miwako's apartment was always nicely air-conditioned and full of freshly delivered flowers. At my aunt's house, we were always damp with humidity and flowerless, prompting my mother to tease: "It is better and cooler to be first mistress."

The seeds sprouted. The bent sprouts shrugged free from the dark soil, showing off their tiny seedcase hats. The rain fell and everything burst open. When her sister returned to Japan my mother registered for night classes at a nearby high school. She studied finance, bookkeeping, public speaking. And, then, with a surge of passion: landscape painting. At age fifty, she dedicated herself to basic survival crafts and, renouncing protections, began to rebuild her life.

It occurs to me now that when she grew food and seeded plants that helped her remember the home she had left, my mother was approaching the land as her own blank slate, without thought for the human, plant and animal nations that predated her arrival. Her garden of exile and renewal may have departed from the pastoral dreams of European settlers, but it was still botanically unsettling to cross oceans bringing small seeds of empire, living inside the dream of another country, another hemisphere. This is the "multiple truths" of it.

SIX:

SHŌSHO

(manageable heat)

AUGUST 25

THIS SAME SENSE OF SURVIVAL-CRAFT WAS WITH HER AS she underwent treatment for the cancerous lump. We were back at the hospital, where a woman with a squeaky trolley and broad Glaswegian accent handed out cookies and knitted hats, *just for you, love*, explaining that volunteers liked to make things for the patients in chemo. My mother eyeballed the woman, up and down. She hated being called "love." She was still recovering from her first surgery and had been scheduled for a second one. The cancer was in her lymph nodes. If her mind was frayed with tension or dread about the future, she never let on. She said no to the pamphlets and the offers of counseling, which, to her mind, belonged to a different culture, a younger generation. But, yes, she would like a knitted hat. She studied the hats professorially and decided the mauve one would be nice. After placing the hat and two packets of cookies in her purse, she fell silent, staring off into the air in a loose, preoccupied manner that had developed in her over the past few months or so.

In the waiting room, before meeting with the geriatric oncologist, I talked to my mother, moving slowly up and down the slopes of her thoughts. To put her at ease, I brought the cupfuls of cold water she requested, dousing whatever fire she imagined burning inside herself. Bullets of ice clattered from a dispenser.

❧

MY MOTHER FOUND out she was pregnant in the second year of her affair. It was August 1969. She asked her older sister for advice but received no clear guidance. She reached out to her childhood friend, who told her she would be there if she chose to terminate the pregnancy. But my mother was still unsure. So my mother touched her palms together and prayed at her altar. She asked Buddha for direction. She asked her female ancestors, who peered out beside incense and candles and a small stack of oranges. If Buddha was the bossy sort, she might have found an answer. But she left the butsudan knowing she would have to guide herself.

What did A. say when you told him about the pregnancy? I asked.

"He said he would marry me."

He proposed?

"I was scared. He was a playboy and much older, in his mid-fifties."

What did he say?

"I don't remember. I just remember I didn't want to hurt your father."

But what did he say?

She shook her head and tilted her chin up, kind of aloof. Her mouth was set in an unfamiliar line and I realized I was having trouble reading her. I was waiting for her to acknowledge that her memories meant something to me, to dig a bit deeper because she loved me and could see I was not at peace with the holes that riddled her story. I was trying to hide what I was really asking: Did he want me?

September 1969, she cabled my father, Michael, who was in Vietnam. She told him a baby was on the way. The telegraph operator misheard my mother so the message he received read: DAVY IS COMING. My father called home, wondering: Who is Davy?

And why is he coming? I don't know if or when she told him the child she was carrying wasn't his, but I imagine that after six years of trying to conceive, this would have been self-evident. I don't know if he was upset, or what he first said, but I know he had many things on his mind.

In early September 1969, ignoring a telegram from North Vietnam advising him not to come to the capital city purportedly *because of flooding*, my father arrived in Hanoi only to discover his arrival had coincided with Ho Chi Minh's death.

As the sole Western journalist present, he reported on the half a million mourners clad in white who queued for hours to see Ho lying in state, his head resting on a soft pillow. It was "a great river of people," said my father in his television report. The temperature hit 107 degrees and kept climbing. He continued traveling through the country, filming the impact of four years of US saturation bombing which the world had never seen. Journeying at night to hide from the bombing, along a route he described in a voice-over as "stitched from broken-down rock, thousands of loose planks and nerve-wracking bamboo platforms bridging the craters and canals," he arrived in the nearly flattened city of Nam Định. "Here for me was Picasso's Guernica in its senseless destruction."

In one of the most devastating scenes of aftermath I have ever seen, he visits orphans inhabiting a jagged and misshapen building adjacent to rice-lands. Three young boys lean against each other, staring at the camera with shy smiles. The moment is wavery. It flickers like heat over asphalt. My father—tall and skinny as a stick, forever ducking to avoid being concussed by doorframes— does not approach the orphans with his elongated arms but with his voice. He reaches out and lifts them up—not as a journalistic savior. He reaches out as a fellow orphan, who long ago saw his foster home destroyed in the Blitz, experiencing the terror of skies opening in battle as bombs and fire cratered his town. He reaches out with sadness and culpability: "What was done here is part of the record of Western civilization."

For weeks, the cratered landscape occupied my father's television reports, seen around the world. On a different day, with fewer real bombs, my mother's news might have landed differently. War is a seismic disturbance, one that made him feel at times helpless and underequipped but one that left a moral and emotional perspective. It is possible the news of a baby, even one by another man, would have felt minor, not even a tiny explosion.

By the time he returned to Hanoi, he knew he wanted to be a father, full of the best intentions and hopes. To mark the moment, he bought a handcrafted lacquer box, which he held on to until the eve of my wedding—the simple but loving ceremony of a father who always made me feel he had eyes on my future. For my mother, he bought a second box inlaid with a sarus crane, a tall soaring bird found in the Mekong Delta that would later be, for a time, doubted to have survived the war. The small hotel where he stayed had a little garden and early each morning, a custodian tended to the plants, dousing, pruning and harvesting. In the note he wrote to my mother, he described this garden as if to counter the idea that a war zone is only one thing.

The man, Michael, who is to me my real father, raised me, remaining with my mother until I was eighteen. My mother stayed with Michael, trusting that his affections might roam but would never move elsewhere entirely. This was the bet she made.

A. divorced and married again—another young Japanese woman. When the news reached her, how did my mother feel? Did she at any point see this collection of Japanese women as evidence that she was not singular but dismayingly interchangeable, repeatable, replaceable?

SITTING IN THE waiting room, she paused, long enough for me to think it was the end of the story, which it was. At least for now. I peeled her an orange and she began chewing on the sectioned fruit as juice dripped quickly onto her lap. I wanted to ask her more questions, but I stopped myself. I told her I was glad she had shared what she had and I would love to hear anything more that she remembered when she was ready, that I would find it helpful.

She looked at me funny, then said, "You know, Michael was really strange, but I miss him because he was always on time."

PRAM

SOME PEOPLE BELIEVE THAT SECRETS ARE A FORM OF deliberate and unforgivable duplicity, that dishonesty is not absolved by remaining undetected. But I don't believe the truth is available to everyone. It was available to my parents for a moment, when they were handed an "Application for a Certified Copy of An Entry in the Births Register"—perfectly blank—and then a door was closed and it stayed closed. Michael signed my birth certificate and declared me his daughter ("the particulars entered above are true to the best of my knowledge and belief"). With this form, with the hard-leaning signature I would come to know so well, he created a solid cover version of my story, erasing the first chapter.

I arrived in a congested ward at Princess Beatrice Hospital, originally built to provide care for the "sick and needy poor," and famously used as the ward where David recovers from a nasty wolf bite in the film *An American Werewolf in London.* The hospital had a small obstetrical unit overlooking a cemetery. My mother was on bed rest for ten days after giving birth. "Lying-in," a mandated postpartum confinement for first-time mothers, was still a standard NHS practice into the 1970s. Every night, I was trundled off to the nursery, fed by nurses in the early hours.

My mother consulted a fortune teller, who examined the shape of my head and peered into my eyes. Michael was called over to listen as the fortune teller endowed me with a good mind and other qualities a father might admire. "She will be clever," the fortune teller said, pointing to my lucky forehead.

Maybe this is the moment it starts: my mother will often need, when it comes to me, appealing prophecies, an outside appraisal. I will somehow always know to earn my keep.

❧

THERE IS A photo of her appearing worn out, standing in a garden near a pram containing her hard-won baby, just home from the hospital. A nanny from Lancashire bends over the pram. My mother stands a few feet away with her hands clasped behind her back, mulling it all over. In almost all the photos from this time, my mother has a glazed and separate look, eyes buggy with exhaustion. Or maybe this is the way all new mothers look when they haven't slept very well or are on the brink of being diagnosed with a postpartum thyroid condition that will require medical treatment for life: like they are ready to sidle away, like a baby meteor has just landed in their life.

I look at the photo. She looks at the pram. It is difficult not to read this photo as a summary.

A. gave my mother the blaze of romance, enticing panoramas—vastness. How did she feel in her small life when it was over? Did he remain in memory a distant oasis? Did she search for him at the casino? What did she see when she looked at me? What did my existence represent? What is the bond between mother and child in such a situation? Who took this picture?

I look at the pram photo and it is not there yet. The fits of fury. The tongue coated in venom. The emotional aftermath of our arguments and care failures. People who witness my mother's cruel and blistering directness do not understand how it is possible for me to fear her while also loving her to death; that this is the devotion that happens under pressure. Even though we seldom agree on anything, immigrant mothers and kids, we kind of stumble together, interlocked, contending very closely. I understand that when she looms up, becoming La Force, and when she deems me The Enemy, it is often when she feels the smallest to herself.

WE WERE SITTING in soft chairs beside the fish tank in the waiting room, staring into the O-breathing mouths of the small fish. We were in a tiny examination room and my mother was resting on a scroll of crinkly paper as we waited for the doctor to arrive. We were in the hospital food court wolfing down refrigerated maki as the woman beside us feverishly turned the pages of her clothbound prayer book. We were leafing through an old pile of magazines looking at Al Pacino's eyes and reading that sea lion mothers squeal uncannily when they watch their babies being eaten by killer whales.

UPON FURTHER QUESTIONING, my mother said my biological father may have met me once. A few minutes later, she changed her mind and said he may not have met me. Or he may have met me several times. He may have held me. In this way, she kept editing, enriching, deleting, offering always-transforming versions of the truth. I asked if she ever saw him again and she let me in on a secret: "Your two fathers began meeting now and then after you were born."

What? I said. Why?

"For drinks."

But why?

"We were broke."

So he gave Daddy money?

"No. A flat to stay in."

My father's gambling and impulsive spending sprees meant there was, at times, an often crushing lack of money, but I was a little flabbergasted by the idea of him spare-changing my other dad at a bar. All the details were juggling about. But the questions remained. When was the last time? Did my biological father depart or let her go out of love, selflessness, indifference? In the years that followed, did she notice qualities in her daughter, both favorable and negative, and think: *she must have absorbed that from him?*

⤝

FOUR AND A HALF years after my birth, my parents packed up their belongings to move to Canada. I remember leaving the garden in England: the old brick wall and the climbing vines. I remember the sunlight streaming across my mother's back as she bent over the flowerbeds one last time. The bleeding hearts bursting, the spent peony petals scattering. I remember families of clouds passing overhead and a ladybird hiking up my arm.

We settled in Tkaronto/Toronto, a place I would much later learn was ancestral Indigenous land. My parents buried their secret and my story many times over. They kept moving, pulling up stakes. It seemed there was nothing permanent in our lives. We lived in so many places; one person always on the cusp of leaving yet never able to pull away. The newness of a packing box, the constant starting over. I was seven, eight, nine, walking home to the wrong house, beginning to lose my bearings, lose track.

My father continued his habit of gambling until he was broke again and borrowing more money. His long work absences made me wonder about his existence and, when he returned, I would shadow him like a dragonfly, fastening myself to his trousered shins until he lifted me up, up, up, to the sky. Maybe it was all the moving that precipitated the gardens, that made my mother resemble that monk I would later meet at Eiheiji temple in Fukui, Japan, the one vigorously assuaging the earth with his bare hands. Maybe she understood that the dukkha of being so perennially unsettled was the nature of human existence. Or maybe she was reaching out her hands to touch something obscured.

For forty years, her secret stayed hidden.

So he gave you a flat to live in?

"No."

But you—

"No. It never happened . . ."

YARROW

AFTER HOURS SPENT AT THE HOSPITAL, I BROUGHT MY mother home to sit and work in the garden. We wanted the certainty of the ground now that the bottom had fallen out of things. My mother studied the soil; earth scored with deep, dark wrinkles. It hadn't rained for weeks but a passerby assured us that during a dry spell, roots prospect for moisture underground, poking around for pockets of gold. *Also*, she said, pointing to herself and to my mother, *look at our hair.* My mother's hair was a wild white nimbus, expanding in the humidity. *Rain is coming.* I chatted with the woman and eventually noticed my mother sucking her teeth and looking vaguely disgusted by my friendliness.

Sometimes I sensed she was relieved to have her story known and accepted. Today she said she was glad the secret was out, glad to see that I finally knew about my birth father. She also said, *I never would have told you.* What she really meant was: Now let's forget it.

When we first spoke of him, I thought I could summon her to tell me everything, that the secrets would tumble out in a disinhibited rush. I imagined us closer, all the occluded parts of ourselves dancing and twirling as freely as ravers. But since that first conversation, she had little more to say. We did what we always did in a bind. We sat and ate. Today it was *omusubi*, a quiet munch of rice and salty plum.

Water, my mother said when she finished her snack, pointing to a limp mound of yarrow, crouching to lift the droopy pink flowers with her arthritic fingers. Deftly, she pressed a bamboo stake into the ground a few inches away from the crown. She could not press down very hard and her fingers shook but she tied the plant to its support, raising the fallen, filigreed leaves, and went to get the hose.

BEAUTY

WE WANT TO STOP LOVING, WE ARE HOLLOW AND TIRED OF loving, how do we keep going? When her heart dimmed, the garden was a pilot light. When the house was too clouded with uneasy feelings and domestic expectations to stay inside for very long, the garden pulled her up and onwards. In the garden, she outfoxed her sadness, out-beautified her disgrace. She laid claim to her outsidedness.

She had always planted but after my parents' marriage ended, my mother became single-minded. Between work and night school, between cooking and cleaning, the woman at the center of the garden was no longer ornamental: she was working.

She didn't own an empire of botany books, use Latin names, steep herself in the romantic genre of gardening prose, or even feel particularly at home with the people who ran the nursery. She never even called herself a gardener. But I watched the way she handled the soil. Eased in, palms open. Tracking damp earth across her forehead. Sweat rolling off her. Her blue cotton dress fading in the sun.

What failed to grow under the influence of the house was able to thrive and prosper in the open air. She took off her fighting gloves. The soil, dark beneath her, seethed with bacteria and insects and all the strange tiny microbes which turned rotted things into more dirt and more plants. The soil was animate and loud, comforting and steadfast. My mother, never one for listening, listened. She heard the crackle of a beetle, the tiny whack of an ant, the choppy rhythm of wind passing through a bush. She loosened the boundary around herself. A tiny rumble saying *future* looped into the caverns of her ears.

In an interview with David Naimon, Alice Oswald says that when you listen to the living world, the interruption makes it difficult "to hold or prioritize human meaning over the meanings that are going on around." Oswald adds: "I love meaning, but I like to be interrupted before it gets too smug, I think."

THERE IS A photo taken the same year my mother began her final garden. 1991. It shows the activist and filmmaker Derek Jarman, who has just started his own sanctuary on the windswept shingles of Dungeness, one of the most salt-beaten places in England. He is crouched over the ground in a faded T-shirt and straw hat. In profile, he squints over a splash of red poppy, focused and maybe a little distracted by the wind whistling around his head. I see my mother in his deep concentration. I see the way she used to disappear, fade into her surroundings.

My mother's ruggedly beautiful garden was not planted on an isolated and inhospitable beach in sight of a looming nuclear power station, but she faced her own unwelcoming conditions as a gardener, trying to find succor in a place that quarreled with her belonging; holding ground under a disapproving gaze. The white neighborhood presented its own arid, desert-like terrain.

My mother's garden was mostly moss, stone, horsetail, shrubs with few flowering plants. Hardy survivors. There were bushes that looked like broom and a general sense of the dry and fibrously prehistoric. There were curious rock arrangements and a pebble river that one could imagine flowing all the way, unbroken, to Japan. Her lumpy, inventive landscape did not weave into the tapestry of English ornamental beds that surrounded us. There was no perfectly mowed lawn. No jaunty blooming borders fed by rotary sprinklers. While the Jewish family who shared our semi-detached house admired my mother's artistry, our other neighbor would patrol the perimeter, sporting a sun hat and connoisseurial attitude, can of iced tea in hand, shaking his head as if encountering a child mid-tantrum. *Shouldn't a Japanese garden be more . . . minimalist? Shouldn't it have good edges?* To unseeing eyes, to our neighbor with his perfect plot, my mother's garden was a Cretaceous heap of undisciplined shrubbery and strangely tattered leafage. Like my mother, it seemed to belong to another ecology altogether.

It is my experience that people who love the Zen garden of Ryōan-ji temple in Kyoto and the spare and soothing neutrality of Tadao Ando's architecture often have a certain angle on Japanese aesthetics, a certain expectation of Japanese people existing quietly and *becoming air*. In other words, what is meant by minimalism is often stylistically conservative; a tone of frictionless restraint that suggests we can transcend the chaos of ourselves and others. As an ethos, it failed to capture or captivate my irreverent mother, who never learned to fold paper the "Japanese way," did not move like "mist on a mountain pass," and always had a knotty relationship to such adjectives as "austere" and "subdued."

My mother did not wish to be a good cultural ambassador or an Elegant Japanese Lady. Immoderate in aesthetics and emotions, she brushed off her critics. "They don't appreciate this Gallery of Plants," she said, while wondering what fascinated them so much about their spring bulbs and new fencing.

Still, the white neighbors who regarded the plants in my mother's garden as "foreign," or even "non-native," were setting a vibe and it was less one of decolonial solidarity than *cordon sanitaire*. Which is to say the line between an "exotic," "imported" and "invasive" species is sometimes a matter of basic horticulture and sometimes a matter of simple xenophobia.

What is vibrant and desirable and what must be brought under control? Who decides?

As Robin Wall Kimmerer, the great Potawatomi elder and scientist, reminds us, there are "non-native" plants that have lived peacefully in the Americas, without infesting or invading habitats. Moss, flowers, dandelions, sorrel, plantain, clovers have existed without issue amongst Indigenous plant worlds. The questions Kimmerer poses of any settler are reminders that conquest is not the only route to survival: How can you be a naturalized, beneficial plant? How can you respect local ways? Who and what is here? What will be your terms of relation?

MY MOTHER PLANTED deep. Digging and grunting, heaving and patting. She turned and turned the dirt like a problem in her mind. She used the soil to numb what could not be mended and to interrupt a battle with the world. She planted when her mother died, she planted to eat, and she gave me this harvest of tenderness in little paper bags. She overturned conformities and rejected the conventionally pretty while showing me that if you looked closely there was weird beauty everywhere. In the creeping sedum and spurge. In a sprawl of common juniper.

As children and adolescents we often gravitate towards glittering surfaces and ornamented affection. I could not always see the beauty or care she showed me. I did not understand there was a species of love that was loose and gestural, that did not resemble typical patterns, that expressed itself through everyday service that tacitly nourished and fortified. I could not always hear her when she said, *You don't need to please*, or understand I could quit the mission: I did not have to please for the both of us.

But I would think of her a few years later, when I was in graduate school and encountered other first-generation, ESL and "minority" kids seeking to prove themselves and justify their parents' sacrifices through the possibility of recognition, the performance of intellectual excellence or the fulfillment of fortune-teller prophecies. The theater of adeptness woke me up to a pattern, but only after it broke me down. On the cusp of beginning my doctoral studies, I crashed. It was my mother who snipped the leash, took my hand and led me out of the cycle of shame and respectability, a cycle she had helped establish through her judgments. I didn't think I was trying to meet some external standard, just wrestling with meaning and self-approval in a more specific and personal way. It was my mother who led me, with her rough hands, to the Ministry of Rest; away from the model minority cage of being "exemplary" and "good," away from a certain fear-based obstacle course of institutional achievement. She held me in her arms tight and close for the first and only time. I felt her flood of baffled affection. The disorientation of intimacy. I wanted to be lovable. I wanted to be a rigorous thinker. I wanted to read Derrida and Deleuze without having to perform them. I wanted to know the difference between what I went for and what I really wanted. I had read so many books. My bones were overeducated, yet I was still unformed. Dropping out meant dropping in to activist and artist-run scenes that would be as vital to my intellectual development as the university.

Neither one of my parents finished high school. There were obvious downsides, but one result is that they discovered the movement of their minds without thought of permission, without an eye on a good grade. From them, I should have known: knowledge is a beautiful sideways and sometimes upward spiral, but a tower of appeasement will not feed you. Merit badges will teach compliance with preset paths but will not teach pathfinding.

❦

I WISH MY mother had met Derek Jarman. I can imagine them sharing thoughts on their preference for "shagginess" and their shared disdain for the overgroomed. They both veered toward an unstructured, untidy life. (Of my mother's "low maintenance" approach to housecleaning, my father once joked: "Soon we will be able to grow potatoes.")

I would like one day to join the cult and make a pilgrimage to Dungeness to visit Jarman's garden in person. I can picture the varying greens of sea kale, gorse and fennel. I've heard that it's like he "just walked out," that there is a sense of him still living there. There is no barrier to cross for visitors. No enclosure. Jarman's oft-quoted words from his beautiful book *Modern Nature*—"My garden's boundaries are the horizon"—are a reminder that some people find solace without fence or border. In fact, creating a garden that merges with the world may be the definition of solace.

I would like to travel back to my mother's last garden to watch the gray-green horsetail clack and wave in the wind and sun. I am startled by the degree to which I dismissed and overlooked it. In its final incarnation, the garden was a showstopper. It became for many visitors the strange gem of a changing and diversifying neighborhood.

When she finally left the house in 2003, the new homeowners tried to maintain the garden but eventually gave up and replaced it with grassy lawn. My mother moved into a small downtown apartment. Her new residence had a concrete balcony and was set among a cramped corridor of office buildings. Everything was vertical. She tried to grow plants and small trees in barrels filled with soil but the windy, sun-deprived balcony was ungardenable. In the end, the management removed the garden for exceeding weight restrictions. Yard tools—rake, shovel, clippers—sat in a pile by the door. She began a plot of houseplants.

I NEVER GAVE much thought to the gardens of my childhood. They did not fit the charming story I was used to hearing about white family farms, or sunny vegetable patches or grandparents passing on horticultural know-how like a permission slip.

I tend the soil for my sons now, to repeat her motions, her infinite actions, the choreography she still plays in her head. I go to ground to feel the quiet energy, the turning of the earth. In my mother's shadow, I am learning how love vacillates—telescoping between the domestic and the earth-encompassing, simultaneously so small and so big. Tending the soil of a small garden is not the same as urban greening or building a commons but my mother's garden, at a crucial moment, inserted her into a larger story of unfolding seasons, cyclical, non-capitalist time.

Every day that my mother knelt down to make her garden, some-one across the world and across time was doing the same, turning to plant abundance to momentarily forget what was meager or confining in their lives. Maybe they were new immigrants joining a community garden, created on thick claggy earth, as a grander act of nourishment, care, respite and self-determination. Maybe they were micro-gardening in a corner of a refugee camp, easing some of their mental anguish by putting down roots, blooming ingenious irrigation systems from water bottles filled with a mix of sand and water. Maybe they were inmates working the Rikers Island jail garden, discovering the wonders of leafy therapy. Maybe they were gardeners of collective incarceration, like the Japanese Americans who cut gardens into the scorched desert, arranging rocks and irrigating rows of vegetables to feed their families. Or maybe, across time, they were formerly enslaved men and women who escaped brutal plantations to build free independent communities, exchanging crop seeds and cuttings to create edible gardens (of taro, okra, beans, rice), the traces of which are said to still exist in the forested interior of Suriname.

Everywhere, the gardens asked, *How can love take root without a true home to ground it?* And all the small green shoots poking through the ground said, *Like this.*

WHEN MY HANDS are dirty, I slit the grime from beneath my nails with tiny tools. Lately, I want my sons to feel like the plants in my mother's garden. I want them to experience the feeling of being tended to, like a briefly touched petal or a gently righted shoot; the unfussy love of being well watered. *You don't need to please.* Lately, my hands are seldom free of dirt. I am passing along missives.

You don't need to please was my mother's way of saying, as Derek Jarman once did: "I have conducted my whole life without fitting in." They both showed that a garden could grow out of precisely that.

CLARITY

WHEN I WRITE ABOUT MY MOTHER I CAN FEEL THE ROOMS
of this story get mossy, vines rounding angles, microbes and fungi
crowding the ground. What seems straightforward reveals itself
to be circuitous and, ultimately, a mess. The questions I ask in
hopes of sorting through the disarray only seem to intensify it. My
mother can shape a garden in her mind, heave great boulders and
shrubs into a stable arrangement, but she cannot shape a story.

In the waiting room I was holding whatever she gave me, meager bits and pieces floating inside me without settling. I needed
a foundation of facts. The degree of my parents' dishonesty had
left me with low-level paranoia, the need to bring my eyes level
with others. The questions spun: *Did my biological father even
know of my existence? Did he walk away? Where was the truth?
Who built the secret?* I needed more from my mother. More memory and more effort to honestly remember together. I did not
feel she was trying with the tossed-out specificities she retracted
moments later.

I tried to transmit my wish for truth, clarity and chronology into
my mother's head by staring at her ear. My wish was met by a dis-
quisition on the moon. She spoke of its fullness. Its phases. She
tried to remember a Buddhist story about a finger pointing at the
moon . . . her sentences ended in ellipses.

Without wearing her out or letting her smell my fear, I was trying to gather everything that might be carried away by her cancer. It may have been an unfitting time to seek answers, but I hoped a new closeness would be born in the hospital, in this pressurized moment; that together we would be able to bring the past into the present and give shape to the forgotten. So far this had not been the case. Whenever we spoke a new story blossomed in her mouth like a bouquet. Every time this happened I held the bouquet with its open petals until the flowers burst apart, as though set off by a tiny grenade buried inside a bud.

Today, she looked at me with bemusement and impatience. What a funny girl. Look at you fixated, wrestling with yourself, nattering on like a talking machine about ancient history. "What's past is pasta," she said, smiling and closing her eyes for a nap. She found it difficult to stay awake, a side effect of Zometa infusions. From under a blanket, she said: "I wonder why you're not a more optimistic person?"

Ten minutes later she was wide awake again. So I picked up where we left off. *"It must have been fun driving around . . ."* It was tone that mattered. Calm. Casual. Disinterested. Optimistic! *"He said that? So what did you do then?"* I recognized a powerful desire in myself to re-enter her words, smooth things over, make particular passages and links clearer.

How difficult could it be to give a simple and consistent account, fully continuous, where certain episodes foretold others, where there was arc and meaning? And if chronology was a challenge—how hard was it to have a motherly idea of how much specificities ("he held you once") might matter, however faint and fallible their order?

I was about to give up for the day when my mother surprised me. She told me she didn't tell my father, Michael, that I wasn't his child until *after* I was born and he had already signed my birth certificate claiming me as his daughter.

But he knew he couldn't have kids, I say.

"That's true."

So he must have known you were hiding something.

(Silence)

Both of us were looking at a small television in the corner. Chagrin in the silence, in the wide ocean between truths. Was my father unaware of the circumstances surrounding my conception? Did he ever learn the truth?

My mother's face was blank and she was behaving like a Remote Lady, brushing past me just as she brushed past the woman offering her a dainty pink ribbon in the hospital lobby.

I gently pressed her to remember how her affair ended, knowing well enough that love, even love that happened yesterday, cannot be easily recalled. Details are lost or censored. The heart does not have a clear windowpane. Love is a hot, wet cocoon. Love is an obscure box trap.

Her answer to the question of when it ended came in sly segues and haphazard loop-de-loops that swirled into restaurant meals, poker games, local celebrities, an unrelated dream. A sentence set out only to be blown in another direction. Today's theme, apparently, was dining out. So: lipstick, the gift of an antique hand mirror, cigarettes, a plate of spiced chicken stew, delicious almond cookies, and a cute saxophonist playing in the corner.

The sentences, I realized, could really be placed in any order. Her smile, now the smile of a stoned stranger, told me it might be willfully disjointed.

IN THE FUTURE, any time I think I am a semi-patient or kind person, I will think back to these days of listening to my mother flounder, digress, lose the thread, while I sit wondering how long she can continue without something revealing or relevant being said. I will think of her wildly orbiting thoughts, her long and detailed reminiscence about meeting RAF officer Peter Townsend or King Hussein of Jordan. I will hear my voice and recognize that it is not patient and does not resemble kindness at all. It is the voice of an overeager loading-dock manager in the middle of shipping and receiving, shouting and waving their lollipop around.

HEART

BECAUSE THE CANCER WAS ON HER LEFT BREAST, THE RADI-ation oncologist told us they would have to take measures to protect her heart. There was a breathing pattern to learn. Twenty seconds of holding every time a new dose was administered. Then release. We went over it once, twice, many times. They told us that by expanding my mother's lungs with air, this breath-hold technique would shift my mother's heart away from the "danger zone" of radiation. There would be six weeks of daily treatments. If done properly she could reduce the amount of radiation to her heart by half, compared with breathing normally.

Before the first radiation session, we practiced at home and in the car. My mother passed the simulation. But on the day of her actual treatment, she could not hold each breath consistently; the transition from breathing to holding needed to be more defined. There needed to be a clear line between contraction and relaxation. The radiologists laid my mother down on her back and raised her arms above her head. The instructions were confusing and exhausting. She kept slipping up. The radiologists in the booth talked to her over a speaker. They used a laser as a visual cue. They rolled back and forth on their little stools and tried and tried but my mother failed to understand their directions and what was supposed to take twenty minutes took nearly two hours. Language was an issue and because of this, they explained, my mother's heart could not be properly protected. "I'm so sorry," the Asian nurse said with a quiet shrug, though it was clear even she found my mother a strain. "They tried their best. She really doesn't listen to instructions very well."

When pressed, they said they would try to shield her from exposure using another method, perhaps by adjusting the intensity of the radiation beams. In other words, adjustments were possible. We would need to practice indirection, but also be precise, when it came to my mother's heart.

MA

WHEN I WAS GROWING UP, MY MOTHER AND I WATCHED MY father on television, listening as he interviewed people for his weekly documentary series. He believed in the power of questions to make a story legible and practiced the values associated with good investigative journalism, pairing persistence with compassion. Sometimes the highest value of a question is to dig up truth and empower people with a sense of agency. I saw that a good question could coax intimacy, trust, even relief. But what I also learned from watching my father's reports was that there would always be a few people who flouted the terms of an interview, who saw the direct question as pushy and disrespectful.

For some people, there were no right questions. Sometimes questioning itself was a problem. In my mother's case, I was coming to understand that questions might yield a few more facts, but would get me no closer to understanding the heart of her story. In fact, my questions were distancing me further, forcing us to speak within uncomfortable transactional limits and roles.

Over the years, I had spoken to my students about the ethics of interviewing, warning against an extractive approach. I had espoused Trinh T. Minh-ha's idea of "speaking nearby," as opposed to speaking over our subjects by imposing a framework for our listening that stopped connections from developing organically or collaboratively. I had called upon Édouard Glissant's concept of the "right to opacity" as an alternative to the objectifying gaze. I had promoted obliquity as a way subjects might hide in plain sight and protect what was private.

And, yet, when it came to my mother, I had become an interrogative bully, training my camera and microphone on her. *What was it like the last time you were together? Was anyone else ever with you?* The questions were terrible because they were trying to close in on something, rather than open something up. Of course, a mother with secrets is hard to pin down in conversation. Yet, when I asked myself why I was so relentless and hectoring, why I tried to strip all ambiguity and mystery from her speech, causing her to be wary and tight-lipped in return, I knew it was not reportorial hunger that drove my questions. It was fear. It was because I had a perpetually alarmed feeling in my body. *If they lied about my paternity, what else did they lie about?* I wanted to see around corners and through walls. I never wanted to be surprised by a fact again.

One day while reading Robin Wall Kimmerer, it dawned on me that the problem with most questions was their forward nature. "It is rude," says Kimmerer, "to prod a sovereign being and ask: How come you're doing that? How come you're living that way? How come you're that color? How come you're that tall? How come you die in the winter?"

There are old arts of inquiring "that are courteous and delicate and don't demand information but instead search for it." Instead of approaching the world with prosecutorial zeal, the trick is to move circuitously. Instead of trying to make our way *toward* something, *through* something, we go to the ground, with delicacy and restraint, and listen.

Let's say we want to know how a particular species of moss responds to drought. Some people would take samples into the lab and drought-stress them, but that's pretty crude, in my opinion. If I want to know how water is important to moss, I'm going to go to wet places and be with the moss, and I'm going to go to dry places and be with the moss, and I'm going to discover whatever I can. I will say to the moss, "I'm not going to snatch you from your home and grind you up to learn your secrets. Instead I will sit at your feet and wait for you to tell me what I need to know." And I'll do so joyfully, appreciating the experience regardless of what data might come from it. A way of learning that's not destructive, that minimizes interference—that's my goal.

I tried better to listen in the weeks that followed; to be very deliberate and hear openly without anticipation, without the engine of my mind shifting my mother's words into my own predetermined pattern or needs, without hauling her back to a possibly painful time in her life. I had been behaving too much like a writer for whom writing was an exorcism, something I needed desperately and impatiently to complete before I could move on. It was time to think more like a wise gardener and see how far along this strange path we could travel.

Quickly, I realized I did not know how to listen to my mother speak on her own terms at all. This was a realization that made my spirit pause. The problem was not that I still kept wishing for her to fill in story gaps, driven by swells of curiosity and impatience and some notion that a finished story would organize my feelings and settle me. I did not know how to tune into the quieter melody of my mother; how to listen beyond what was plainly "said" for the underthings.

The filmmaker Hayao Miyazaki would call this quieter melody "*ma*." In Japanese, *ma* is the word for pause, interval or even emptiness. There is no direct translation, but the kanji characters that form the word show a sun peeking out in the space between two gates. In an interview with Roger Ebert, Miyazaki once illustrated the concept to Ebert by clapping. "The time in between my clapping is *ma*. If you just have non-stop action with no breathing space at all, it's just busyness. But if you take a moment, then the tension building in the film can grow into a wider dimension." According to Miyazaki, American movies with their frantic pace and obsession with plot are often afraid of that silence, that *ma*. Yet life is filled with empty spaces and details that aren't directly "useful" to the story but have their own emotional brio. That is what Miyazaki is always telling us with the lulls and quiet moments in his films. Two characters riding a train in stillness, silently watching a landscape at sunset or observing the slow performance of a spinning leaf remind us that dialogue is not the only way people talk.

I have always loved how Hayao Miyazaki does rain. How Terrence Malick does grass and Andrei Tarkovsky does wind. I love the lovingness toward the long image and the plotless moments when ground overtakes figure and, zooming out, we're suddenly allowed to see human drama in its proper proportions. Instead of every moment being dictated by the human story, this scaling up of the overlooked is a great reminder that we are, in fact, minuscule in the cosmic scheme of things, just one part and particle of a larger picture.

There is no real proxy to the moving, mute camera in written text. Silence must be declared through words that sometimes sit on the page with too much presence. Silence proclaims itself as "thick," "fleeting," "heavy" or "noisy." It is not the sinuous and indeterminate silence of film; a silence that can be subliminal and suggestive rather than stated. To appreciate filmic silence, imagine the nervous clatter of dishes or other quiet incidental sounds taking place outside a room while a family sits down for an awkward meal. Feel the emotional pressure and renderings that carry into wordless, unvocalized space.

Whether we call this a quieter melody or *ma*, it is powerful to feel the presence of what is not openly declared, what lies beyond persona's grip, the promise and possibilities on the outskirts of any story. If the gap, particularly the gap between self and other, is intrinsic to the story, it is possible something is lost when we fill it with supposition, chatter, conjecture, even artistic flourish. But what is it? What is lost when we dissolve a gap for the sake of smooth tale-telling?

Ma is frequently equated with "negative space." I have also seen it described nicely by Jerrold McGrath as a "free zone that allows for dissimilar things to co-exist." Likewise, it can refer to the distance between two fighters. In karate, knowing the safe or suitable distance (*"ai"*) between oneself and an opponent based on their reach is considered "understanding *ma-ai*."

One weekend, I sat with *ma* and did not ask a single question. I did not try to tug up my mother's memories by their pointed tips or forage her life. My mother and I watched several Miyazaki films together. Her favorite was *My Neighbor Totoro*. Maybe it was the way Miyazaki stopped to take in the view or how he made a character of trees, sky, insects, water. Maybe it was how he pointed to the ghosts living easily within daily life. Or maybe it was just all the flowers.

A garbage truck rudely shook us awake the next morning. Sun flooded the plant room where my mother had slept and where she now watered pots on the windowsill. The hedges in the garden sang a song that sounded like starling, that sounded like truce, and I briefly pictured two birds waging a lifelong battle to love each other better.

❧

LATER, WHILE WE waited for my mother's daily radiation treatment, sitting side by side on a slippery gray couch, my mother freewheeled through the day's topic: "Places I have visited." She laughed often.

Sitting beside my mother, the gap between us was at times simple and at times painfully full. I tried to experience it as one might a grassy field but I was not sure how to fix things if I had to minimize my feelings and swallow my thoughts. I could not get away from an image of the grass growing taller until we disappeared into yards of thick green.

❧

BUT MAYBE THAT grassland, inside our bodies and lives, was where we met up rather than separated. Maybe it was where we let the unknown in each other brush together in a windy surf. Four weeks into my mother's radiation treatment, there was a two-day reprieve over Labor Day, so we left the city and headed north for rolling hills and river valleys; tallgrass prairie and oak savanna. We stood on a moraine, in the wave zone of history. Around us were immense boulders and debris, left by the retreating ice sheets of an ancient glacier. Oaks and bones and rivers. The glacier had crushed this region. We were on the treaty territory of the Michi

Saagiig and Chippewa Nations. The air was filled with raspy crickets. Whistle and strum of wings.

We walked along an easy trail, a winding path fringed with bloomy stands of black-eyed Susan, echinacea and aster. The garden rolled without apparent edge. There were fat pods of milkweed everywhere, waiting to burst open with their seeded silk. A cool breeze shook a sunflower and the purple-blue flowers growing on twining vetch vines. I followed my mother who had brought her cane, walking slowly behind her, affirming her footfalls even when she wandered off trail, even when I was certain there was a more sensible, less constricted route. Her hand reached for mine when the path was uneven but she had an attitude of indomitability, moving in directions she was drawn to rather than follow routes recommended by any plan.

The path my mother had chosen was now fringed with chicory. Crooked stems exploded with light-blue flowers. In the distance, we saw an abandoned farm overtaken by a large meadow. We had been walking in silence for many happy minutes, the *ma* space in us gleaming like glitter, filled with boisterous birds. We are finally getting somewhere, I thought—all we needed was a full-circle path.

On the walk back to our car, the noise of a trillion questions filled my head. It was a condition, I realized. Until I cured myself of it, I would dig small holes in the garden, hollows in the dirt, rather than let the gaps swallow me up. I would dig to reach her. I would spend hours teasing out roots and nestling tiny lives into the ground like hair transplant follicles to forget myself with this simple, difficult work. But I would not forget. Many of the plants would stay thin and tiny, before expiring under a toxic black walnut tree.

A garden will tell you, rudely, when you've planted something in the wrong place. It will laugh at your rage for ordering things. It will upturn any earnest utopian impulse. But this was my detour from the narrow path of paper and ink. If you are at risk of floating away, it is hands in black soil that might anchor you, even if you have never been so bad at anything in your life. This is the work of staying attached to the earth. If you water a hole for long enough, narrative drowns.

SEVEN:

HAKURO

(white dew)

PLANT WITNESS

THERE'S A SIMPLE TRICK I LEARNED IN ART SCHOOL. IF YOU cut out the central figure of a painting, you immediately reinforce the background. Anything surrounding the white negated space will assume new significance. John Baldessari was famous for his cuts, reducing figures to silhouettes and flat outlines, inviting the eye to turn to the context for clues. The thing about this technique, as you will know if you've ever cut an ex-lover out of a group photo, is that banishing a person only emphasizes their power and presence. It is hard to ignore a scissored void. It jolts. The scene around the void becomes something else completely: a testament to deletion.

In 1966 or 1967, my mother began a lengthy affair with an older married man. She hooked up with him because she had a chance or fell in love. There was an accident, a decision, a capitulation, or a mutual passion. He was the love of her life or the enemy of her happiness or a momentary diversion. His disappearance from my mother's life was total. It was also, in all ways, fertile.

If you were a documentary filmmaker, you might try to reconstruct what happened by turning to photos and evidence from the archive. There might be stock footage to provide context. There might be interviews with witnesses and an authoritative voice-over, bringing what was out of focus into the realm of intelligibility. Gradually, the missing figure might emerge from shapeless static.

But how would you proceed if the photos and records were completely absent or erased? How, without falling, do you leap over a gaping space?

For the children of cutouts, the imageless void is a place of imagination and improvisation. To render visible, we must fabulate.

I begin by assembling existing pictures, but the image of a white man and an Asian woman received through the crates and circuits of 1960s mass culture is too heavily scripted, or kitsch, to stand in. So I take two separate photos and place them side by side. My biological father. My mother. It looks odd.

I draw them as white space, blinding light, blurred and blown out.

I scour photos of my mother for the shadows of unseen people, study the way the shadows fall, the aim of her smile. Following Baldessari, I try to imagine what streams around, between and through the missing figures. The air and atmosphere. It's full of content. The background is full of truth.

ONE DAY, my mother tells me about an eight-hundred-year-old banyan tree she saw while traveling with A. in Tangiers. A missing photo. "Me and the tree. We were both wearing white skirts," she says. When I ask what she means, she tells me the trunk was painted with white limewash to protect it from disease and sunburn. She then describes the tree with its aerial roots sprawling in many directions.

As she recounts the strolls they took through leafy foreign streets where there was little chance of running into anyone they knew, it occurs to me there *were* living witnesses. I imagine placing lapel microphones on the trees that lined their way. Green canopies stretching into the summer sky.

> ME: Please tell me what happened.
> TREES: We can't.
> ME: But you were there.
> TREES: We were busy.
> ME: But they stood right under you. *Please* tell me what you heard.

WE WITNESS TREES but the opposite is also true: they witness us. This witnessing is rarely simple and sometimes terrible. Think of Georges Didi-Huberman's attempt to interrogate the birch trees surrounding Auschwitz-Birkenau about what they might remember of his murdered family members. Think of the giant sequoias and knotted oaks that bore the "strange fruit" of American racial terrorism. Or the olive groves uprooted for the sake of a separation wall in the occupied Palestinian territories.

Often, plants and trees are not mere survivors of events, but also ongoing agents, burying or transforming the evidence and terrain. In the Demilitarized Zone (DMZ) of the Korean peninsula, an unexpected haven for wildlife has appeared over the past few decades. Unrestrained plants and vines engulf the land, swallowing fortified fences, land mines and listening posts. Undisturbed roots push into brick and chain link. Trees hide bullets they have absorbed beneath new layers of wood and bark. And vigorous lilacs and sweet briar mend the visible scars of craters.

THE GROUND OF our stories is rolling and alive. My mother has always known this. She once tried to describe to me a scene from *The Godfather: Part II*, a movie she has watched many times. It is the scene where nine-year-old Vito is in Don Ciccio's garden with his mother, who is pleading for his life, right before she is gunned down. What my mother remembered was all the flowers and palm trees asserting themselves. *Such a beautiful, normal day and then . . . bang!* When I later re-watched the film, I saw something else she had noticed: how much the cactus in Ciccio's garden grows from Vito's first visit to the moment he comes back years later to avenge his family.

OBSESSED, INFATUATED, I begin researching plants that grew in the places where A. and my mother visited. I want to touch a past that is otherwise beyond my reach. What was growing that season? I study the plants that bloom on the flat land of Tangiers and the hilly land of northern France. I picture the twisted rosebush branches and towering sunflowers, the geranium boxes and the rhododendron. I see the moon and a line of black cypress. I picture a profusion of lavender in their midst. It's a world of heady fragrance. I convince myself they sat under every kind of tree— black walnut, fig, cherry, pear, cedar, apple, apricot. I conjure their world from an arboreal perspective—peering into their windows, overlooking their al fresco dinners, the dissolve of bodies on a mattress, following their car as it moves cinematically through a loose and romantic fog.

I see it vividly through the filter of my mind's eye, the time they spent together, their ways of walking and sitting. In my reconstruction, I feel the light, shadow, temperature and sounds, that changed the ways they moved, thought, felt. I build evidence of a relationship deliberately kept from sight, knowing that this is what they wanted: to roll through in a wild rush, unseen. My amorous and amorphous father begins to feel more real.

To imagine my parents' story in plant time is to consider what happens when we're not here. How quickly we become blip and obscurity in the living world. How minuscule the fate of individual human activity, how swiftly we dissolve into the shadows of the trees, our imprints lost in the whispering grass, our stories just pale traces in the story of the wide world.

Here is one last image, found among my mother's other photos. A picture with no one in it, that could actually have everything in it.

TREES: SATISFIED?
   ME: Yes. Thank you, trees.

GIVERNY

IN HER EARLY FIFTIES, AFTER HER HUSBAND LEFT AND when she felt at the edge of the earth, about to fall off, my mother traveled to Giverny. She wanted to see the inspiration for Claude Monet's *Nymphéas*. To say that these were challenging days for my mother would be an understatement. A marriage is a counterweight, and while she had never been compliantly or happily married, it was frightening to her, unimaginable, to suddenly spring forth into the world. This was not the future she had expected for herself or the tale she had inhabited for decades. She decided, impulsively, to use some of her savings to go to Giverny at the very moment she was being asked to forge a completely new life, to assume another form.

Monet's work became an obsession; his loose, almost abstract paintings of lily pads grabbed hold of her. I have spent most of my life wondering why people love what and whom they do, why we fasten onto certain others. To me, Monet's paintings had always seemed too pretty, exuding an air of powdery sweetness that reminded me of Yardley soap. As a child, toted along on museum pilgrimages, I preferred the heavy lines and geometrical shapes of Joan Miró and Paul Klee. I didn't understand my mother's washy tastes, her appetite for dissolving and sparkling landscapes. All that echoing light. There was no center to these swirling and frothing paintings! Any time I tried to find a place to focus, my eyes were drawn everywhere around. But maybe that was the point and a clue to the effect they had on her. Here was art you could disappear inside. Here was a place to lose yourself, a place to gaze rather than be gazed upon. Of course, I am speculating. No one teaches you to see through your mother's eyes.

For my mother, it wasn't just Monet. She loved J. M. W. Turner for his watercolor sketches of the sea. Shiko Munakata for his trees. Joan Mitchell for her sunflowers. What entranced her were paintings that tossed the viewer into a big absorbing picture space where the world became less solid, more atmospheric. The artists she most admired seemed to share a common understanding: it isn't always easy to set down what you see or say what you mean. I found it almost unbearable as a child not to know what I was looking at but if I said so, she would simply reply: *It's paint.*

Monet moved to Giverny, forty-five miles outside Paris, in 1883, at the exact midpoint of his life. He had been looking for a place that combined water, field and light. He immediately set about gardening, planting weeping willows by the water and, of course, water lilies in the pond. He arrayed the garden with pink roses, red geraniums, deep-purple pansies, impatiens, lavender and peonies. In an area where people cultivated land for food and not for apparent pleasure, Monet's horticultural choices were regarded with suspicion.

When my mother arrived at Giverny, it was a late-August afternoon; clouds were moving in. Her small tour group was rushed directly inside to see the water lilies before the garden closed for the day. My mother took a slow walk by the lily pond. In the summer sun, the pond was a simple reflective blue. Then the sky darkened—a cloud passed in front of the sun—and the pond and the lilies trembled and changed.

Monet's eyesight began to fail not long after he moved to Giverny. Cloudy with cataracts, his eyes would approach blindness in his later years. By 1922, when he looked at the pond he would describe it as seeing "through a fog." It became "more vast and chartless the closer [Monet's] gaze approached," writes the art historian Kirk Varnedoe.

My mother stood in the spitting rain, the prickled pond now the purple-gray of irises. She was prepared to stay by her marriage, just as Monet had stood by that pond growing a wild white beard to his knees, returning to the same subject over and over. She was prepared to stay in that tempestuous, tender, painful, destabilizing relationship, a union built on loyalty that defied reason, until the end of her days. Then it disintegrated and the world became less solid, more wavering.

My mother stood by the pond as the rain fell faster—soft speedy droplets. She stood where the artist had painted his famous *Nymphéas*, paintings that tried and tried again, capturing the nature of light vaporizing form and narrative. Monet worked on the water lilies as World War I flared around him, as the sound of artillery erupted in the distance and his son and stepson were sent to the front to fight for France.

Monet's paintings, which conveyed a painter's decomposing reality, were derided by some, including Paul Cézanne, for their insufficient and formless sense of structure. For other critics, the structure was there even if it was not painted or expressed directly. It was present in the mood of softness bordered by solidity, in a view of a world edged by turbulence, in brushstrokes that registered perceptual upheaval, a canvas recording forces and feelings beyond pure light and weather. A man turns inward while feeling the storm at his back.

My mother walked around Giverny. This was how she chose to mark her independence.

To what do we commit ourselves and for how long? Monet painted the *Nymphéas* two hundred and forty-seven times. "It took me some time to understand my water lilies," he wrote. The older I get the more I understand this impulse toward reduction and repetition; the more I understand there is infinitude in a spartan focus, in Agnes Martin's geometries, in Giorgio Morandi's vases. Focalizing can be regenerative even for those of us who believe the sprawling clamor of the world demands our promiscuous attention.

Two hundred and forty-seven times. A marriage may have as many incarnations, some more satisfying, some more frustrating than others. Love can be revised and resurrected after a long dormancy. It is possible, when a couple finally collapses, to grieve the better incarnations that are also dissolved.

There is a photograph of Derek Jarman by the pond at Giverny, standing on the small, arched Japanese bridge against a blooming bank of wisteria. Jarman visited many famous gardens, but this was to be his final excursion before his death from AIDS complications in 1994. Like Monet, his sight was failing, and perhaps this deepened the bond he felt with the earlier artist. In his book *Smiling in Slow Motion*, Jarman describes Giverny as a "delight" and "the shaggiest garden in the world," surely a compliment for a place tended by ten full-time gardeners and coming from an artist-plantsman who celebrated shagginess as coup against the monotony of too much human agency. ("If a garden isn't shaggy, forget it.")

Giverny is a garden that verges in areas on Orientalist kitsch. Jarman was called there just as my mother was called there, as if summoned by a courtesy phone. They had no adjoining or mutual story but they shared an eagerness to stand by a lily pond. Perhaps Giverny is where you go when you need a measure of hope or are trying to make a transformation endurable. Maybe it is a place to mark death—whether the demise of a marriage, the passing of a life stage, or a more literal ending. Joan Mitchell was "trying to get out of a violent phase and into something else," she said in 1964, a few years before moving to Vétheuil, just up the hill from Monet's house.

The visitors were told they had twenty more minutes. The rain was now a light drizzle, the pond cloaked in wet floating mist. My mother chose to spend her last moment by the bamboo grove, which she felt was all the more special because it was an area of the garden Monet never painted. Then she shook drops from her sleeves, went to the gift shop and bought a single blue-and-yellow dinner plate and a fridge magnet. When she returned from Giverny, after she had stood on the Japanese bridge, looking upon the wisteria and water lilies, she allowed her life to become abundant and untamed. The shagginess of Monet's garden was so different from the paintings. Time had made it so.

Monet once said, "For me, it is only the surrounding atmosphere which gives subjects their true value." I would like to be a writer who, if I cannot convey things in themselves, captures the air as it touches the world. If I cannot tell my mother's story, I want to tell her atmosphere.

❦

MANY YEARS AFTER my mother visited Monet's garden, I return to it through Ja'Tovia Gary's short film *Giverny I (Négresse Impériale)*. Shot in the summer of 2016, the film shows Gary, a young Black woman in a brightly colored dress, blending into the vibrant flowers and lush foliage of Giverny. In an early scene she is a reclining nude against a flattering backdrop. Her presence in this oasis is interrupted by images of Black men killed by the state—including a video recording taken by Diamond Reynolds immediately after her boyfriend Philando Castile was killed by a police officer in Minnesota on July 6, 2016. At a later moment, footage of Monet painting in his garden is juxtaposed with a speech by the slain Black Panther Party leader Fred Hampton while a remix of Louis Armstrong's *La Vie en Rose* (1950) plays.

What kind of privilege is it to sit in a quiet garden, painting water lilies, surrounded by blooming flowers, while the world burns? What kind of necessity? The questions go unanswered or are unanswerable, but Gary does not spare herself from scrutiny.

At the heart of the film is footage of Gary running through the greenery and screaming in resistance while standing on the Japanese bridge, the bridge my mother once crossed. Gary traveled to France for an artist residency and stood in that same spot by Monet's pond.

"There are moments of deep vulnerability," Gary said of her conflicted time in Giverny, a place built on the lavish illusion of retreat and innocence. "The environment as a whole was a really unique experience that forced me to reckon with my body and identity as a woman, as a Black person, but also as an artist."

SEPTEMBER 9

IT HAD BEEN THREE MONTHS SINCE I DISCOVERED THAT A Jewish racecar driver was my father. To receive a new father so deep into life is a bit like being born again. So, I was a baby. But in caring for my mother, I was also tasked with being very adult. So, I was both very young and very old—an ancient infant. At the hospital I could hear the receptionist opening and closing drawers. Somewhere a hammer was hammering. A rolling chair creaked beneath a long metal desk. A cleaner went back and forth with a spritz bottle. Footsteps receded, a door closed, a laugh behind the door.

Today, the volunteer circling with the juice and cookie trolley was an Asian woman, very tender with my mum, almost saintly. She offered her a sparkly beanie to glamorize her head. She said to me, "There was a time when we were small and our mothers were large and strong. Now . . ." She drew a huge moon in the air with her arms. "Full circle of caregiving."

Few people are as willing to engage with strangers as my mother. If friendship is a marathon, she prefers sprints of infatuation. Today, she left me and sidled up to a woman of her age seated alone in a corner, bald and barefaced with the exception of a black winged line drawn dramatically on each eyelid. Soon the woman was enraptured and they were laughing and exchanging banter with a younger man who moments earlier was sullenly thumbing the crucifix around his neck. "What's so funny?" I asked with a smile. They giggled more.

"Oh wow, your mother!" said the woman, a few minutes later. "What a marvelous girl!"

Sometimes I eavesdropped on her waiting room conversations. No one seemed to mind her opening gambit: *"What's your problem?"*

Pancreatic cancer.

Leukemia.

Brain cancer.

The women she approached seemed mostly relieved to have someone interested in them or their states, eager to shake any private sense of illness away from their skin. They talked of "back home" and shared tips on how to treat skin scarred and blistered by radiation. My mother handed out Kleenexes from her purse. She was, in these brief moments, a vivacious listener and natural consoler, nodding thoughtfully. Her usual combativeness dissolved into a shy sense of reciprocity. She was a vigilante, eager to protect others. I could see she was worried about the women, worried for herself, worried about the whole waiting room.

The mother in my head, the one rebuffing her offspring's intimate questions, was different from the open and ardent person offering her seatmates cinnamon chewing gum and bottomless care.

UNTOWARD

THE CANCER TREATMENTS SHE HAD BEEN RECEIVING, WHICH
had included six weeks of radiation, were winding down. The doctors and technicians had done what they could to stop the seeds
of my mother's cancer from proliferating. But today a geriatric
oncologist tugged my elbow and drew me to her side. She wanted
to speak with me, privately, while my mother remained in the
waiting room.

There were two residents already in her office, one seated and
the other standing. After a few preliminaries, the doctor asked if
I had noticed any changes in my mother's memory. *Anything
untoward?* As she tilted her head sympathetically, I thought of the
time after my mother's first surgery when she left the door open
to her hospital room, waiting for her daughter to arrive; how she
looked at me and said "hi, daughter" as I entered and introduced
me to her roommate—before telling me to leave the door open for
her daughter.

"No, not really," I said.

The doctor exchanged a quick look with the residents and then
asked if there had been any notable "incidents of forgetting."

I thought of recent conversations with my mother, the ones
that looped along a track in a slow but hypnotizing circle like an
airport luggage carousel; how the luggage we wanted was seldom
on this track.

"No. I mean, not more than usual," I said, with a laugh.

My laugh was not echoed. The standing resident looked down and shifted his weight from one foot to the other and back again.

I explained that she had always had an unreliable and elusive memory. She was not an organized person. "There have always been a lot of things she can't keep track of."

I thought of the recent looseness with detail I had chosen to see as her new conversational style; her powerful genius in dodging a question; the cognitive acrobatics. I thought of her fridge, chaotically filled with bricks of Dubliner cheese and containers of desiccated bean salad that rattled like maracas. I did not want to list all the leaks. Or mention all the things that had been filed in the wrong place. I wanted to show them her hands and how they still knew what to do; all the painting, knitting and planting she did without apparent effort.

"So, no incidents of forgetting?"

Yes. No. Yes. No. Yes.

I was about to say no, then changed my mind. "Well, sometimes she forgets to lie."

The room fell quiet as I mentally flicked through images of my father in the last few years of his life. I wanted them to know the culprit of her memory loss could not be too serious because my father had suffered from vascular dementia—an insidious disease that gradually erased his memory and language, leaving him shipwrecked in the middle of thoughts and sentences—and I had resolved not to travel to the center of that ocean again. Also, could they not see my mother was indestructible? I repeated her surgeon's theory that it was possible there was some lingering delirium from the general anesthetic, that the second operation might have set her mind a bit off, distorting her sense of time, but the surgeon had been confident that any confusion would resolve soon. A muscular sense of worry filled my limbs as I spoke.

What I didn't say was that I suspected I was responsible for her recent unspooling. By unearthing her story, I had created a disturbance, called in the ghosts. Willfully or not, sometimes a wire is tripped that tells us to forget; that tells us it's better not to examine the past, especially if you don't have a way to manage what comes up.

They read my face and stopped asking questions. The resident who had been taking notes put down her chipped clipboard. The other resident delicately suggested a CT scan and a test at the memory clinic—"We'll put her on the wait-list, just to be sure." The doctor agreed it was a good idea and told me her own mother in Cairo was having similar struggles. "We are sometimes unable to see that we're already at sea, it happens so gradually." I nodded at her ominous words and offered my gratitude and sympathy. They all offered me a handshake at the end of the appointment.

When I returned to the waiting room, my mother was sitting with a woman in a blue ripstop jumpsuit. The woman looked enrapt. A parachutist, possibly.

❦

WHEN I RETURNED home, I could smell the garden beginning to turn and ferment. Inside the house, the plants now occupied every available window. I carried the tropical ones to the bathroom and turned on a hot shower to conjure their equatorial memories. I sat on a footstool surrounded by pots as the mirror steamed and tears began to fall. The steam was soothing. I understood something even as I knew I was late in doing so. It had something to do with our assumptions about truth and healing, about secret-keeping and release, all those clichés that map one's way back from grief, that imagine doors opening onto crisp clarity. Who does not dream of emerging from a difficult transition feeling as clear as cold rain, restored by new insight? The crying was my body saying to me it had seen the future coming and it did not like the look of it.

My husband returned home and I walked into his studio covered in thin, clammy mist. If I stepped any closer, moisture would collect on his glasses and we would dissolve in the land of "no clear story."

EIGHT:

KANRO

(cold dew)

NIGHT GARDEN

IN THE NIGHT GARDEN, MY YOUNGER SON JOINS ME, THE
one who has always been nocturnal, who lives in the greens of his
mind. He dreams of a laid-back Eden as we slowly convert the
lawn into a pollen-heavy garden, all bait and enticement. He
plants milkweed, coneflower and catmint under the inky blue sky.
I watch him work, dumping soil and barely making a sound.
When he cuts into the ground with the shovel it goes in cleanly.
When he smashes the soil flat it is with soft, even smacks. We
aim by feel. Our garden is only a sliver of city-owned land, but at
night we get lost in it.

In the night garden, we meet the strollers. The romantic, the homeless, the dog-besotted, the stoned, the bored. One woman waits
for the dark to slowly rise, then rattles through our trash bin and
offers morsels of advice. A glow of skin, flash of white marking a
smile. A longtime resident on the street stops to remark on a pre-
vious owner's orange lilies, causing us to consider the parade of
tenants that have passed through, leaving behind wishes and traces
deep in the soil. To grow something is to consider what will still
be here long after you have moved on but also to touch the history
of what was here before. We dig deeper and find a flattened pop
can, a Spanish coin, toys and plastic pegs, a chocolate bar wrapper,
the tiny bones of a bird, a cosmos of channeling creatures.
Suddenly the night feels full of ghosts and possible unburyings.

The neighborhood cats are very hepped up. There is a ginger one that swirls around our legs like high tide, possibly spurred by the full moon. A moon can change everything, pulling moisture upward in the earth itself. When we water the sweet woodruff, the flowers shine like tiny stars.

The day gardeners cannot understand the allure. What are we doing? How do we manage after the sun has set? Are there sensors in our gloves? *Yes*, we say. *There are.* What we don't say: at night we can hide our lack of method. Our mistakes. We can plant questions in the soil where they bloom into a very skinny gingko tree and then a patch of wild bergamot and tufts of little bluestem, which encircle the house. At night, we can scatter the day's confusions and worries and hear them all go to seed. We can send a photo of a glowingly blurred limelight hydrangea to a new half brother to prove we are not loveless strangers and have him write back, wishing us *Shana Tova um'tukah!*

When you walk through a garden at night, says Alice Oswald, "the plants come right up to the edges of their names, and then beyond them."

SECRETING

WHAT WAS THAT DRIPPING NOISE? WAS IT THE SOUND OF the secret secreting? Could I crawl down to its source? Was the worry about my mother's memory why I was sleeping poorly, why I dreamt when I did sleep that we were trying to lift an enormous sculpture onto a loading pallet? Who made this bulging sculpture with its gaping hole? Barbara Hepworth? Should I consult an art historian or a therapist? Would I rest better if I stopped sleeping with my head facing north, as my mother was always suggesting?

I read a study co-written by four psychologists about how secrets may be experienced as physical burdens. "People have this curious way of talking about secrets as laying them down," writes the lead researcher, Michael Slepian. According to the study's "burden-someness index," the weight of a secret is not just metaphorical. When people are preoccupied with an important secret they tend to perceive distances to be farther, hills to be steeper, and generally see physical tasks as requiring more effort.

I imagine my mother carrying her secret on her back, like a baby wolf in a cloth *onbuhimo*. Over time, it grows bigger, altering her gait, causing her to slouch. It is a lot of work. Her stooped shuffle says: a secret is not a one-time load, adjustments have to be made as time goes by, one may need to build a stronger frame.

The question I ask myself a thousand times over: *Why?* Why did my parents decide to keep carrying this burden? Why did they continue to mislead me?

DEAR PARENTS

I WOULD LIKE TO KNOW IF IT WAS BECAUSE YOU WERE PART of the "hiding things" generation, children of the 1940s and 1950s who were taught to withhold information—cancers, addictions, crimes, affairs, illegitimate children—and practice compulsory amnesia for life?

Was it because the moment when it felt "right" to tell the truth passed too quickly? You could have told me at age five, when I was least introspective; at age eleven, when I was old enough to understand but my identity was still pretty much up for grabs. You could have presented the information at many points during my childhood, but maybe you were distracted or nervous so you didn't and then, suddenly, it was too late to share the truth in a factual, non-emotional, unthreatening way. Is this what happened?

Dear parents, I know you are not the first to hide something immense. Cai Chongda writes of growing up in a rural fishing village in Fujian Province with parents who tried to hide the ocean from him. The ocean! They were afraid Cai would run into the water and that something bad would happen. "They had their own pain, and they wanted to shelter me, out of love. When I heard the ocean crashing in the distance, I always assumed it was just the wind. When I smelled the salt air blowing in from the coast, I always assumed it was coming from the fertilizer plant. But the ocean rose and fell without me, and it kept shining, and it kept calling to me."

Dear parents, was it because you forgot you can't hide the ocean? Did you forget that when an ocean is hidden there is a risk a child will grow up "fanatically devoted" to the sea and all that was hidden, all that was unceasingly rising and falling?

Dear parents, was it because of the rope? Do you know of the two performance artists (Linda Montano and Tehching Hsieh) who spent a year tied together at the waist by an eight-foot rope without touching? I ask, because you, in your own way, did that for almost fifty years, bound yourselves to each other with a secret, twenty-four hours a day. Conjoined this way, did you channel your differences into performance art, forming an unusual and creative dependence?

Was it because you feared gossip? The loaded smiles of those who would have spoken about you, not in your hearing? Was it out of habit (like smoking and gambling, which you also did)?

Was it because you had the secrecy bug? I remember you making unnecessary secrets of so many things. Eventually the secret would come out and I would think: *What was the point of keeping that under wraps?!* I remember you kept the death of my favorite Japanese uncle from me for two years, only telling me on the eve of my departure for Tokyo. ("By the way, best not to mention J.-san . . .")

Was it because the "burdensome index" does not account for people who train their minds not to wander back to the secret? Because through ongoing suppression there may come a point of unknowing?

Was it because *memory makes what it needs to make* (Anne Carson)?

Dear parents, I would like to know: Was it because you always liked wearing jackets with inside pockets?

Or was it because a secret can feel erotic—and not just like betrayal—as it passes through the body, building pressure to escape?

Was it because you could not predict what damage might occur when the truth was released like a meltwater river? Or how it might overrun our lives?

Dear parents, I am no longer certain about the world—its seasons and facts, its rules and goodwill. I do not trust my feelings because I am filled with both too much and nothing at all.

Dear parents, I have told only my closest friends about this secret. A feeling of dissociation and emotional emptiness moved through me when I repeated what I knew. Stories are carried in the body and edited each time they are shared aloud. Some stories may seem soft on the outside but have an inner wall. The version I told sounded rehearsed, like it was being spoken by a smooth and suave proxy. It was a story that seemed eager to be hospitable and not appear unhinged. I did not believe in the coherent face it was selling. I felt I was now in another country from the people I loved, and we were speaking on tin-can phones across an ocean.

My closest friends looked at me with worried eyes as I smooth-talked. They did not buy the story either. Or my deluded hospitality. Their worried eyes said: *Just stop it.*

The hospitality of a story is not about *hygge*. It is not about fluffing yourself up or restaging life events for resale. *Stop it*, their worried eyes said. *Stop treating us like we are your audience or your readers. We are here for you and your heart, not for the reassurance or entertainment of a story.*

Okay, I'll stop it.

Dear parents, when I told another friend about my discovery, he said, "Is this why you married a Jewish man? Why you've had other Jewish . . ." I stopped him before he could continue. He was speaking of the pull of lineage, an inborn impulse we have to love our own or at least those we have been taught to think of as our own. He was speaking of ancestry's signature on our hearts and desires. Its atavistic flame. My friend is not Jewish. He was raised by mixed-race parents. His last three lovers have been East Asian. I lift my eyebrow, to remind him: we are not interested in the ethnonationalism or kinship of sameness that DNA promises us.

But maybe all he was saying was: we are composed of what we have forgotten, too: unconscious and embodied memories.

Dear parents, the deep knowledge you tried to bury and erase still managed to leave something behind.

HIDING

"OUR FATHER WAS A VERY PRIVATE MAN," MY HALF BROTHERS
had both repeated to me. They told me he would shake off any
questions to do with his past. I pictured an affable man but a man
who did not pull his weight in social situations. A man who did
not believe in sharing nuggets of family lore. A man who smiled
serenely while filtering out questions. Neither of them knew
whether he had always been this way or whether he became more
discreet and cautious over time. His omissions were presented as
the mark of a modest, even delicate person.

I wondered if he confided in anyone about me or whether I
was kept completely secret, to protect his family but also himself
from the consequence of his affair. My older half brother, D.,
suspected there were other secret relationships and admitted no
one could confirm for certain how many children there were. The
last child we knew of, our half brother born in 1981, was raised in
the Algarve, where our father lived until his death in 2002, all but
disappearing from his former British life.

What else had he disavowed of his past? Months after discovering his identity, there was so much I wanted to know, but one of
the puzzles that preoccupied me most was his name.

IN JANUARY 1939, my biological father married for the first time;
a Jewish woman named Sylvia. His family name, Cohen, appears

on the marriage certificate. I know a little bit about the name Cohen. I know it is one of the most common Jewish surnames and is traditionally associated with hereditary priests directly descended from the biblical Aaron, brother of Moses. Not every Cohen can claim to be a descendant of the priestly class. For example, looking it up, I see there were Jews in Imperial Russia who wisely adopted the last name Cohen to avoid the required twenty-five years of military service, on the grounds that members of the clergy were exempt. But, either way, Cohen is an indisputably Jewish name.

A year after my father married, he had his first child: my half sister, S., born in July 1940. On the birth certificate, registered in the London borough of Hendon, "Cohen" is listed as her family name. But, dated the same year, there is a second certificate that gives me pause. On this document, her surname has been changed to one of Welsh origin. It is a name that means "well-born" or "noble." My father's family name as it appears on the certificate has also been changed, anglicized from the Ashkenazic. So has his first name. The given name "Isidore" has been erased and replaced with the middle name "A."

There are other name changes that I can see on the family tree. As multiple languages were adopted throughout the Jewish diaspora, surnames acquired dozens of variants. Rapske became Rabski/Rabsky and even Ressler. Cohen also appears as Kohen and Kogen. Some first names have been changed, like a hat or a hairstyle, to appear modern or even glamorous. But this new surname is different. It will work as a disguise.

1940. Fascism is on the rise. Belgium, the Netherlands, Luxembourg all fall to Hitler in a matter of weeks. France collapses by the end of June. With most of Europe conquered, the German Luftwaffe begins an intense bombing campaign across Britain. Looking up at the sky, my father Isidore would have seen planes with swastikas bombing London and he would have heard the drone that Virginia Woolf compared to "the zoom of a hornet, which may at any moment sting you to death." Around him, Jewish refugees are arriving in Hendon, escaping the terrors of Nazism and Hitler's program to make Europe *judenrein*, a continent free of Jews. Many of these new arrivals do not speak English and can barely communicate. Many are pale with hunger. Some have left behind relatives who will be killed in the death camps. Meanwhile, anti-Semitism is spiking around England, with Jews blamed for their own plight. Jews are accosted in the streets. British Ministry of Information director Cyril Radcliffe attributes the increased hostility to Jewish "errors of conduct" and "their peculiar qualities . . . such as their commercial initiative and drive and their determination to preserve themselves as an independent community." In Jewish experience, words like "initiative" and "drive" are seldom compliments. Being considered "peculiar" generally ends badly. It is important not to stick out. "Hide your traditions" is the advice given to terrorized Jews wishing for invisibility.

1940. At age twenty-five, my biological father makes a decision to start again with a new name. It seems a fitting time to assimilate and protect your first-born child from rising uncertainty. A pattern begins. It is a pattern of deletion, secrecy and constant self-reinvention. This is the moment he begins to carry a private world alongside the public one. The private world is the one he won't much discuss, composed of all the things he wishes to leave behind. Am I reading too much into this?

In her essay "Split at the Root," Adrienne Rich breaks the silence of her father's assimilated Jewishness while grappling with the "daily, mundane anti-Semitisms" that shaped his and her entire life. "We—my sister, mother, and I—were constantly urged to speak quietly in public, to dress without ostentation, to repress all vividness or spontaneity . . . the Rich women were always tuned down to some WASP level my father believed, surely, would protect us all—maybe also make us unrecognizable to the 'real Jews' who wanted to seize us, drag us back to the *shtetl*, the ghetto, in its many manifestations."

I don't know if my father ever reflected on the loss of his name during the war when so many died for the right to be Jewish and to proudly bear their Jewish identities and symbols. I don't know if he would have even experienced it in these terms or if he felt any psychic anxiety or sadness as he performed the labor of melting into the gentile world, achieving anonymity and possible protection by making his Jewishness invisible. But I cannot help but wonder: Did he feel it was a very bad bargain, this gift of disguise? Maybe an impossibility? To prove that Jews are not really assimilable, after all, has been the eternal project of anti-Semitism, much like the project of anti-Asian racism, which says no matter how many generations have passed, or what perfect, exacting efforts have been taken to be "essentially English" or a "model minority," belonging will always be beyond reach.

Did he worry how very little it would take to be ousted from respectability and hiding?

Assimilation is tricky. One must be different enough to be likable and interesting, but not so different as to be threatening or to "invite" harassment. One can be anti-assimilationist at home and festively cultural while encouraged to be politically and publicly integrated so as to "reduce" social friction.

I think of my "disobedient" mother who refused to fall in line or learn her place, who saw there was no lasting refuge to be found in proximity to whiteness or the "dissolving of difference." When she arrived in Canada in 1974, racism was considered an aberration, seldom recognized as a crucial part of the Canadian story. My mother recognized it, pointed at it, refused to be "nice" or apologetic or to peg her self-worth to white mercy. Living with my father gave her a front row seat to the amplitude offered white people. It was a form of going undercover that I would recognize the first time I saw Eddie Murphy's mockumentary "White Like Me" on *Saturday Night Live*. What do you do when you witness such daily variance and audacity, when the stratified terms of the world are so intimately experienced? My mother became a wave maker, a rogue force, towering and dramatically declaring her worth and style. *A perpetual foreigner, an angry minority.* Certainly, the wrong match for my biological father, a man who wished for a quiet, pale integration.

⇜

I ASKED MY BROTHERS, *Was he a practicing Jew?* "No." *Did they observe the high holidays?* "No, never, no." *Did you feel Jewish growing up?* "There were some ideas he taught me. Like *tikkun olam.*" And: "Our grandmother Pollie insisted my two older brothers have a bar mitzvah, but she died before I turned thirteen." *Do you feel Jewish now?* The question produced a quizzical silence from my older brother. "That's interesting, but no."

"As the word implies, 'passing' is gradual: it moves like a wave over generations . . . and always in one direction, toward the foamy crest of whiteness," notes Namwali Serpell in an essay on the fantasy of racial transformation.

It was time to move against that momentum, returning names and people to a story that in 1940 was altered—an altering made troubling by the pressures of history, occurring under the sign of transports. It was time to pull family findings out of the vault and release the knotted energies directed at concealment. Until I did so, I would not know how to move away from the murky orbit of the secret or understand how the past continued to travel in and through me. Let it rise.

SUMMON

FLOATING BETWEEN SLEEPING AND WAKING ONE NIGHT, I had the strange feeling that there were many people in my bed. I woke my husband and said, "There are at least seven people here!"

"There are seven people here," I repeated, kicking the covers into a twisted mess by our feet. Rain was drumming on the roof. My husband clearly had no idea what I was talking about. But I knew. I had summoned the ancestors. Through fervid Googling, the kinfolk had been alerted and were now rising from archives and databases, seeking to make our bedroom a meeting place.

This was what happened when you mailed your DNA to a private company that bragged about its matchmaking abilities. Now that we were matched, the "we" of my forebearers were looking to imprint themselves on memory foam; waiting to sink into me. In that moment, I believed in these ghosts even if I still did not know how they traveled through me. I tried to relax my limbs, making myself pliant to their resonance. I waited for them to move and breathe and walk toward me.

It had been many weeks since I looked at the family tree. I had been waiting for a moment when my heart felt quieter to meet this family of strangers, to study the branches that had sprung up from nowhere, simultaneously, as if on a single long day. Looking again, I saw the tree had authority but it was a skeleton. The records could only tell me about the family's bare bones, how people appeared and disappeared in time and space; not the stories of how they made it through their days, or where they put their love and laundry, how they managed their mistakes and shame, their joy and pleasure, or their most desperate longings. It could not tell me about the leaves that had fallen or the gaps on branches. Not the most important things.

SUKKOT

MY FATHER ISIDORE WAS BORN IN 1915 IN LAMBETH, SOUTH London, the first in his family to be born into English from a Yiddish-speaking family. His father, Hyman Cohen or "Harry," was an immigrant draper by trade but was also rumored to have been a trumpet player with the Ambrose Orchestra. Isidore's mother, Pauline Rapske or "Pollie," was a refugee whose family had fled Russian pogroms in 1895, when she was about five. From their mud-caked shtetl, the Rapskes trekked the refugee trails of Europe, finally making a temporary home in Lodz, Poland.

Autumn. Somewhere in Toronto, I am helping build a sukkah in the back of my best friend's house, where the garden is wild and full-blown and gone to seed. We are seven years old. It is the weeklong festival of Sukkot, the Jewish harvest holiday. My friend's father has fashioned a simple wooden frame of two-by-fours. Mr. B. He is handsome and saunters around in a fitted T-shirt and bell-bottoms offering us palm fronds, fanning us like a cheerful cabana boy. We cover the roof of the sukkah with leaves and branches, leaving spaces in the thick canopy so we can see the sky and the stars. This is to remind us of the awesomeness and majesty of Hashem. It is Hashem, Mr. B. says, who watched out for the Jews in the wilderness when they were freed from slavery in Egypt. For forty years they wandered in exile, resting where they could amid flying sand and gale-force desert winds. This is what we are celebrating with our symbolic shelter. Refuge. How to survive in diaspora. I notice one star moving very slowly across the sky. A satellite.

When the Rapskes arrived in Lodz, it was a booming center for the textile industry, nicknamed "the Manchester of Poland." They worked twelve-hour shifts six days a week in noisy, gaslit factories. Air churning with ash. They snipped and starched and ironed and serged and sewed, joining the city's growing Jewish population; a population that was nearing 100,000 in 1897; a population still haunted by the possibility of ethnic cleansings across continents and centuries. Forty-three years later, their worst fears would be realized when German troops invaded Poland. By early 1940, Jews living in Lodz were forced into a sealed and segregated ghetto—164,000 people dwelling in an area of 1.5 square miles—an urban prison set up to deliver residents, ultimately, to the death camps.

We are remembering, on Sukkot, a journey through the desert and we are remembering the agrarian roots of the Jewish tradition. We are remembering, through ceremony, how temporary huts protected wandering ancestors and how little separates the world's housed and housed-nots. Mr. B. invites us to decorate the sukkah with plants from the garden, to see the makings of a home in the world around us; to feel in the brisk air and the smell of dying leaves how we might be sheltered by the place where we live.

The Rapskes arrived in England in 1900, into a world of oil lamps, dirt roads and horse-drawn carts. It mustn't have felt too far from Russia and the shtetl. They believed that upon reaching England, they would be freer. In London, they lived in shabby housing in Stepney, jammed into a crowded warren of streets, alleys and courts. This is where many of London's poor Jews lodged, earning their living in sweatshops and warehouses, working in the informal economy of the old-clothes trade and as peddlers. The Cohens also worked in the clothing trade.

Did they experience community in this cramped Jewish ghetto? Did they feel the fabled warmth of immigrant Jewish life? When food and money were meager, did Pollie's parents, my great-grandparents Solomon and Eva, whisper promises of plenteousness in her ear? The *1911 England Census (London/Shadwell)*, written in elegant script, records only five surviving children out of eight. I think of all the pain and dashed hope but also about the times they felt okay and even happy for a moment. As Maira Kalman writes of her mother Sara Berman's journey from Belarus, "Yes, there were Pogroms. Yes, there was deprivation. But Life was not all bad."

Mr. B. arranges two inflatable mattresses and duvets in the sukkah each night. We eat outside with a view of the moon, folding fresh pita with dollops of hummus into our mouths. I think of my mother, who claims Jews are the only white people who do not give her a stomachache. There are foods she knows well, a comfort that melts her. She will continue to source the perfect beets and nicest broths and the best smoked meat. Not because it is in her blood, but because it is her first experience of welcome.

My grandmother Pollie went to Betts Street School in Stepney (a school that, in 1900, was described as "all Jewish or being Judaized"). Her father, Solomon, became a mineral water manufacturer. By 1910, Pollie is registered as a milliner at 152 Commercial Road in Whitechapel. At some point, Pollie met my grandfather Harry, whom she married in 1911 at the Great Synagogue. The oldest center of Jewish life in London, the synagogue dates back to 1690, when Jews returned after more than 350 years of expulsion from England. Pollie was twenty-one on the day of her wedding and deeply devoted to Judaism. Thirty years after Pollie and Harry's wedding, the synagogue would be destroyed during one of the last major raids of the Blitz, a mangled chandelier left hanging amidst timber and rubble in the roofless shell.

It should be provisional, transportable and somewhat open to the elements beneath its roof of organic material; an unquestionably temporary shelter. In a sukkah, there are often only three walls. As my best friend and I recline on the inflatable mattresses, I have a string of feelings. I am happy because I am not trapped inside, and this allows me to relax enough to feel loved.

Seventy-seven years after Pollie's marriage, I marry a man with a muddled and erratic relationship to his Jewish identity. He is a secular Jew who remains attached to the philosophical ground-work and cantorial traditions of his ancient religion but who rejects the ideological springs of Zionism and is horrified by the violent unhousing and displacement of Palestinians in his name. There are certain colonial blueprints for kinship he deems abhorrent. In this light, the practice of "loving one's own" feels increasingly inde-cent. The first time I meet his mother, she invites me to a weekly vigil led by a group called the Jewish Women's Committee to End the Occupation. She gives me bottles of Zatoun olive oil from Palestine. "Our job as Jews," she says, "is to speak out as often as we can." She speaks out even when a pro-Israeli protestor spits at her and tells her she should have died in the gas chambers. She speaks out when another woman, yelling "traitor," bashes into her legs with a baby stroller. She speaks out. This is the expression of her inheritance: rejecting the fear impulse to close in, to close gates against those banished as "not kin." This is a legacy of Jewish radicalism arcing toward a Jewish futurity where, in the words of Solomon Brager, "assimilation and exclusion have no quarter." She refuses to support settler borders that will result in multigenerational refugees. Violence done to "us" must never be leveraged to justify violence done to the other. *Not in my name.* The answer to a history of obliteration is not further obliteration but justice and creation.

Mr. B. says he wants to adopt me and gives me a Hebrew name. It is a name that means *springlike.* I say yes to the Hebrew name when he gives me a bag of jelly beans even though my eagerness feels disloyal—a confirmation that I've secretly wanted all along to slip into another family. Despite his apparent solidity, it turns out Mr. B. is not a man who will stick around; one morning when I meet my friend on our daily walk to school she tells me he is returning to England, the country of his birth. Her parents are divorcing and her mother will have full custody. When I begin to cry, she is watchful but then laughs in a worldly way: "Why are *you* crying?"

I can't put words to it. I am shocked. *How can a family come down so fast? What is constant if every story is waiting to collapse?*

She laughs at me, at my innocence, at my absurd self-pity. To be our age, seven, and be unaware that "people divorce" and "bad things happen." Years later, I will think of her poise and matter-of-factness as I watch Buster Keaton's most famous film stunt, the legendary scene in *Steamboat Bill, Jr.* where the facade of an actual house falls all around Keaton while he stands in the exact right place to pass through the open attic window instead of being flattened.

"A sukkah is built to emphasize the truth about any of our buildings; that they may fall at any minute, that we may be made to dwell in uncertainty before we have a story to explain what has happened," writes Samantha M. Shapiro. I think of my best friend and me nibbling mandelbrot we have stored in our pockets, reclining happily in a structure meant to represent the breakability of all structures.

Throughout my childhood my mother will have an ability to find the only Jews on whatever street we live on, finding commonality in their outsiderness in the neighborhood. Their homes and observances will come to have a familiar, *heimish* quality. We will be invited to weekly Sunday night dinners at China House, where kosher "Chinese-Canadian" dishes revolve on an enormous lazy Susan. Does my mother contrive this, even subliminally, ensuring I will never experience a sense of cultural loss that accompanies being raised in a non-Jewish family?

With my sons, one autumn, I make an ungainly sukkah in a nearby park with their secular shule. The hut is structurally dubious. We labor obsessively over the roof, creating a shelter no one would ever willingly enter, piling on greenery as if function and symmetry are irrelevant to us. One son is a maximalist, carrying voluminous armfuls of palm; the other a minimalist, holding thin husks. Our sukkah is aesthetically indecisive.

With these pages, I am making a sukkah and bringing back the names of my refugee ancestors, saying them aloud, to recognize the ways my life is woven with the journeys of strangers and wanderers, with those who were unhomed in the past and those who are unhomed now.

"Ghosts, too, are susceptible to the wear and tear of time," writes Etel Adnan.

To bring back the names of these ancestors, saying them aloud, is also to say there are ghost traces and restless spirits in me. My genetic story revealed many things I already knew—that I am predisposed to fear heights, prefer chocolate over vanilla, experience motion sickness, have poor musical pitch, and tend to be a restless and light sleeper—but not why I have problems with attachment and love.

We are full of epigenetic mysteries, a "living collage" of our predecessors, as my friend M. puts it. We carry phantom habits, gestures, phobias, flaws and talents. But heredity is not a simple matter of dooming or freeing future generations. The deep past may live and persist in our bodies, but we are also all precisely and particularly ourselves and of our present worlds.

I may have lost the thread of family, but I have the milliner in me. I have the tailor. I have stitched together names and embroidered events to fashion a story. I have inadvertently honored my ancestors, over the years, with Yiddish lullabies, Hanukah candles, wobbly Hebrew prayers, secular socialist seders and a Haggadah that bows to the international working class. Somehow a raft bearing the millennia-old Ashkenazic traditions of Eastern Europe has wended its way into my life.

When my husband sings the Kol Nidre, the walls of my body vibrate. But also when he sings "God Blessed Our Love" and "Let's Get It On."

I often wonder what it means to be writing about family when my own thoughts about kinship are so complicated.

I do not believe in blood memory or the cultural determinism of DNA, but I believe I am a descendant. I believe we are aftermath. The more I think about this, the more sense it makes. The more I see I am here because somebody else ingeniously struggled, traveled, risked, resisted, labored, created, often defying probability and hairline margins of survival. I was born of and through others and nowhere does this feel more true than when I think of my literary and art ancestors, a long pulse and complex provenance that reminds me I am not of the only-now. I am enmeshed with words and images I house like kin. To paraphrase poet Jericho Brown, *I think of myself as a descendant of traditions whether or not their bearers would have wanted me.*

This lineage, this reminder that we are for and from others, is not, as Ross Gay notes, "without a little ambivalence sometimes in the world-destroying horseshit capitalist nightmare fantasy of the individual." The mantra of *the beholden*, of the descendant: "Oh shit, it's all been given to me. It's all been given to me. Oh. O. Thank you."

The festival, or practice, of Sukkot ends at sundown on the eighth day and afterward the huts are dismantled. When my mother-in-law N. dies suddenly in the pandemic days of autumn 2020—a week after Sukkot, when she seemed perfectly fine—she will have left us a beautiful, wide idea of what it means to be descended, beholden, sheltering *family*. Not family as a fixed or fossilized artifact. Not family as boast-record of achievement. (She always said: *Don't worry about being good and accomplished. Don't worry about doing stuff or not doing stuff. I love you no matter what.*) Not family as an act of convenient closure. Hundreds of people will gather for her online memorial; an immense crew of chosen relatives not genetically connected but bound by communal care, willful entanglement and queer improvisational grace. We will reach toward each other, sobbing and laughing and sharing stories, wondering how we are going to make it through our shock and mourning, knowing we are prodigiously blessed; that our dearest N., our Laureate of Love, bequeathed us the *how*, gave us this outward-looking, extralegal, unofficial, kin-making model. This utopian horizon. This wider way to be. For surely in this world, there is solace without walls. There is balm beyond the bubble. There is a place for friends and even strangers who do not have a sukkah of their own.

How will you receive? How will you be received? It is said the *ushpizin*, the honored biblical guests or spiritual ancestors of the Jewish diaspora, would refuse to enter a sukkah where the poor or those on the move were not welcome. The same week my mother-in-law dies, a Toronto carpenter named Khaleel Seivwright will be at work building tiny insulated shelters for the growing number of unhoused people living in makeshift encampments across the city since the pandemic began. On the side of each shelter, roughly one hundred in total, will be taped a note: "Anyone is welcome to stay here." A deep idea of habitat. In the park where my sons and I once built our sukkah in the memory of ancestral homemaking and defiant survival, we will pass one of Seivwright's wooden structures—roughly four feet by eight feet—colorfully painted with the words: SOMEONE LIVES HERE. A temporary refuge for a woman, recently evicted; a structure of architectural *restoration*, in the truest regenerative sense of the word. This is what it means to tend our home and our garden.

During the Occupy encampment at Zuccotti Park back in September 2011, the first tent to successfully challenge the NYPD ban on structures was a sukkah replete with a portrait of Jewish anarchist Emma Goldman. In the middle of the night as the skies opened with rain, a voice echoed: MIC CHECK! MIC CHECK! TONIGHT WE ARE ALL JEWS! BUILD YOURSELF A SUKKAH TO SLEEP IN! And, so, the tent city began. And, so, it continues.

My sons sit on a couch with their father on the night after their grandmother dies watching the Marx Brothers, sending laughter and tears through the house.

DESCENDANT

I AM A DESCENDANT OF MY FATHER, MICHAEL, TOO. MY father who was four years old when he first felt unsheltered, whose earliest memory was of being left by his single mother with a strange family, of locking himself upon arrival in a garden out-house in terror. A foundling. He was coaxed from his hiding spot by an unfamiliar sound, a mewling. The family's black cat, puddled under a tree, watched over his arrival with a kindness, or a kind indifference, that felt like love. The story of this early moment would acquire the dimensions of a foundational myth.

For the rest of his childhood, my father would board with the Burns family and their seven biological kids, all older. They lived in the semi-pastoral world of Kent and later, when they were bombed out of their home during a 1940 air attack, they moved to council housing in Beckenham. He would never live with his mother again and would always, at some deep level, see himself as a little boy left behind, awaiting her return—a mother who did nothing wrong except fail to have the things needed to be a good parent: adequate housing, food in the fridge, nursery provision, a helpful family. A mother who came up against a cruelly common situation that was not for unsupported women and children.

When I first saw a cat through the slats of a crib, I am told I too felt love. Our family cat in London, so orange, so soft, could only mesmerize me, could only enthrall with the relaxed and lavish swish of its tail. At some point, very early on, I understood my father as cat-smitten, always keenly sensitive to the small, stray and unowned. Within my parents' marriage, I noticed cats were a site of détente and joint delight. I can still see my parents' hands meeting on the back of a new rescue cat, stretched between them on the sofa. My father using his long fingers to trace the line of the spine, my mother rubbing its ears. ("I never had a cat before I met Daddy. I didn't like cats," she told me once, bowing low to the ground as one does when crouching small against a hurricane, or when preparing for a tabby-human heart-to-heart.)

Even when his earnings were meager, my father continued to send large yearly donations to a rescue shelter. I did not know this was a ripple, a tremor of my father's childhood in him. But in the last months of his life, when he began to power down, it did not surprise me to see him happiest lying in a sunbeam with our self-contented rescue cats knotted at his side.

Beyond explaining to us the origins of his cat devotion, my father refused to talk about what had happened to him as a child. Any time I probed too much, I would end up feeling sick with regret that I had caused him pain, so I learned to keep a heedful distance from family history. The one time he spoke candidly was in an interview I did with him on the publication of my second novel. *A bruised childhood. A twisted childhood.* These were the words he used. He recognized his foster parents, the Burnses, didn't have much—the father a traveling salesman who peddled vacuum cleaners; the mother a schoolteacher who struggled with gout and rheumatoid arthritis. He had landed with a decent lot but I know it hurt that they never adopted him, which might have given him a surer sense of belonging. It is possible his mother refused to sign the relinquishment papers that would have made adoption possible. It is possible the Burnses were adamant about not wanting another permanent child. Not a single photo exists of him from that time, no evidence to show he was beheld or cherished. He grew up believing he could always be sent away if the money for his boarding didn't arrive. *This*, he told me, is why he folded himself into books. To disappear. To limit his footprint within a family and life that did not belong to him. This is why he left at age fourteen to work as an errand boy on Fleet Street and live on his own. This is why he turned to the act of writing, believing it could house him, that he would never again be unstoried.

I remember everything he told me during that interview. I remember and think back to how my first son once cried for fear of the night and how my second son once cried for fear of an impending house move. I remember and think of my sons because they were four years old when they held those fears and that's how old my father was when he arrived at his foster home. Four years old.

In her book *Stranger Care*, Sarah Sentilles chronicles her experience of becoming a foster parent through the foster care system. "[A] social worker led us through an exercise during which she asked us to brainstorm the emotions a child taken out of his home and placed in a foster home might be feeling. She wrote words on a poster at the front of the classroom as we shouted them: *fear, confusion, shame, guilt, relief, anger.*"

In his late teens, my father had brief reunions with his mother. But they never went well, never erased the trauma of their early separation or the feeling there was something wrong with him that had caused her to leave him. At age seventeen, he was also reunited with his biological father for the first time, a man who had hidden his son's existence upon remarrying and fathering two other sons. His relationship with his birth father, of whom he had zero expectations, went better.

What he carried—an early distrust of blood bonds, a memory of upsetting estrangements—flared sometimes, without warning. It somehow infused everything. It whispered in his books, yelled in his reports, keened in his photographs. Throughout his career, his most compelling reports would continue to include children who had been orphaned or displaced and sewn into new family arrangements. Children who had been treated, in some essential sense, as waste. Children as unwanted as he thought himself to be.

This, then, was the context in which I was born and raised.

This is perhaps why he needed me to feel I belonged, indisputably. This is why he gave me the middle name *Iona*—a small Scottish island but also a flag-planting homophone of his possessive parental attitude. This is why he wanted to grant me the gift of an uncomplicated story. I know his childhood cannot explain everything, but it was a piece of who he became: a father who wanted his daughter to know she was permanent.

In his eighties, the sadness he felt at being abandoned resurfaced. Layers of defense peeled away to uncover old hurts.

When a child is traumatically separated from their parents at a young age, their body releases a flood of stress hormones that kill off neurons and dendrites in the brain, resulting in permanent physical and psychological changes—or what Karla Cornejo Villavicencio describes as a brain that looks like "a tree without branches."

He could not have been more exactly the father I wanted. I could not have loved him more fiercely and tenderly or truly, in the deepest sense, cared less about my biological patrimony. He became mine and I became his through an infinity of actions. But that does not mean I didn't have the right to know the truth.

When those close to me ask, *Do you wish you could have met him, your other father?* I remember that it was a possibility; that before my birth father died, my first-born son could have met him too. And that glimpse into the alternate life hurts to consider.

At some point, after his first stroke, after his cancer, but before the diagnosis of vascular dementia, I became a mother figure to my father. As a mother figure, I was never enough. A missing mother will carve a need out of you as deep as a cave. He was on edge any time we were apart; always worried that those close to him might simply slip away never to be seen again. But then he eased. Returned to a state of vulnerability, he looked around and saw, to his surprise and joy, that he was encircled by unshakable love. He felt his mother love him fiercely, from beyond the grave. We loosened the grip of an ancient and destructive story. Caring for him became effortless.

It would have been unbearable, I think, for him to imagine me thinking of another father out there, thinking *what was he like* and *did he remember my birthday* and so on. It is possible he lived with the worry that I might be "reclaimed" and taken from him, that our intimacy might be retracted, his parenting and our lives erased. As it was, he struggled, humorously, painfully, irrationally, with anyone he feared might diminish my affection. There were possessive outbursts on the eve of my wedding and immediately after the births of my two sons, as if he could not bear the idea that my affection might be atomically split. Even toward my mother, after they separated, there were several, unexpected fits of jealousy. (Why was she out all the time? Who was she with?) Only a person who had experienced love-rationing as a child reacts this way, sees proliferation as subtraction, sees every opening as a risk.

So my father did something very kind for me. He gave me a far steadier foundation than he himself had enjoyed. He cut my awkward origin story away, pruning that part of my past, so I would never feel abandoned or unwanted, I would always feel loved, securely, no matter what. But in hindsight, I think I was being asked to do something for him—quite a few things, actually, in return.

As my mother said to me, with surprising clarity, when I asked why she chose to stay with Michael: *Your biological father was a very warmhearted man, but Michael needed you. He loved you. He saved your life. You saved his life. So why be fussy about it?*

As a child, I watched my father Michael cry twice. The first time was one evening when I was about six. I walked into his office and heard the crying in his voice first and then saw the tears glazing his face, though he never revealed why he was so sad. The second time was a few years later, after the funeral of his father, whom he had known only as an adult. The funeral took place in England. My father returned home from the airport in the late afternoon. He walked across the threshold of our home, a threshold my mother had scattered with salt in a ritual of purification, according to Japanese ceremonial custom. He proceeded to his favorite chair and, placing his face in his hands, began shaking. Salty tears poured from his eyes. This was not a man who could stop the pour. This was not a man who could make a dry and clean break from his past. I remember my mother backing away like someone encountering a suspicious parcel. I remember gold sunlight coming into the room, brightness hitting every surface. I walked slowly toward him with the cat glowing in my nine-year-old arms and lowered myself until his face lifted to meet mine, our heads in a warm slant of light. Even his eyes had a little beam in them. I remember he let me comfort him as the room brightened and darkened, turning from gold to rose, as clouds passed.

I remember my mother opened another blind and my father turned his head, heliotropic.

"He cried more than any of us," my uncle A. later said of the funeral.

NINE:

SŌKŌ

(frost falls)

DECAY

ALL THE FINAL FLOWERS OF AUTUMN WERE FALLING. MY
mother sounded the gong at the hospital, a big brass gong to cel-
ebrate the end of her treatment. The gong's purpose was to let
her "courage and determination resonate." She rang it loudly, as
though warning her village of an oncoming flood or enemy attack.
Then she released the wooden mallet while the staff and patients
in the unit gathered and clapped; and she shrugged, a little bash-
ful. Outside the hospital, the story that had been forming since
spring was coming apart. Night fell earlier and the evenings grew
colder and every day the leaves pivoted in the wind, in a rustling
and crackling ballet. As the energy of the plants traveled downward, back into the earth, and the floating seeds finally slipped
into the black soil, my mother declared it was the time of year to
eat things that grow in the ground. *Gobo, daikon, naga-imo, renkon.*
It was time to cue our own bodies into moving slower; settle ourselves down, down, into the roots and circulatory system of winter.

I walked around the city, looking at fall gardens, rebuilding a relationship with decline. Sag, decay, collapse. I loved the beauty and
the coming apart of beauty; the Duras-ian "ravaged" look the
plants had when they were openly aging, when they had seen too
much, when the color was slowly draining out of everything. *I
prefer your face as it is now,* I said to the black nubs of petal-less

flowers. Spring is the season of love, but any time I have been infatuated it has been the fall.

A few days after my mother's final treatment, while we were still awaiting her CT scan and memory test, I returned to the greenhouse to hear a talk by a well-known "plant influencer." The talk was held in a glass room known as the children's conservatory. The plant influencer was a former engineer with well over half a million Instagram followers. He was a warm but shy speaker, keeping his gaze low on the podium. *Plant care is not a recipe, it is a relationship . . . Relating to a plant beyond decor means celebrating its maturity and livingness, rather than worrying whether it complements your vintage lamp . . . True plant love means moving beyond human centrism, surrendering a controlling mindset for a caring one.*

My mind wandered while members of the audience asked about fertilizing trays, watering timers, light meters. Then I heard a gravelly voice from the back. "Can I ask a philosophical question?"

I turned and spotted the speaker, an elderly white man with a scraggly beard, slowly rising to his feet. "I have been thinking about the interdependence of the forest, the way trees will keep a five-hundred-year-old stump alive by sending it nutrients." People shifted in their seats, phones lit up, and I noticed the woman beside me tap in a search for seaweed fertilizer, then scroll through the reviews. The man continued, "I want to know, do plants do that? Do they know when their roots are self or stranger? Will plants of different species be happy in the same pot? Will they care for each other?" He continued, speaking in sweeping circles about root space and parasitic plants that feed from the bodies of other plants, about competition versus companionship. The plant influencer tried to prune the questions down into a kind of coherence. Then he politely thanked everyone for coming, and wished us all a good night.

Walking home it was still light. I picked up fallen leaves that were yellow-haloed, amber-mottled, Technicolor.

That night, I prepared a pot of *kenchin-jiru* for my mother. Peeling and cutting the daikon, taro and burdock root, gently slicing konjac and tearing aburaage with my fingers until soup was simmering on the stove. *Kenchin-jiru* is an earthy dish, originally created as a Buddhist temple staple. The steam tufted from our bowls as we ladled the broth over our rice.

I fell asleep to winter wind rattling the window.

A FEW DAYS LATER, the plant influencer posted photos he had taken at the greenhouse, explaining he had, with intention, arrived *before* the professional gardeners began their daily rounds to see how many imperfections he could observe.

Traditional houseplant care is heavily focused on looking at visible plant imperfections and suggesting some change in your care routine, he wrote. *This perspective gives the impression that any and all signs of decay are "bad things," which are preventable and correctable. On a higher level, it also creates the illusion that your actions have a larger role than the environment in determining the plant's fate/success. Notice how we casually say "I killed the plant" or "she has a green-thumb," which are human-centered statements as opposed to "it died" or "the conditions are ideal for growth."*

GOODBYE

WHEN MY FATHER WAS IN THE WEAKENED LAST WEEKS OF his life, he began asking for my mother. My parents had not been alone in the same room together in nearly two years. On the last occasion, my father had collapsed while sorting bills and letters for her and, unable to stand up again, had crawled to a wall waiting for the paramedics to arrive. The shock of his fall, followed by his uncertain recovery, proved to be too much for my mother. She gave herself permission to turn her back on him once and for all. To turn her back on him at his weakest point was to say she had given him everything she was prepared to give. And just like that: I was on my own.

I knew my father missed my mother's presence. He would ask after her now and then but in the last week, when it became an effort for him to speak at all, he began to ask for her persistently. *Where is she? Where is Mariko?* he asked, using her artist name.

Whatever conflicts there had been between them had been forgotten by my father. In his mind, they were still legally married and so he was still her husband. Often, I could feel him conjuring her from memory, from much earlier recollection. *Where is Mariko?* Every time he asked, I stared at my feet and said, *She'll visit soon,* even though I knew she would not be coming. Finally, when he seemed to need more than my empty reassurances and when I sensed his eyes actively scouring the room for her, I made a promise: "She'll be here in two days. On Christmas." As soon as I said that, my father's breathing evened out and his face softened.

We often lay beside each other quietly in those last weeks, using our eyes to communicate. We were alone, without family to gather around, but never lonely. Sometimes I fell asleep and would awaken to see him looking at me. Restless. Occasionally he took my hand in his as if he wanted to tell me something. That day, when I made the promise about my mother's visit, he looked completely calm.

Like a child who cannot stop trying to reconcile her parents, I convinced my mother to come see my father on Christmas. When she arrived, I walked her into his bedroom, where he had been lying down for almost a week losing kidney function, where I had administered oxygen and drained his catheter because the paperwork for palliative care was still being processed, stuck in a holiday queue. I was too tired to be tense and towering so I sat in a corner. I had prepared a chair right beside the bed. My mother, never one for ceremony, moved the chair away from the bed, then she moved it further back again. She did not know what to do by a deathbed, did not know that a held hand could give shape to the part of you that was too sorrowful to speak. Either she did not know or she did not want to know. This is why she needed the chair to be near the doorway, three meters from my father, from his dying flame.

My father, whose eyes had been open just before she arrived, did not open them during her entire visit. She thought he was being remote and unreachable, but I knew he had become an astronaut. He was in all places and no place. He was wheeling among the planets. She asked him if he remembered her. She said, *Maybe if I raise my voice, you'll know who it is. Maybe if I am yelling and yelling, you will say A-ha!* My father smiled and I quietly chuckled at that. But she wouldn't get physically close. The light inside the room darkened as the sun set and shadows traveled across our faces. She kept talking, combative and tender, leaning forward: *Open your eyes, Michael, it's me. It's Mariko.*

Watching him remember her, as she sat there speaking in her fierce-caring way, while his organs and his brain were slowly shutting down, was one of the most difficult and strangely loving moments I have ever witnessed. The fury dimmed. The infidelities and grievances lost their sting. The unyielding yielded. Was this what happened when two retired fighters had outlived their wars? For a minute I did not wonder how such dissimilar people had spent even one afternoon together, let alone years. Instead, I imagined what might have been possible had they cast off the old dubious forms and false protection of coupled domesticity to openly improvise something new.

"A piece of me is gone forever," said George Foreman, when asked to remember his famed opponent Muhammad Ali after a lifetime of contending.

I watched my father's breath rise up the wall and curve onto the ceiling, a sinuous twine. I watched it thread back down the wall, sink through the floor, into the ground, returning to the earth.

Finally, my father spoke: *Bye-bye, Mariko.*

❧

AS SOON AS my mother left, my father opened his eyes. He looked unimaginably peaceful. I nodded and smoothed his hair. It was Christmas and someone had brought crème caramel, so I offered him a small slip on a spoon. I adjusted the green oxygen cylinder and the tube in his nose, watched the now-smooth rise and fall of his breath. I turned on the television to a Christmas NBA game, muting the volume and watching my father's brightly lucid eyes scan the court as he followed LeBron James with the ball. I thought we still had time when Klay Thompson missed a jump shot. I did not know we were in the time of last breaths when Andre Ingram stood at the free throw line. My father's fingers were busily pleating his sheets. He was always so meticulous. I did not know this was his way of tending and preparing, or that he was already leaving.

Then we held hands. He gave mine a squeeze.

My father died two hours later.

BLUE

I STAYED WITH MY FATHER'S BODY THROUGH THE NIGHT.
For the first few hours, he did not appear dead. There was an after-
glow. Only gradually did I feel the air subtly alter as the room
emptied of his presence. It was like a light of him-ness going out
very, very slowly before fading altogether. His face eased, became
the face of a young man or a man of no-age. Everything went still
and very quiet.

The next morning, when the undertakers arrived wearing
black ankle-length cloaks, when his him-ness felt to me so
clearly gone, I grabbed his unopened mail and rushed to the
residence laundry room to hide. The thought of seeing his body
removed was too frightening. I waited, leaning against the gently
rocking dryer, while my husband graciously met the gurney. I
thought my crying would be masked by the noise. Two of my
father's neighbors, Ruth and Anna, came to find me. Ruth entered
first. "Hello, dear," she said, as if we had arranged to meet. She was
wearing a bicycle helmet to protect her head from epileptic sei-
zures. "Your father was a gentleman, and I was always glad to see
him," she said in a no-nonsense voice. Anna came in next, took
my father's mail from my hands and hugged me in a way that
felt like slow dancing. She stroked my hair as she swayed me
from side to side, moving to the damp revolving whir of the
washing machine.

Ruth was ninety-two. Anna was ninety-four. They did not say

he lived a long life or pleat their brows with pity. "You are strong enough," said Anna, simply, while Ruth, touching the hem of my shirt, told me about the Jewish mourning ritual of Kriah. She told me, with his death, my father was ready to be a good ancestor. "You were sweet with him," she said. "It made me miss my own father." Before I could ask, she began to tear up and added, "Fifty-two years. That's how long he has been gone."

Two days later, steeped in death bureaucracy and in a fit of wanting, I ordered ten antique apothecary bottles online, bottles discovered in a heavily blitzed part of England, the area of my father's childhood. They looked convincing in the photos, like they had just been pulled from the rubble of German raids, mucked with the soot of bomb sites.

A small case of chipped blue glassware arrived. Odd and bubbly, the color of a summer sea, the color of incoming waves. I arranged them in a way I thought my father might have appreciated. He always kept his apartment like a tidy shrine, with a soothing feeling of evenness and contemplation, everything placed just so. One of my best friends filled the bottles with flowers.

As a child of the Blitz, my father saw great meadows of fireweed bloom between jagged blocks of stone and in the crevices of fallen buildings. He saw what could grow from wasteland and knew that dangerous places could also have pretty views. He described seeing areas of "bomb alley" that were carpeted with self-seeded flowers. What can a flower do but regenerate?

It was not in his character to tell me about the flowers as proof of an indefatigable planet or life's capacity to rebound. I believe he was trying to communicate something more complicated: that the site of injury, even when left unhealed, can sometimes be where the most growth occurs.

❦

WHEN HE DIED, I did not like glib sayings about silver linings or the long sharing of personal death memories I received. But I did like the notes that were brief and instructional ("get a massage"), the off-kilter and unvarnished wisdom of old women, the resilient hijinks of children. I liked the spores of unencountered information about my father—hearing any new thing, receiving any unseen photo.

I did like, and appreciated, my care bully and best friend, N., who left me soup, often along with one of her gorgeous paintings, divining when my heart was about to close shop. Having years of behavioral evidence as support, she was always right in her timing, telepathic when she stormed the place with broth and beauty. The moment I felt myself reaching for the iron shutters, I would receive a call or a text: *soup?*

I did like the easy warmth and comradery I felt from my minyan of friends with dead fathers. R., B., M., S., K., C., J., M., N., H. And the one who burst with laughter after she said: *Don't wish this life stage away because who knows what comes next?!*

I liked the illusion of blurring—the days, the conversations, the faces, that seemed to lose focus immediately, dissolving into vapor. "Do you ever feel a haziness?" I asked an acquaintance, whose face at that moment resembled a human cloud. "I don't mean blurry vision. I mean fuzzy, edgeless, metaphysically unfocused," I clarified.

"No," she replied, politely. "I don't think so."

It wasn't a bad feeling. It was as if Gerhard Richter had been called in to smudge out unimportant information with a benevolent squeegee.

SPOON

ANNA CAME TO SPEAK TO ME AS WE PACKED UP MY FATHER'S apartment. She did not know my father as a man whose mind was once in constant motion but as a man who often sat in a gentle aphasiac silence, observing his surroundings. But there were things she wanted to share.

She confided, with unwelcome candor, that some of the other white residents had judged my father for marrying "outside his race." "Some people wondered why you look so Asian, and not so much like your father. I told them to mind their own business."

Anna also told me my dad had once mistaken a spoon for a pen while signing a petition demanding the city create an ambulance parking spot outside the residence.

When she left, I continued sorting through my father's books. I looked at his chair and remembered him once staring at his bobbing knee, wondering if it was truly his own leg. I looked at his wardrobe and remembered how he tried to repay me for the orange juice I'd brought, retrieving two folded undershirts instead of his wallet, laying them down before me, saying: "This should cover it."

What did it matter? Did the spoon care it was not a pen?

I thought of all the times we sat in the garden or dining room, how he would always introduce me to people, beaming: "My daughter. This is my daughter." He could not say it enough. I thought of the woman in the residence who sometimes mistook me for her own child, just as she confused the trellis in the garden for a friend and wished it "very well." When she reached for my hand in the elevator, I used to glance behind me until one day I began holding her hand, joining in when she loudly announced all the floors we passed to reach the ground. Clarification was unnecessary, even when a mother was holding the hand of the wrong daughter. Family is sometimes just an approximation, a shape in your heart.

I thought of my father beholding a spoon as a pen, without apology, watching it clatter to the floor; all his muddling, all his mistakes, all his gall and malfeasance, all the misguided literalism transcended, all his love.

LOOP

I WON'T BE FUSSY ABOUT IT BUT I USED TO HAVE ONE FATHER, then I had two, but now, really, I had none. My unmet father died in Portugal in 2002. Only two of his four known and surviving children attended the funeral. He was buried in a mausoleum in a cemitério along the southern coast of the Algarve. I am told the tomb is large and one can walk around inside. Such was his fifth wife's love for him, she would have built a towering memorial to him with her bare hands.

He lived and died for me, was found and lost, in the same moment of discovery. There were no personal possessions to sort through, no stories or keepsakes, just a few belated photos and short, fuzzy film clips, sent to me by my older half brother. *To give you a sense of how he moved.*

I have watched the footage countless times. In one clip, racing cars speed along a winding road in a rural village. My father, foot on the accelerator, hurtles through space. I picture his eyes looking through the turns, a green blur of trees as he flies. I try to get close to him, this whizzing ghost of a father, by imagining what this roaring speed feels like in his body, what it's like to be unrattled by risk, constantly courting danger. I imagine whooshing, whistling, a soft hiss, even though the film is soundless.

In another clip, he is a short, handsome man with sunglasses, walking with his hands clasped behind his back. Cool Windsor knot and white shirt under a dark, round-neck jumper. I absorb it all, the physicality of this person, the Chaplinesque gait of a father as the light flickers over him. He appears to be on a farm, a place with abundant wildlife. He adjusts his collar, a gesture so specific and small, and even though he avoids meeting the gaze of the camera I imagine him preening, knowing he will one day be watched by his daughter, a daughter searching for some vestige and trace of what she may have missed.

Another floating newsreel fragment from Pathé: this one an unending race on a stretch of motorway. The sportscar is a single-seater Cooper Climax T45, designed for forward flying, for those who feel steadier on the go. Watching it at first soothes me and then makes me anxious. Racecar driving is a perilous performance requiring ultimate control. I brace for a sudden screech and collision. In the 1960 Italian Grand Prix, I have read, my father crashed on the first lap when his brakes failed as he turned. Back then, Monza had famously lethal banked corners. In the 1962 Macau Grand Prix, he also crashed early in the race. In the 1963 Japanese Grand Prix, he finished third, so I guess he got better. Watching the car whiz around on the newsreel, all I hear is nothing, the loudest nothing I know. Breath held. Each time the clip ends, I exhale and press PLAY and off he goes again, ceaselessly, soundlessly. There is no language. What's missing is a voice, his voice.

Lately, my mother says he definitely saw me more than once after I was born, meeting her at the flat in Chelsea. I cannot substantiate these facts, but this is the version of the story I want to believe. I want to believe it because it grants me a father who may have been interested, may have felt a bit of loss and regret when I left England, too young to even form a memory of him.

I press her to elaborate but she doesn't, unaware that a child who has been adopted might feel love but also hurt. "The windy place right at the core of my heart" is how Jackie Kay describes this hurt place. What I want is a shared recognition of facts. Some confirmation of the weight of them, so I can stop second-guessing myself.

Did he sometimes think of a day when we would sit down together and he would say, "Okay, tell me what I missed"?

"Do you remember what he said about me?" I ask my mother, again and again. Looping.

I quarrel with my elusive father in my head, I slam a door, I dole out crazed adolescent behavior. I sit with him and ask all my ugly, burning questions. I smash his black box of secrecy. Then I apologize; because, at some level, the seed of deep privacy within me understands his desire to keep a part of himself shaded. All I really want is the tiniest, most banal exchange. Maybe a little flattery. All I want is to live out a story with him. Again and again, I watch the clips, hoping one day he will meet my eye, wondering if there are other secret children like me busily searching for him in the archive. It is possible I will meet them at some point, that there will be a constant flow of new relatives. "The number of lives that enter our own is incalculable," writes John Berger at the beginning of his book of memories, in which the past overruns the present and the dead mix with the living. I think of the secret kiosk of surprise kin, always on the brink of shaking things up.

My first father will always remain dimly realized, but I keep watching him zip through narrow country roads—an apparition—fierce and fast, appearing and vanishing.

GRAVE

I VISITED MY TRUE FATHER'S GRAVE. IT WAS NEITHER TOMB nor mausoleum. Just a flat marker the size of a large laptop that did not rise above the ground itself. Nine months after he died, the earth still looked newly turned but there was a fringe of clover and a few blowsy white dandelions growing around the stone. I dug a small hole and planted some thyme I had uprooted from our yard. I went to the car where my mother was waiting and opened the trunk and placed the dark stones I had brought into the hammock of my skirt and walked back to the grave. A small pile to keep his soul anchored. I knelt on the grass and asked him the important things. I told him what had grown from the seed of his death and saw that the grave was thirsty.

I had to say a lot of things at once, like *I miss you* and *I love you* and *I am writing about you*, and *I could really use a hand*. And as I said that last part I was grinning a bit, because I knew my dad would be raising an eyebrow and smiling in a way that said: "Even now, in my rest, you are asking me to help you with your homework."

My dad, reflecting on his days as a war correspondent, once told me: "Sometimes you have to bury the feeling to give a report." In his last decade, when he began making more personal films, he said: "Sometimes you have to bury the facts to give a feeling." Both of us knew, from experience, that everything buried, every feeling and every fact, is spring-loaded.

My mother was still sitting in the car. I asked her to wait a little longer while I went to fill a bottle from an outdoor faucet. The metal faucet creaked and sputtered as I turned the knob and a gang of pigeons exploded up from the ground.

When I returned to the grave, my mother was in an awkward crouch, watering the ground with tepid tea from her thermos. She kept looking over her shoulder as if she were doing something sneaky, like slipping my dad a little extra when no one was looking. I watched the dampness of the tea darken the beige dirt. Her fingers loosened the soil. Wiggling them around, she plucked out a small round stone and added it to the pile.

On the way back to the car, my mother stopped to examine a familiar flat white flower head with a tiny drop of blood-like red in the center. The big flower was made up of groups of little flowers. And each little flower had five petals. And each petal was a tiny mittened hand saying, *Hello*.

TEN:

RITTŌ

(beginning of winter)

HOLDING

IN LATE OCTOBER, MY MOTHER FELL TWICE. SHE HAD taken too many sleeping pills. No one said what this was. No one used the words *accidentally* or *deliberately*. I watched her closely, trying to read her rambling and agitated air. Her jolted sentences like black coffee, double shot. Did she see her own death coming? I moved her into our guest room, where the breeze stirred the curtains and made a glass of water shiver. I needed to hold her steady, remind her who she was and get rid of the unfamiliar person who wanted to die, the one who had replaced my mother.

My mother spent hours in the guest room, moving plants around, observing how they surged, as though pointing to where they wanted to sit next. My view from the third-floor loft was of my mother playing a game of Busby Berkeley with a slow-swirling flurry of choreographed pots.

Seeing how happy this made her, her easy absorption, I began adopting more plants. One day, I walked a small fiddle-leaf fig home from a convenience store, where I had found it dying beside a stack of Wonder Bread. I walked for fifteen blocks through sweet-smelling vape clouds, past strangers sweetly smiling at me and my strange plant-child.

A few days later, I went to a nearby pottery studio and began making vessels. My mother used to do this to "sweep the clouds" from her mind. I still remember shelves filled with her unfired pots. I kneaded the clay. I punched and pounded it until the pottery teacher said, *Whoa*. My pots were thick and lopsided. We tried to guess at what they could hold.

The pottery teacher gently encouraged me to create "multiples," in case one project didn't work out. She watched as I kneaded the clay and pushed my overgrown bangs out of my eyes, making ugly pot after ugly pot.

I liked pottery, I told her, because it felt like I was learning something tangible that might help me in the rest of my life, where I seemed to be working toward something less holding. "Hold-able?"

It was now mid-November and the gingko tree in our yard was still golden, but then the leaves fell all at once, in one complete cold-night shedding. The next morning when we stepped outside on our way to see the geriatric oncologist, the ground was a golden puddle.

In the hospital, the geriatric oncologist briefly touched my hand and said, *Let's talk.*

REPORT

ACCORDING TO THE DAUGHTER, THE PATIENT HAS EXPERI-
enced a slow decline in her memory over the past year. She has
lost some money, misplaced her health card today, as well as she
lost around five credit cards.

SHORT-TERM MEMORY: There is clear defect in this domain.
The patient repeats herself and sometimes forgets events.

ORIENTATION: Sometimes she loses track of the date and
day of the week.

LONG-TERM MEMORY: She remembers birthdays, wedding
dates, as well as her retirement history and the death of her
ex-husband.

LANGUAGE: She did not have difficulty with word-finding or
a shrinking of vocabulary but she is repetitive in conversation.

RECOGNITION: She is still able to recognize familiar faces
and objects (her daughter, son-in-law, grandsons, concierge
and the people in her building, as well as any object in her
apartment).

She was born in Japan and immigrated to UK in 1963, then after that from London UK to Toronto Canada in 1974. She worked as a tour guide in London, England. She was smoking before; however, she quit. Her smoking history was over 42 years with 3-packs per day. She is not drinking alcohol and she is swimming on a regular basis.

She scored 12/30 on the MoCA. She has signs of progressive memory loss, particularly with short-term memory and orientation issues. We suggested brain imaging which was done. She had a head CT which confirmed ███████████████████████ ███████████████████████████████ An MRI was subsequently done which further showed ████████████ ████████████

The patient and her daughter were informed about the diagnosis and management.

DRAWING

MY FRIEND DREW ME A PICTURE. IT SHOWED A BALL OF grief inside a box. On one wall of the box was a pain button. When the ball of grief was new it was very large and pressed against the pain button all the time, but as time passed the ball grew smaller. She told me: *Now, it takes a new grief or a sad movie or a certain smell to set the ball of grief moving again, bouncing against the pain button.*

My husband drew a lopsided oval with two eyes and a speech bubble: "What do you call a Buddhist potato?" The answer: "A medi-tater."

The resident doctor drew a picture of the neural path between my mother's eyes and her brain. He explained, *This area is choked with weeds.* Staring at the snarling lines, I wondered who would be the gardener of my mother's head. Who would be her head gardener?

The nurse drew circles drifting across a page and told me to breathe. *Imagine you are holding a bubble wand. Breathe in deeply and then, as you breathe out slowly and gently, imagine you are blowing bubbles into the room. As you keep breathing slowly and blowing your imaginary bubbles, feel your body become calm and relaxed.*

My mother, on request, drew a picture of a perfect clock set to 2:30. *Why are you crying?* she asked.

PRESS

THE ONCOLOGY NURSE TOOK ME INTO THE HALLWAY AND pressed me to her chest. It was more than a hug. It was formidable. It caught me just as my body stiffened, right as my feelings were about to ice over. She pressed into me her comfort, heat, courage, and the experience of others who had stood where I was standing.

When I was seven, my mother showed me how to press flowers in books using my father's heavy *Oxford English Dictionary* and his ancient world atlas. We would take bits of fern and sprigs of flower from a nearby park, harvesting them just before their peak. I remember blanketing pages with small wind-fallen blossoms and imagining the flowers rustling and growing between all the words, waiting to push their way out again, once the book was closed. I knew they would spring free eventually. There was nothing dead about a flower that tilted its head as it listened and waited for the right moment to surprise us; nothing stagnant about a book that spilled new treasures, every time.

Standing in the hospital corridor, I could not stop crying. I pressed myself to the wall, trying to steady myself enough to explain. "*It's just that, it's just that . . .*" But I couldn't get the words out. Eventually, the nurse nodded and said, "I know, I know. *It's just that* it's hard to fully accept something is wrong when you've already traveled down this path with one parent, and the thought of doing so again makes your heart sink into your boots."

⇜

DEMENTIA IS AN erosive illness. Erosion can be slow but it is unstoppable and irreversible. My father did not want to erode, so he skirted detection for as long as possible. When his MRI results were finally in hand, the doctors marveled at how long my father had been compensating for his declining memory—a testament to the brain's plasticity but also to the cunning and overdrive of a man used to forging his own way. *A hard-working bloke*, was the way one doctor put it. When people learned of my father's diagnosis, there was a "titan toppled" attitude to the news. Many of his colleagues and friends could not bear to see him disappear this way, losing his beautiful words, so they performed a disappearing trick of their own, in some ways a crueler tragedy. A handful of friends stuck around and for them we were grateful. Even at the peak of his illness, when the features of his "public self" had been nearly washed away, my father, with undimmed awareness, understood who was coming and going.

Erosion may be incremental but there are landmarks. Knowing how lucid he remained, I could not bear people who spoke over him, saying his name as if he wasn't present, or who raised and slowed their voices unnecessarily. IT'S TIME FOR DIN DIN. ISN'T THAT RIGHT, MICHAEL? My father, giant and gray as a mountain, always responded with a raised eyebrow: *Why is everyone yelling here?*

But the protectiveness I now felt toward my mother, and her personhood, was different. All my life, I had witnessed the tenuous grasp she had on visibility, the obvious pattern of store clerks showing her limited patience and people behaving as if she were hard of hearing, incoherent, or not there at all. I had watched her confront open derision ("ah so, no speaky Engrish"), and even outright rejection. I feared this diagnosis would simply be another reason for others to dismiss her as deficient. Being belittled when you are already considered little is a serious form of shrinkage. All I wanted was to protect her. When I finally managed to say this, the nurse bit her lower lip and nodded.

Now she was crying a bit too and pulling tissues from a box, *swish swish*, like a magician. I blew my nose. She blew hers. I could not fathom her sympathy. Talk stopped for a moment. Then she told me it wasn't my situation's uniqueness that moved her but its ordinariness. She told me she became a nurse to follow in the footsteps of her immigrant grandmother and mother, the former of whom had suffered from breast cancer and struggled within the healthcare system, revealing to her granddaughter the humanizing attention nurses can bring to lives already socially diminished. "I wish I could offer you some rum. Why don't I grab us some juice?"

It was not surprising when I later discovered she had won awards for her kindness. We need more kindness awards in this world of frequent breaking, I thought as I read her award citation. We need more people whose job is the work of reassembly and holding on to things and people.

I listened through the examination room door as I waited for the nurse to return. My mother was busy talking with the doctor and the residents. She had either forgotten or chosen to ignore their diagnosis. She was telling them about her time at hairstyling school.

I could hear it was all they could do to keep track. I pictured them looking at her like she was an Erratic Rascal of Memory. Her free associations and weird refrains: was it all just clinical?

"I can imagine it was difficult when you were growing up," the nurse said, handing me a plastic juice cup. "I mean, because your mother seems to lack . . ." She tapered off.

"Inhibition?" I offered with a smile. "Consistency? Compliance?"

"Yes," she smiled, "all of that."

❧

A MAN WITH a walker was slowly making his way down the hall-way. He was wearing a Montreal Canadiens sweater and stopped to bless us. He had a sore right foot but was otherwise fine.

"I'm ninety. I'm getting old and dumb. Old, old, old."

The nurse chimed in, "Old is Gold!"

❧

THE TEARS STARTED again. I told the nurse there were things I still needed to learn from my mother. Stories. Important ones.

I had dreamt of a memory migration, from my mother to me, like a smooth and seamless flock. But now the birds could not come, now they were a broken cloud, unable to decide which tree to land in, flying without focus to one tree, then another, then back again. In and out of time.

❧

IN THE YEAR of his diagnosis, my father worried over his memory loss and saw it as a form of widening amnesia. "I am getting soft in the head," he told me often. Witnessing his confusion and courage, there were many days I had to conceal my tears. He felt he was losing a vital thread of logic that made him who he was. The fixed patterns were breaking up. He leaned on us for verbal scaffolding. Often his fingers would pinch the air or gently worry the fabric of his trousers as if extracting the structure he needed. He kept trying to pull together the story-shape of his life, kept trying to remake a self with predictable and worthy seams.

It was only in the last year of his life that I saw him relax, accepting the dissolving boundaries of his world. Like the father in Raymond Antrobus's poem "Dementia," the illness became a "tender syndrome" which "simplified a complicated man." He was Sisyphus turning his back on the stone. There was a new vitality in him. Light filtered in. No longer at the heroic center of the story, he became a person who just wanted to sit silently in the day, uninterrupted and unembellished; released from deadlines, insecurity, haste, envy, prestige, released from all the things that had inflated and deflated his ego, that had fed his anxiety, his driven nature. It wasn't some kind of enlightened or spiritual silence. It was the way it was. This was how he ripened. This was the weird and contented bloom he became. Snapping to his favorite ABBA tunes, perfectly in time. Crying and openly exclaiming when he watched a film about the ocean.

The forgetting was still upsetting but I began to wonder if there was a positive form of self-forgetfulness that came with forgetting one's own habits of mind. I wondered why no one talked about this. Dementia stole many things away, but it broke my father out of a possession by plot that had ruled his work and life. Unpressed, letting go of the self in this way, making way for other selves, released my father from his human constrictions into an elusive happiness. People thought my father's brain had died but

I saw that it was only a part—and maybe not the best or most beneficent part.

Even before her illness, my mother's sense of selfhood was comparatively less bordered. She did not seem to mind or even particularly notice her erratic memory. She was not invested in her biographical presence or a reputation she did not socially possess. Maybe this was a result of years of being denied selfhood or an ego defending against repressed material; but if there was a vital thread, she seemed prepared to release it.

ALL THOSE DAYS I had sought direct answers to demanding questions. All those days, struck by her deflections, I questioned my sanity. All those days I felt we were racing against a different escalating illness. All those days she seemed serenely indifferent to the pressures of sequence and arc. All those days my mother was disappearing down alleyways, cutting through underbrush, escaping, fast and light on her feet.

All those days . . . My mother's brain was telling me she was not a specimen. She was not a flower I could place between the covers of a book. Her story would not remain where it was placed, pressed down to the page.

My mother veered, my mother declaimed, my mother lost track, my mother unbound the tightly held book called "My Story"— the most locked of forms—and let the papers and flowers fly.

At some point I stopped crying to the oncology nurse. I thanked her with a hug and went to get my mother, who was now ravenous and ready to eat. We made our way to the outdoor parking lot, crossing the street to meet my husband, who had just arrived.

A man with an IV pole wearing a hospital gown and white leather shoes with no socks was blocking the driveway, repeating, *All I want is a comfortable chair.*

All I want is a comfortable chair.

An e-bike zipped by, precariously close.

"What seems to be the trouble?" asked the attendant.

The man in the hospital gown shrugged. "I don't know, sir. Maybe I'm a little anxious."

TSUYOKU

IT IS A CURSE SOMETIMES TO CARRY UNFORGETTABLE THINGS. But, as Lewis Hyde puts it in *A Primer for Forgetting: Getting Past the Past*, "to praise forgetting is not, of course, the same as speaking against memory."

My cousin in Tokyo sent me a note the day after I shared the news of my mother's diagnosis with her. She had attached photos of city trees propped up with timber beams and wood supports. Red Pine. Cherry. Everyday Tokyo trees on everyday Tokyo streets. I looked at the photos and considered how many crutches it took to assist a weak limb or to help a young tree grow to maturity.

The daughters must be a good support for the mothers, wrote my cousin, whom I knew to be very dutiful but also a little lonely, although there was no way of confirming that these two traits were connected. *Tsuyoku shite kudasai*, she wrote again a few days later, adding a "flexed bicep" emoji.

444

THE CLOCK ON THE DASHBOARD READ 4:44. THIS WAS NOT a problem for anyone in the car but me. My husband noticed I was quietly studying the time and reached for my hand, held it until the clock changed to 4:45. My ravenous mother, in the backseat, ate a rice ball and then another, unaware of any eerie occurrence. She seemed to have already put the strangeness of the hospital appointment behind her. It was not clear if she had fully grasped the situation.

In many East Asian cultures, the number 4 is deemed unlucky. In Japanese, 4 is homophonous with the word "death." As I had traveled deeper into my family secret, the number 444 kept appearing everywhere I looked—clocks, registration plates, streetcars, ovens, receipts—filling me with dread.

I decided to consult my mystic uncle R., the one who'd set me on this journey in the first place. There were many strange things about my uncle and his spiritual intuitions, but also many nice things—including his unperturbed reply when I told him I was being pursued by 4s.

My uncle, who believes in the truths of numerology and horoscopes, and other maps for charting the ineffable, suspected I was seeing the triple 4 because a spirit of some kind was trying to communicate with me. 444 is a number of protection and encouragement.

It was possible the ghost of someone who had died was trying to let me know I was currently following the right path.

He consulted his Swiss psychic friend for a second opinion. His friend read my birth chart, compared it with my father Michael's chart, and replied: "The frequent seeing of 444 is a reminder that guardian angels are afoot and will protect her from all negativity." She said this was *incredibly fortuitous*. She added that if we tallied my father Michael's number with my own, it equaled 10 and therefore 1. "This resonates with new beginnings and positivity. His higher self chose that he should take his role in her life and her higher self chose him too. *It was meant to be.*"

The stars can bring people together, belief can change a path. I was generally not one for supernatural consolations, and I was clearly being confronted with battling numerical opinions, but in the presence of this fine new story, the 444s became bright and beautiful providence. In that moment, I was a believer. A predestinarian. Even the grouchy cynic in me could not refute the image of our higher selves meeting one another and saying: *You.*

It's true, I thought quietly. It was cosmically mapped. Planetarily planned.

This fable of ordained choice began to preoccupy me.

It would lead me to take my next step.

DECEMBER 2019—AUGUST 2020

ELEVEN:

TŌJI
(winter solstice)

WINTERESE

I SPEAK TO MY MOTHER IN JAPANESE, WHICH DESPITE MY passable accent is not the flowing song I want to hear. I have been brushing up with a language-learning app during aimless night walks around the neighborhood, trying to unbury dormant words while reminding my stubborn tongue of its original speech, speech that now sounds to my ear either infantile or starchily official. Having never learned Japanese as "vocabulary" or "grammar," I feel it sit inside me, an ungraspable cloud.

It is humbling, preparatory work. The geriatric oncologist has warned me it is not uncommon for people to return to their "mother tongue" as dementia progresses. Some people lose languages they acquired as adults and return to the reassuring cadences of the words they spoke as children. If this happens, I wonder, who will be left to communicate with my mother? I am recovering my Japanese to bring her familiarity, to bring her home to her long-ago memories. I use words and phrases I re-learn, readying myself for linguistic emergencies, but she puckers her forehead and replies in perfectly clear English.

Instead, my mother goes outside and answers my stammering attempts by speaking the garden. She speaks the shabby foliage and flat, grainy gloom. She speaks the seed heads that have been left for the birds; the ghostly ironweed skeletons. She speaks the slumbering roots, coiled and quiet beneath the ground.

The plants are soft brown, straw, rust and dun. They are breaking down, entering the crucible of the life cycle. Color has seeped away but there are still dahlias straying at the edge of winter, smothering fences down the street. My mother speaks dahlia!

I follow her and try to speak the garden, as well.

Do not tidy, she says, when she sees me holding shears to chop the old growth. *Who will be elders next spring if you chop, how will sprigs know how to grow?* She teaches me to speak husk, bone and winter stem. We listen to the wind churning the last five leaves off a maple. We speak the dinginess of ground covered in mush, the reek of nourishing rot. We speak air, full of compost, smell of wet iron and blood. We touch the un-languageable.

And for a moment I believe the decomposition of the garden, in practical terms, will help me accept the breakdown of my mother. I hear the dead flowers offering essential counsel. I don't care if this is the lie of a pretty scene, the dishonesty of attractive ruins, frosted with light snow.

All those times she said *Nihongo wa hanashimasen ka?!* All the times I thought I disappointed her with my faltering words. I assumed she wanted me to speak with the fluency of a professor or a poet; now I see all she wanted was to share something we could call *ours*.

SIDE LOVES

MY FATHER MICHAEL PLACED THOSE WHO LOVED HIM IN separate rooms. Then he died and the walls separating us began coming down. People stepped out from behind skimpy partitions to explain the role they had played in his life. I reached out to other people I knew only by name, determined to make a loft of his partitioned life.

Many months before, when I had met my father's final mistress, she had mentioned that my father had two other important lovers. She had given me the name of one—J. In early winter, I reached out to J. and asked if she would meet me for coffee. I had delayed this meeting, worried that uninvited information might come my way and throw my already flimsy understanding into havoc. There were things I wanted to know but I was not sure I could cope with the stress of the unasked-for.

This was the second "other woman" I would be meeting in person, but any feelings of disloyalty to my mother had subsided. With my mother's own infidelity lifted into the light of day, she was now cast in a less innocent role. She had transgressed. I was proof. There was no moral high ground when you had been on both sides of the story—aggrieved and aggrieving.

Still, I felt nervous. I half hoped that J. would not show up. I fought the urge to cancel. But my friends pushed me to go. *It might be helpful*, they said. *She might know something.* It was true. The story I had uncovered was so strange and unreal and deeply buried, there had been days when I doubted my perception at every turn and thought I might be losing a toehold in reality. At the very least, I thought, J. will confirm my surprise and confusion. And at best? At best, she would have answers to the questions that had troubled me: Did Michael really know I was someone else's child? Did he freely choose to raise me?

My mother had promised he knew the truth but I could not rely on her promises. Every time I broached the subject, her replies shifted. It still seemed possible that my father had been fooled or had even fooled himself. He could easily have convinced himself that the doctor on Harley Street had been wrong about his sterility.

I met J. near the university campus, at a popular student café. A cashier took my order from behind a tower of French pastry and then a voice from behind called me over to a quiet table. Still glamorous in her early seventies, J. was exactly as she had looked at my father's memorial, tall and willowy, eyes soft with kindness. But now there was a hint of reserve. "So," she said, after we had lumbered through a bit of small talk. The look on her face was tentative, expectant. I realized she had been readying herself for what I had to say.

I took a deep breath and began to share the story of what I had discovered, beginning with the DNA test. She grew very still as I spoke. When I finished, I told her I needed her help determining what my father knew and did not know. I could feel her gentle scrutiny, eyes now sweeping my face.

"*Entre nous*," she said, finally. "I don't want you to put this down on paper."

"Of course not," I said, quickly.

Then she began to speak, what I was to hear but not repeat. She told me she met my father through work soon after she arrived in London on September 28, 1972, "the day Paul Henderson scored the winning goal in the 1972 Canada-Russia hockey series." She provided little information about the few years they spent together but she made it clear that the initial intensity of their relationship—he was forty-two and she was twenty-five—soon passed into a devoted, long-lasting friendship.

She confirmed my father knew I was not his child, that he had shared with her the story of my mother calling him with the news of her pregnancy when he was in Vietnam. As she spoke, I found myself nodding, bobble-headed, saying, *oh, oh, oh* . . . the dots finally connecting. J. was the first person to verify what my dad knew and possibly felt. This was all the more remarkable because it was not at all in my father's character to confide something so personal. She was special.

I asked if he had ever considered telling me the truth and she said he was conflicted. "Every few years we would discuss it and he would decide it was not the time." They had agreed sometimes it was kinder to keep a secret, my dad and his secret confidante.

In *Secrets: On the Ethics of Concealment and Revelation*, Sissela Bok writes that secrets may bring misery or benefit:

> [T]he myth of Pandora's box unfolds interweaving layers of secrecy and revelation. It is one of the many tales of calamities befalling those who uncover what is concealed and thereby release dangerous forces that should have been left in darkness and silence. Other myths tell of secrets that are destructive only so long as they *remain* concealed. Not until someone penetrates them can their evil power be defeated.

This distinction, between misery and benefit, ignores a thorny truth: sometimes one doesn't know what will happen when a secret is spoken. What seems initially destructive ends up being beneficial. Or vice versa. My father was a thoughtful man, a man who valued craft and control. He would have studied the physics of his secret—the distance from the ground, the speed of the fall. He would have shaken his head at the possibility of a violent landing and worried how I would judge my mother, how our already fragile relationship might shatter.

I realized J. was looking at me. She repeated her question. "Does it help?"

I looked back at her.

"Does it help to know all of this?" she said again.

"I think so."

J. smiled a careful smile, then she looked away. Even though she was being supportive, I could see I made her uneasy. How could I not? I was on a quest, wandering through the emotional landscape of my father's life. She held papers I needed, papers my father had wished to remain hidden. It was not just that they had a secret relationship. She was my father's accomplice. A part of me felt shocked and excluded by this bond.

"Is there anything else I can tell you?" she asked.

There was a finality to her tone that told me once we left the café, there would be no future meetings. *What else did I need to know?*

"There's something I can't stop wondering," I said. "What do you think held them together?"

My father said many times that he and my mother had a complicated love, but he never adequately explained the bond they shared, a bond so intangible I could not recall the slightest display of open affection between my parents. Not a single embrace or loving utterance. Or was I misremembering their dynamic? I thought of water gushing from the faucet as my mother filled the kettle for my father's favorite Nescafé every morning. The soft cotton shirts she always bought him. The brief, adoring gesture of a slipped shawl lifted back onto a shoulder. The small, specific tendernesses.

What held them? I wanted J.'s opinion. Was it guilt, sentimentality, grief over a lost mother?

"Well, I think your father genuinely cared about your mother," she said.

"Yes."

"But." *Here it comes*, I thought.

What she told me next shifted many of the things I had worked out to that point. She explained that my father left for periods of time when I was very young but he always came back, drawn by my mother's litany of threats—including a warning that she would tell me the truth when I was old enough to understand. Over and over, I became a weapon, wielded any time my father fell out of line or failed to do what my mother wished. The secret, in other words, did not lie quietly undisturbed. It moved through the house, a fierce electric wire with the power to mute and control.

"But she tried to leave him too," I said finally. "And every time she tried to leave, she said he would pull her back . . ."

"Because he worried he would never see you again. And he worried that you would be alone. With your mother."

J.'s revelation silenced me. I could hear her take a sip of coffee, swallow, the cup gently clinking on the saucer. I had no reason to disbelieve her. I knew my mother's penchant for threats. In my memory, I saw the leather steamer trunk she had always kept packed, telling me both directly and indirectly, *If you are not a good daughter to me, I will leave you and return to Japan.* This threat was used any time I disappointed her or disagreed too strongly, any time she felt that mothering was too much trouble or her anger bubbled over about her lot in life. Back then I assumed other mothers had a trunk. Eventually I learned to hear what a packed trunk was really saying, *I want to go home.* But as a child I simply accepted that love was inconstant, varying in volume. I allowed my mother's threats to pass as normal. Just as I accepted her strange promises, including the promise she made on several occasions that she would hide me in a cave if there was ever a need, a promise that came from the scene in *The Sound of Music* where the nuns shelter the Von Trapps from the Nazis in the Abbey crypt. I may have shrugged as I imagined her ushering me to safety, but it never occurred to me to ask, *What cave? What Nazis?*

"So he stayed to protect me, like a human shield," I echoed numbly. "To protect me from my mother."

If this was true, was it worth it?

IT WAS A difficult story to tell: how my white father came to my rescue, how he always wanted me to have more love, wanted me to love my mother more, wanted me to be free, fulfilled and mighty, while my mother, robbed of better circumstances, often seemed to want less for me.

But J. was not entirely right about my parents' bond. In fact, I thought she was wrong. Even if they were locked together by a lie, a current of devotion had lasted between them, something as simple as a commitment to not giving up or turning away. This was not just something I wished to believe as their child. In fact, I am inclined to think life would have been easier without that current. But I had seen it.

My mother did not always like the closeness my father and I shared. In his later years, and especially when he was weakened by the metastatic cancer that would eventually kill him, she asked me repeatedly why I took *his side*. Why did I care so much what happened to him? *How could you be loyal to him when he betrayed me?* But, after his death when I uncovered their secret, her anger disappeared. Sensing that my feelings for my father had been jeopardized, she began polishing and buffing his memory. At the very moment she could have demonized him, convincing me that he had forced her to collude in secrecy or even engineered their deception, she let her grievances go.

Don't judge him, she told me. *He loved you. He always wanted to keep you safe*. She used words like *nice gift* to describe the impact we had on each other. She told me, repeatedly, how he saved my life when I was a baby, removing me from the Hospital for Tropical Diseases where a fever had been misdiagnosed and I was not getting any better. *He saved your life*, she said. *He saved your life!*

They protected each other. A fidelity persisted in the absence of marital faithfulness—a fidelity maybe only possible in a situation of mutual betrayal.

➤

WE WERE STILL in the café. There was a sort of cool barrier around J. but I could feel it dissolving ever so slightly as she noticed me looking downward. She stopped and, very tenderly, asked, "Are you alright?"

I looked up and saw with a bit of awe how perfectly she sat with her hands in her lap—the freshly cut and colored hair, the voice steady, any emotion withheld, so unlike my mother. I wondered what she knew about my mother beyond her role as

"Michael's wife." I thought of two women who were mainly outlines to each other and how difficult it was to fill in the needs or desires of an adversary.

I could hear the warmth in her voice but a ring of caution encircled me. I think I felt slightly humiliated. I did not know what to think of this stranger who had known very personal things about me for a very long time, this keeper of our secrets, who was perhaps my last gateway to family memory as my mother's memory decomposed into fragments and dust.

I knew I would regret walking away but it was a relief to say goodbye.

MY TWO BEST friends met me for lunch that day. I tried to tell them what I had learned but my thoughts and emotions were knocking around wildly inside me. I rambled to them about a book I had just finished reading about a man, a former speechwriter for Barack Obama, who grew up with an emotionally unstable and manipulative mother; a man who also learned in adulthood that his dad was not his biological father. *The recognition as he described his mother's rages, the psychological chaos, his own forbidden anger, all the times he had to tuck it away because the air was already crowded with his mother's awful wrath* . . . I told them I didn't know if I could even look at my mother anymore. When I said this, one of my friends warned me to *create boundaries, right away*, but the other just shook her head and said quietly: *She can't.*

She was right. Boundaries had never been my mother's strong suit. And, anyway, we were well past that point.

THE WATER FLOWS

MY MOTHER SAYS 水に流す. SHE SAYS, "*MIZU NI NAGASU*. DO you know its meaning?"

Yes. I repeat it: *Mizu ni nagasu.*

The water flows. Let the river carry what is unneeded away.

I AM INSPECTING the clothes in my mother's wardrobe, touching her folded sweaters, looking for something I might wear on a windy bike ride home. She says, *mine mine mine.*

It is not so much possessiveness, I think, as an effort to keep track. Every morning she places her thoughts on hangers in her closet.

"You should keep everything chained up," she says, showing me the complicated tract of stretchy coils, lanyards, hooks and bells that kept her belongings tethered inside her purse.

"That's good advice, Ma."

She likes it when I play the role of the impractical daughter accepting guidance. Lately, she has taken to prefacing her advice with "*wake up*" statements. Such as, *Wake up*:

It's a white man's world.

English is the language of money.

Men do not like women with a baggy uterus.

Nothing lasts for long.

If you care too much, it will die.

"What will die, Ma?"

"The plant. Stop watering. Leave it alone and it knows how to grow."

"I'm just preparing. I have to leave for a couple of weeks."

Back in the mountains, I head into the woods. My students and I stand among tall, swaying evergreens while the leader of our medicine walk pours us tiny cupfuls of tea. I worry about my mother but I also know she has been folded into my husband's vast, queer, multiracial family, a family that had been enacting new modes of relation since the 1960s when a few Americans traveled north to Canada to protest the Vietnam War and counsel other draft dodgers.

In my residency room, the phone rings through the night, every few hours or minutes. Twenty-two straight calls. My mother is unanchored by my absence. Her voice tumbles into the quiet in the form of random questions and statements. *Wake up.* At 4 a.m., unable to settle back to sleep, I blurrily scroll through my phone—a whiplash of content that does nothing to soothe my twitching mind. The salty chocolate pudding is very good. Australia is burning . . .

Blood-orange skies and pink Martian suns. Blazing forests and trees reduced to charcoal poles. It is an otherworldly scene. *Omnicide* will be the word used by Danielle Celermajer, a professor of sociology at the University of Sydney, to describe the previously unwitnessed horror of Australia's 2019–2020 bushfire season. "[H]umans, animals, trees, insects, fungi, ecosystems, forests, rivers (and on and on) being killed . . . in recent years, environmentalists have coined the term *ecocide*, the killing of eco-systems—but this is something more. This is the killing of everything." *Wake up*.

"IT'S THE DETACHMENT," my photographer uncle A. says, when he emails me old pictures of my parents and me. He has an eye and notices things like the hint of intimacy or aloofness in a gap between two bodies. The mini proofs of affection and distance.

"Note the cool demeanor," Uncle A. writes. "Her shoulder turned slightly away, barely perceptible. Her eyes elsewhere . . . not upon him, or even you. The odd sense of mutual alienation . . ."

My mother continues to leave voicemails through the night: *Wake up, Kyo-chan / Honest is very important / That's what Oscar Wilde said a long time ago / I don't know what to say / English is my second language / Kawaii Kyo-chan / I know you were a sweetie-pie / I brought you up almost by myself / And daddy he loved you / You know I mean Michael / I think you believe friends and students are more important than family / But I have a big question mark about that / I try to do my best / Okay desu / Please call mummy. Arigatou / I'm getting crazy about these things / Why don't you call / Why do you have to speak in English? / Don't you remember who I am?*

I return home to find my mother has jerry-rigged a complicated scaffold for our amaryllis with chopsticks and twist ties. The full moon tampers with our hearts. Across the city, the moon gleams over the greenhouse and somewhere inside it, pressed to glass, are five amaryllis keening for their cousins in Australia. All those plants down under are gobbling up the poison in the sky. Amaryllis can survive fire but how much fire and for how long?

It will be months before plant shoots begin to push out of the scorched ground and from charred trunks, tiny tendrils of growth.

Wake up.

WE ARE SITTING together, scrolling through photos of my trip, when I come across a picture I have saved on my phone of A., smiling and stylish in his old age. I am about to swipe left but my mother lifts her hand: *Stop.* There he is in his tortoiseshell glasses in a warm beam of sun. I feel a pang, a feeling I can't pin down as my own.

"When you see this photo of A., do you think of what might have happened? Do you think . . ."

"Yes," my mother says quietly.

WAKE UP

ONE DAY, TOWARD THE END OF MY TENTH YEAR, I WENT TO
a big department store in Toronto with my mother. We were walking around when we heard a strange voice coming from store
speakers. My mother walked up to the cashier and asked, *What
is that?* The cashier handed her a cassette tape. On the cover was
a black-and-white photograph of her old friend with her eyes
closed, kissing her husband. *I'll take it,* said my mother.

The album by the Japanese artist and the English musician was
released in the middle of November 1980, and the first reviews
were almost uniformly negative. "Critics moaned about the album's
unevenness and self-involvement," writes Hanif Abdurraqib.

My mother and I listened to the cassette in her bedroom with my
nineteen-year-old Japanese cousin who was living with us at the
time. I remember sitting on the carpet. The first song was already
familiar from the radio. Breezy and up-tempo. Then we got to
the second track. It started quietly with Y. softly whispering in
Japanese: *Darling, hold me.* But by the end of the song, when the
English lyrics had faded out, Y.'s moaning and panting had reached
a peak. She called out to her lover to make love to her stronger and
faster. She called out in Japanese, in the full throes of pleasure. Or
was it pain?

My mother's eyes widened. My cousin looked at the tops of her slippers in silent horror.

More, more, demanded the Japanese artist in Japanese. My mother started giggling. My cousin did too. "I like that," my cousin said, laughing louder. "I like that a lot."

I remember the look of shock on my mother's face shifting into something else: admiration. The Japanese artist's voice was commanding, loud and unashamed. She was all the things the Asian women who raised me had been to me. But, in white circles, under the stress of adapting to a new culture and country, they had learned to quieten themselves.

I was only ten. My breasts were two tiny hills and the Japanese artist's confidence, the possibility of becoming an unbridled adult, seemed remote. I was so shy I could barely confide my desires and wants to myself for many years, but somewhere I tucked away the sonic promise of her moaning. Socialized by her orgasmic screaming, mothered by her music and outspokenness, I learned the possibility of unapologetic desire. The power of becoming an unbecoming woman. A woman demanding *more*.

"There is the sound of a woman coming to a climax on it, and she is crying out to be held, to be touched," Y. explained to *Playboy* when the album was released. "It will be controversial, because people still feel it's less natural to hear the sounds of a woman's lovemaking than, say, the sound of a Concorde, killing the atmosphere and polluting nature."

The Japanese artist was disparaged for the six songs she contributed to the collaborative album. But that all changed a month later after her husband's murder. She was now a widow. "Once-negative reviews . . . were pulled, or never run, and then later adjusted," writes Abdurraqib.

A year after the English musician was murdered, my mother and I were visiting New York City. She took me to the Japanese artist's apartment, just off Central Park. She wanted to leave a note for her old friend with the doorman. "I am very sorry about your husband," she wrote. "I hope you have found your daughter."

TWO YEARS AFTER her husband's murder, the Japanese artist released a song called "Wake Up." It is a song about starting again and being unafraid to accept the love and good of the world.

BACKSTAGE

WHEN I FINALLY MET Y. FOR THE FIRST TIME, I WAS IN UNI-
versity. It was March 1996 and a wrecking ball had crashed through
our family home, bursting my parents' marriage wide open. Y.
had recently released her "comeback" album and was on a multi-
city tour that brought her to Toronto for a small, sold-out
performance.

When the concert finished, I was standing at a sticky bar
counter chatting with the drummer when my friend mentioned
to him that my mother had been friends with the Japanese artist.
The drummer asked us to wait a moment and disappeared. When
he returned, he waved, *Follow me.*

A few minutes later, I was sitting backstage with Y. in a small
greenroom. There was a buzzing energy around her but when I
knelt down by her feet she became subdued. She took my hands
and lowered her face toward me as one would during a benedic-
tion. "Tell your mother I still haven't found our daughter," she said.

Her eyes were soft and kind and after she told me I had a nice
face she began to tell me the story of my mother wanting to adopt
her little girl. "I was making art and scraping together a life . . . I
never thought your mother and father could have a child of their
own." She explained that my parents had tried to conceive for a
long time. And when they finally did . . . "Your mother named you
after my daughter."

I gently pulled my hands away, suddenly overheated in my wool duffle coat. At this point, I had no idea there was another daughter my mother had wanted with all her heart and that this wanting was carved into my name.

If Y. noticed the ripple her words had created, she didn't openly acknowledge it. Or maybe she did. Just as I was thinking our conversation was over, she let out a sigh and pointed to my stomach. "*Onaka ga sukimashita ka?*" she asked. I nodded.

At the restaurant, seated among a dozen or so people, I felt her watching me from across the large table, nodding kindly, affirming something. She seemed to grow more contemplative and withdrawn as the night went on, perhaps exhausted by the demands of touring. The plates of Italian food kept arriving. She gestured, *eat*, reminding me of the Asian mums and aunties who always offered food when a moment was difficult, when talking just made things worse.

I ate what was offered, I ate too much, listening to the chatter around me. For years, my parents tried and failed to have a baby. This was a secret. I didn't allow myself to know it at the time. By the time the meal was over, I had let that information dissolve and joined my friends at an after-dinner hotel party.

ENVY

AND SO, I MISUNDERSTOOD, OR SIMPLIFIED, THE NATURE OF my mother's envy. For years, I thought it was tied to the Japanese artist's happy marriage. Her fame. Her artistic notoriety. Her wealth. I thought what she resented about Y. was her stuntwoman willingness to roll through the flames of public scorn. I thought maybe their friendship would have lasted longer under different circumstances. Maybe it was to be expected: the breakdown of love between two friends who were not loved by the wider culture.

When asked, my mother's most consistent complaint was that her friend *took and took and never gave*. In my mother's view, her friend's artistic ambition lent her a cruel, unmotherly focus. She became too separate a self.

When Y.'s daughter was kidnapped, my mother felt terrible for her friend. She never called it karma or punishment. Only once, when she sensed I was being too admiring of Y.'s work, did she suggest that losing your daughter was what happened when you didn't want it.

Want what, Ma?

My mother's envy was multilayered, charged by her own feelings of frustrated agency, but it was also rooted in something very simple. In my mother's eyes, the Japanese artist possessed what my mother had wanted most. *That daughter.* The one that was not hers.

IT IS ONLY years later, when I am pondering names for my first child, that I think how strange it is to choose a name preloaded with memories and comparisons; a name to be worn like a borrowed garment. I wonder if my namesake grew up to be happy and independent; if she found her own way. I know she was reunited with her mother in the late 1990s and, shortly after, made brief contact with my mother to let her know she was safe and well.

A brief online search leads me to an artist statement by the daughter, accompanying an exhibition of eleven erupting ceramic spheres in Iceland: "My pieces are heads exploding with ideas while also struggling to contain identity. They are vaginas and wombs, beautiful in their release and in their reservation. Lately, I've been dealing with my personal history. The past will come out whether we allow it or not."

SPILL

WE WERE SITTING TOGETHER AT THE KITCHEN TABLE, THE wind blowing into and out of the room through an open door. We had been drawing with ink when a strong gust toppled the tiniest and narrowest ink bottle, leaving a long lean of blue across a roll of white paper. We watched with a sense of distance as the ink pooled prettily into a soft puddle before I righted the bottle again. I was finding it hard to make eye contact with my mother. She kept turning her shoulders and her head away, refusing to return my look. She was still mad at me for traveling and leaving her, although she wouldn't say it directly.

I always know when she is upset because when I am most unguarded and distracted, she likes to drop "truth" bombs of information.

"Let me tell you something," she said, her voice suddenly energetic and frank. I braced myself.

"Let me tell you something," she said again, this time leaning in. "He wanted me to get rid of you. He gave me money and said, 'Take care of it.'"

I knew immediately she was referring to A. I looked at my husband, whose eyes had widened. I took a deep breath and slowly exhaled.

"Do you understand?" she said, her voice cold.

"Ma," I said, meaning *we don't have to go back there*.

"Do you want to know what he said?" My husband was shaking his head fast. *No, no, no*.

But she kept going. "He said, 'You must have an abortion.' He told me, 'Get rid of it.'"

My husband and I caught eyes. What kind of story was this? Was it a tale of rescue?

My mother continued, "I told him, 'I can do this alone.' Maybe I shouldn't have."

"Shouldn't have?" A familiar burble of anxiety rose in my chest. "This is a new story, Ma. Are you sure you're remembering correctly? Why are you telling me this now?"

"There's nothing wrong with my memory! Do you understand?"

I understood. *Maybe she shouldn't have*. It was a terrible thing to say to me. That's why she said it.

Of all the scenarios she had planted in my head, all the origin stories whispered and blurted and confidentially explained, which was the most ripened and true? Which version could be trusted? Was it the consoling scenario where my birth father came to see me when I was three years old, a secret but proud dad slipping into the back aisle of the Adelphi Theatre where I was performing in *The King and I*? Was it the one where he never knew of my existence, never suspected anything at all? Or was it this scenario? What was the truth?

I rolled up the paper with the ink stain very slowly, while an icy feeling filled my limbs. As she prepared to be driven home, I heard my mother, who was still not making eye contact or acknowledging me, tell my husband that while her daughter might be "clever" (she made a dismissive gesture), he was definitely "smarter" than I was. She was smiling as she left and seemed, if not quite happy or triumphant, unfazed.

≫

"THERE WERE OTHERS, before and after," my husband said, when he returned. We were standing in the kitchen. "Your mother just told me in the car. She had other boyfriends during her marriage."

"So it wasn't all sacrifice or standing at the sink, ruefully?"

"Apparently not."

"What is wrong with her?"

"Hey," he said. He watched me with a kind, sad look on his face. "Please. Try not to take it personally."

"When she says she should have aborted me?"

"It's not her, it's the dementia. The confusion, the stories that change, her gift for accidentally saying horrible things, it's her illness speaking."

I shook my head.

He reminded me that people of all kinds, even ambivalent fathers, fall head over heels for their children, no matter what dramas led to their birth. In other words, even if this latest story was true, I should not assume that my birth father's feelings would have remained the same. He was trying to pull me out of a dangerous vortex.

"You have to be prepared," he said, making a rollercoaster motion with his hand. For a long time he had been constructing a mute button in my mind, something to press when my mother and I launched into *old dynamics*.

"For what?"

"For the variations to keep arriving. For the details to keep changing."

My sons came into the kitchen and we stood in a half circle around the table. "What happened now?" they asked.

"It might be nothing," I said.

"Nothing," my husband said.

Press it, he was saying. Press the mute button.

A FEW DAYS later I asked my mother about her other boyfriends, but she denied having ever said such a thing.

That night I told myself: Do not be frightened of your mother's head. Step inside and listen to what she is actually telling you. What she says, maybe it is unreliable and upsetting, but it is also passionate. Sink down to the heart of things and hear what she is always saying: *No one will protect you like I do. Stop waiting to be acknowledged by your fathers. They are not the main narrative. I am not the background to the fathers.*

I was working very hard to keep a safe distance from the impact of my mother's words. But something inside me was still pulling itself to standing, still struggling to understand and forgive.

The truth: when she dropped this particular bomb, hoping to disassemble me with her feigned or real regret, she made me the background to *her* story, inflating herself as a martyr, demanding I recede.

WHEN MY MOTHER STARTED FORGETTING, AND I BECAME her remembering daughter, she moved into a retirement residence near us with full-time nursing staff. The first week there, she tried to put food on the plate of a woman seated at a neighboring table. The woman, Eileen, had confided in my mother that she was lonely. My mother gave her a baked potato as a friendship offering. The management misunderstood this gesture of affection and called it "food dumping." The truth was my mother seldom went out of her way to share and she didn't like potatoes, so they had a point.

They wanted my assurance she could behave decorously and live without assistance on the independent-living floor. Could my mother, a woman loaded with sparks and personality, observe basic etiquette? Could she be a neatly packaged human? I didn't know. Even if I could have answered with certainty at that moment, I didn't know what kind of person she would become as her inner life spilled out, turning everything that was solid into a faltering, otherworldly version of itself.

What she needs, I said, turning the tables, *is understanding*. She wasn't good with unquestioned authority or rules she found nonsensical. Forget the regimental paternalism that was often confused for "help." She wouldn't put up with phony cheer or care lords lording over her.

Got it? Good.

TOUCH

WHEN MY MOTHER STARTED FORGETTING AND HER THOUGHTS fell like anarchic rainfall, I became a protective daughter. I tried to protect her flow and independence but it overwhelmed me, her unstoppability. She wandered and freely crossed the worlds of the real and the dreamt, the present and the past. There was sometimes no sharp line where a day bordered night, or one emotion separated from another.

I tried to lead her to a place where she could flow with secure edges. I wanted for her a river-rush toward life but also safeguards and a raft.

Touch is its own sorcery and when I bumped or leaned into my mother, I noticed she was often becalmed. When we went for walks, I began holding her forearm with a touch that was gentle but straightforward. I took her hand with its veins of a leaf and felt the tension evaporate. When she rested in bed, I touched her feet and felt her let go. Psychologists have a term for our need for touch. It's called "skin hunger." The touch was for her. It was for me. A form of corroboration. *We exist.*

I noticed my mother enjoyed it most when the touch did not feel directed.

It is harder than it seems to touch someone in a directionless way, but I put myself in my mother's feet, creating genial patterns with my hand, up and down, circling, an infinity loop, trying to remove my brain from my fingertips and touch in a way that did not appear to be caring overly much. Comfort can be weirdly triggering. Somewhere in our cells, old apprehensions awaken. If I wanted to impart a message, I knew it had to be of a general nature.

One day, I felt a breakthrough. The room was still and, for a brief moment, I sensed an unfamiliar energy in the particles of the air; there was an emotional lightness, as if the particles had decided we had struggled enough, all the years we had moved through space together. A shift. I could feel her, she was there, as I was here. Calm hearts. She was silent, then looked up. "It's gone," she said.

Even though I didn't know exactly what she meant or if we meant the same thing, I smiled and nodded.

LISTING

WHEN MY MOTHER STARTED FORGETTING, AND I WAS HER daughter touching her feet in Toronto, my brother in Shanghai wrote to tell me about a virus that had reached his city. He attached a map showing his home, a blue dot, and nearby a red dot to signal a confirmed infection. In his apartment, the elevator buttons, now potential "virus transmitters," were covered in cellophane. Someone had placed a cup full of wooden toothpicks ("non-contact sticks") beside the buttons. At the grocery store, he photographed the fronted shelves, just one layer of product and behind that nothing. A Potemkin village of tinned fish and vegetables caught in a hygienic glare.

The virus had landed *over there* and I was at my mother's place, sitting on a chair slipcovered with a giant beach towel to protect it from dust. The television was on as it had been for my entire visit, the unstoppable January news coming out of it. But the news of the virus was still remote. Even when my brother sent advice for "when the virus hits," suggesting I source medical masks immediately, the warning felt improbable; an overreaction.

Only slowly did it dawn. And then, into the transformations of spring, as slow-stirring seeds leapt to life, the virus that was *over there* hopped on a plane or stowed away on a ship or drove across a border and it was *here*.

As the virus spread in March 2020 and we entered lockdown along with much of the world, I began making lists. I made lists because it was the start of a pandemic and we were in an unfamiliar orbit, churned by fears of contagion, spiraling in loose circles, experiencing moments without linear order or clear direction. "Listing" is a nautical term to describe when a vessel takes on water and tilts to one side. I had been out of balance, inside a roiling feeling of unknowing for long enough that the uncertainty did not alarm me as it might have others. The world went vague but the lists, edged with unbalancing and lolling mist, were anchoring.

My sons were fifteen and nineteen. My older son's girlfriend moved in and joined our pod. The pantomime of online school with its ideas of goals and competence, which had never entirely convinced my sons, was quickly jettisoned.

With an outbreak at her residence in April, my mother also came to stay with us. *Was she incubating the illness? Were we?* The public health nurse called every day to monitor our situation. *Open the windows in all your rooms*, he advised. We located a thermometer, stocked up on vitamins and magical thinking, gargled with apple cider vinegar and, before every meal, practiced ten rounds of deep breathing to expand our lung capacity—a loop of air in the chest, in the diaphragm, in the alveoli.

Months before Black Lives Matter burst open the lie of a safe and insulated quarantine, before the health crisis transformed into a political uprising against the ongoing murders of Black people by the police, before the surge of anti-Asian violence, we could not stop tracking breath.

A warm afternoon in early spring, I watched the street from our second-floor window, noting the passersby. There was the boy who zoomed up to strangers on his trike in a doomed performance of social distancing. The little girl who liked to trace her fingers along fences and up poles in a daydreamy way, oblivious to sterilities. There was my fifty-five-year-old next-door neighbor who limped to catch the bus to his factory job. Through the same window a year later, I would watch two paramedics carry his blue body (sudden death by heart attack) towards an ambulance as his brother wept unstoppably. There was the white man who always gave me and the Asian man on the corner a farcically wide berth when he passed us on the street—a reminder of what happens when you assign a virus a nationality. There was the woman with the impeccable white-and-gold Adidas, the woman darting precisely past the mail carrier, the one panic-planting tomato seedlings in the velvet darkness of her garden. I had questions for all of them. *What is your shelf of plenty? What is your essential? Who are the kin in your tightly sealed bunkers? Have you chosen well and generously?*

No fever. Good appetite. No cough, I reported when the public health nurse called to check on my mother every morning. The bubble families I now witnessed on my night walks embodied a vision of intense absorption; the beauty of our most atomic, cocooning selves but also a mordant narrowness and unnatural self-sufficiency, defined by the threat outside.

But in spring, at our most separated and privatized, I came across another, more bounteous vision. One morning, I read of Pina Andelora and her partner Angelo Picone, two street musicians and community activists living in Naples. When the city became a ghost town and soup kitchens closed, they began to prepare meals for their homeless neighbors. Observing social distance, they relied on an old Neapolitan custom by lowering food baskets from their balcony. In the basket, along with the food, a notecard: "you can take and you can add."

If the pandemic gave respectability to the worst impulses of retreat and ownership, if, as Lydia Davis would have it, it was a difficult "prologue" or "dress rehearsal" for future emergency response, there were anti-isolationist beacons who refused to retreat to the smallest, most neurotic and boundaried version of kin; what the UK-based Care Collective decried in its beautiful manifesto as "paranoid and chauvinist caring imaginaries." Instead of contraction and overly particularized love: a dilation, a widening attention to others.

To live tightly might be medically sound but it is no way to live, ethically or planetarily speaking. To lift care out of the bubble is to reveal the not-so-subtle violence behind any idea of limited caring capacity. Months later, the lesson of vaccine apartheid as variants hopped across oceans: no one is safe without an abundant internationalism, without the will to make life truly livable for all.

One of my best friends put it this way in a magazine interview: "Scarcity love [as opposed to abundance love] justifies barbarism. It can play out at a familial level or a neighborhood level, a national level or a race level, but the governing ethos is out of my love for my own, however 'my own' is defined. I justify whatever it takes to protect my own." This same friend, on the first Father's Day following my genetic discovery, forwarded an "Alternative Father's Day Reading List," a mindset-change to remind me that the most important question about paternity is not the tightly clenched *Who is the father?* but the more loosely held *Who or what do you want them to be?*

"People out shopping for groceries now stop by our baskets and leave something inside," Picone, in Naples, told one reporter. "Pasta, sugar, coffee and cans of tuna."

While local larder gestures are no substitute for state support or a redistributive economy, and while it might seem a form of lopsided charity to offer a basket from on high, I was taken by the possibility of unobliterable reciprocity. Of care as a different kind of super-spreader event. Of a care-giver becoming a care-taker, by which I mean a recipient of care, in the contact dance between unseen strangers. In this act of poetic hospitality, I found a small reminder that a family can be a much larger and swirling aggregate; that well-being and security are more than banked capital.

In placing food in a basket, I communed with the stranger who long ago fed my hungry father when he was a boy and told him he would be okay. The gesture of the *panaro solidale*, or "the suspended basket," had a meaning that could be renewed daily, across decades. Like the seed libraries and the mutual aid groups that sprang up around the city. Like a lesson in basic ecology. These acts of solidarity echoed what natural scientists and Indigenous botanists have long known: individual species can only exist in concert with other living organisms, in a cacophony of mutualism or convivial giving, across deep time.

We are choral, said the balcony musicians with their nightly concerts, said the birds each dawn as they carried away the night and the lie of hyper-individualism. *We are choral. Not soloists.*

Oblivious to the global time-stop, the branches budded and, in the streets, cherry trees and lilac bushes blossomed in a lysergic parlor trick of life.

Everywhere, suddenly, the growers—planting wild edibles, building food sovereignty, sharing seeds, or just giving a touch-hungry, futurist "hello" to little patches of soil.

Scrubbing myself of dirt after a few hours in our yard made the ritual of handwashing mundane again, stripped the action of panic. The tight-fisted buds of an old peony plant had returned, red stems thrusting from bare soil, dark-green knots loosening into layers of papery, faint-pink blush. It was good to be in a great green room, even if it was just a narrow rectangle of earth. *Goodnight worms, goodnight insects, goodnight microbiome.*

Was the theme "forgetting yourself in the garden"? Was it "nature as vital tether"? Was it "positive anticipation"? Was it balm, sustenance, pastime, remedy, reprieve, song?

"We have never seen anything like it," a shopkeeper told me a few days later. He was transforming an old auto shop into a large garden center to keep up with the demand, the new biophilia, one of three new plant shops to open in our neighborhood that month.

Walking one day, I began photographing the windows of empty restaurants and shuttered businesses, sills thronged with abandoned plant life.

If there had been war effort posters announcing our civic duty, they might have said: We can do it! We can make a Family of Stir Craziness. A Family of Stoical Feeling. A Family of the Bougie Lucky Ones.

Plants sprouted all over Instagram, providing a glimpse into the blooming intricacies of closed public gardens but also a view of fecund fire escapes. The gardeners I followed tracked the "breaking leaves of quince by the pond," indulged in puns (#stayplanted), chided a spring blossom for its flamboyance ("Jeez, spring. Read the room."). A self-dubbed "Gangsta Gardener" showed how to build beautiful soil while @countrygentlemancooks in North Carolina shared his knowledge of pokeweed.

"The plants shift beneath you regardless," writes Ali Smith, which could mean many things.

But after the police killings of Breonna Taylor and George Floyd, in the wake of more murder, the shifting of plants hung heavy. To a gardening community hiding in flowerbeds and litely carrying on "as normal" while ignoring the racial reckoning taking place around the world, BIPOC British food grower Claire Ratinon responded: "Black Lives Matter: Fuck your fucking French beans."

What is gardening content? Gardener and activist Sui Kee Searle set up the Instagram account @decolonisethegarden to widen the possibilities. Her question: "Is it too much to ask that this year, we garden to learn and remember, not to forget?"

Gardening content was vast and wormy and sly and long-memoried. It was Jenna Wortham steeped in a "deep network of Black, Latino and nonbinary herbalists around the country . . . sharing their ancestral knowledge of plants online to care for their communities and help them cope with the waves of grief, anxiety and depression." It was Imani Perry with her soul-saving microgreens watching her "friends and family on screens as they delighted in collards, berries, tomatoes, and chives. Small joys as death rolled by."

Gardening content was the history of violent settlement and the enclosure of common land. It was land justice and food sovereignty. It was complicity in unfettered growth beyond rightful means. It was the ethics of wild food foraging on stolen Indigenous lands and the nettled politics of "protected" species. It was prospering weeds and "world-building" moments where flora in quietened cities reclaimed itself as paramount. It was the work of soil amendment that sank us into deep relation with those who preceded us, with the dead, the more-than-human, with the earth. It was a legacy that reached back before any "English garden tradition" to the Assyrian gardens in Nimrud and the Islamic paradise gardens of the Alhambra.

Pollen in the air. Eyes streaming with allergy tears. I took a long bike ride through the city, passing playgrounds blocked off with yellow police tape, where swings had been wound up and knotted to prevent use and where a man who looked like Calvin of Calvin and Hobbes sat alone on a bench, staring at an overturned tricycle in the middle of an empty wading pool as if surveying a crime scene. I felt the wave form of Frank Ocean from a passing car window, then, from another car, a bass line so loud it filled my stomach and beat under my breastbone. I kept riding, a boosting wind at my back.

Passing the greenhouse on my way to deliver groceries to my mother-in-law, months before her sudden death, I stopped to peer inside and found the plants pressing their clammy hands against the glass, foreheads to the cool steamed windows, colors warped by condensation and sunlight. I saw blurry trees. I imagined the silence and my pale-green grief inside. That night I wrote to the head gardener asking whether it was lonely for the growers working inside the glass dome, watering and maintaining the collection in that great aquarium of quiet, and he replied no. *There's no loneliness.*

I thought I could grow closer to my mother during the intimate days of quarantine when the city's soundtrack hushed, when the earth purportedly shook less, and we were forced to think about a closer horizon. I thought I could become a connoisseur of her eccentricity and strength. What better time to get reacquainted than during a plague that stops the world, reducing seismic noise? But we were not made to stand still together, housebound, without the quick escapes we were so used to in life. By the second month, my mother prowled the hallway in her plush pink bathrobe like a caged animal doing lengths. *Why can't I come and go as I please?* No matter how many times I explained, she never remembered. *Why do I have to be in prison?* Some nights the pantheresque pacing continued until 3 a.m. I would toss in bed to the sound of flip-flops angrily slapping against the hallway floor.

How could anyone function on so little rest, I wondered as I watched her rise pertly each morning, spritzing and watering plants around her room, singing "Bésame Mucho" to the newly sprouting leaves, rescuing the fallen tendril of a flowering oxalis which seemed to shimmy and spindle toward the tender voice she reserved for plants and cats. "What does 'Bésame' mean?" *Kiss me.* "And 'Bésame Mucho'?" *Kiss me a lot.*

One afternoon my mother walked over to an open window and pointed to a pile of old leaf matter in the yard that had taken the shape of a decaying heart. My mother had been at our house for two months and she was now a person dead set against her captivity, a woman ventriloquizing her grievances through compost. Strong smell of mulch and softened wood, wet heat of decomposition already underway. Palette of mud.

She growled at the softly padding soles of my feet.

My husband's leg danced nervously under the table. His leg said, *No drama.* He brought us cupfuls of herbal tea to douse us, to bland our incendiary extremes. I tipped the tea to my lips because I felt sorry for him, and I loved him and I worried for his frayed nerves.

You must prune unhealthy leaves because they draw energy and nutrients a plant needs to flourish. A little pile of wilted and brown plant matter appeared on a coffee table. As soon as my mother was finished, the plants with their remaining green leaves looked refreshed.

She kept pacing through the night. I didn't understand why she couldn't be happy. Her pacing irked. Her daily judgments made me overly defensive. *The Opera of Old Dynamics.*

My husband made the sign for *For God's sake, just say "I agree with you" or "You're right, Ma."* He made the sign for *Try looking out the window at something very far away.*

He pointed to the door and I was obliged to go outside and take deep, de-escalating breaths in the yard.

We awoke one morning to a freak spring snowfall. My mother had disappeared. When we called her mobile phone, she was waiting at a bus stop, on her way back to her residence. Jailbreak. She was done with our barracks. The snow was falling quickly, fashioning a white cap on her head and epaulets on her shoulders.

We had become so unwandering in my mother's presence, so protectively closed in on ourselves, but after my mother left, following her wish to be independent and return to her residence, we began to take longer walks. We modified our errand routes to pass through alleys and unfamiliar roads. One day we came across "HANK'S GARDEN" in a paved alley off a main street. Spilling out from a small concrete stoop onto the sidewalk was a collection of potted plants containing blazing orange and hot-pink annuals; barrels overflowing with forget-me-nots and beamy sunflowers. To stand on the street was to be inside Hank's garden and its gift of tiny opulence. Around the corner, inside a small community garden, we met a man nurturing scallions and tomatoes in a yellow mop pail. "Free for the taking." Surrounding him were recycled basins crowded with leafy bouquets of rainbow Swiss chard, fragrant skeins of fresh rosemary, chives and basil. The more we looked, the more we encountered these errant fragments of paradise around the city. It was doubtful they could make a dent in local food insecurity, but food was not really, or not only, what was being planted. "When you make a garden," says my friend H., "more than the seeds you sowed will grow."

The boys were growing too. In a frenzy. Their anklebones poked out from under their pant hems as they shot up, beyond me, reaching fervidly for the sun. My younger son leaned on my head: *Hey, what happened to you, Mini-Mum?*

The first visit after her return to the residence we sat across from each other in the garden's assigned visitor area. Our chairs were placed six feet apart, blue tape marking the required distance. We were both masked, staring into each other's eyes. She was Marina Abramović, sitting silently, unblinking, her back straight. The roar of a building vent above our heads vacated my thoughts. A thousand minutes passed. I thought there ought to be music. Something.

"I feel awkward," she said finally, kicking off her mint-colored sneakers, calling an end to the long-durational performance. I nodded, looking toward a bush. I felt awkward, too. Overwhelmed. Even with our masks, it was too much, to be face to face, in disorienting up-closeness, without any buffer or distraction. She pulled her purse onto her lap and retrieved a small bottle of honey lotion. She dabbed a little onto her palm and, reaching forward, placed a small dollop onto my outstretched palm. We lathered our hands. I kicked off my sandals. Then we stretched out our knees and calves, our eyes still locked but smiling now, eyebrows lifted.

In this honeyed cloud, drunk on sweetness and teasing attention, I wanted to ask if we were ready to be a different family, less withholding, aggrieved, mistrustful. One that could embrace the ways we stretched far and farther. I wanted to know about our years of unspeaking and the secret she had kept from me. But my mother, a grand evader of questions, transcended conversation. She pointed to another Japanese woman sitting across from her visiting daughter in the garden. The daughter was a professor of biomedical engineering. I waved hello to the important and successful daughter, to the mother whose sacrifices had not been in vain. Hi! And they waved back at the daughter of missed potential.

As I rode home, a thousand insects flew over a thousand flowers; a thousand cannabis stores awaited a thousand customers; a thousand people stood at a thousand green lights, forgetting to cross.

EDOARDO

WHEN MY MOTHER STARTED FORGETTING, AND I WAS A daughter who did not yet have a name for her mother's inability to remember, a daughter lying at night in the skew of things, I made plans to meet "the family." My "homecoming" was arranged for June 2020, the fresh days of summer, when my older son and I were booked to board a plane for England. The plan was to meet my brother S., a few cousins, and possibly my two "lost brothers," and finally outfox the secrets that had kept us separate. From London, we would travel with S. to the Algarve for a few days to visit my father's burial site.

The yearly anniversary of a loved one's death is called *yahrzeit* in Yiddish. It is a time for reflection and introspection. On the day of the yahrzeit, one lights a twenty-four-hour candle to commemorate the departure of the loved one. On the one-year anniversary of learning of my other father's existence and his death, I hoped to light a candle at his grave in Portugal and mark the place on the earth's surface that held his remains. But by February 2020, with a pandemic in global emergence, we doubted the wisdom of continuing with our trip as planned. By March, when borders began to close, we watched our plans crumple. After a lifetime of distance, and months of virtual kinship, I was prepared to wait a little longer to meet my brother in real life, but I could not completely shake my disappointment.

My father was not essential. I was no longer a child and did not need him in any straightforward way. Still, I had convinced myself that seeing where my father lay would stop him from haunting me. It seemed simple enough. I would visit his grave and all the shapeless, swirling and swamping feelings I had about this unmet and unbodied person, a human who was my blood and bone but also *just air*, would finally settle down in the solid grounds of a cemetery that marked his final place in the world. After this ceremony, I could feel affection for his ghost and carry on.

I needed to figure out a new route that would allow me to go where my body could not.

"Let's make another ceremony," said my older son.

I reached out to a man in Faro named Edoardo. We had been in touch several months before when I made a booking to join his botanical tour of the Algarve. With Portugal's borders closed to nonessential travelers, Edoardo was now out of work. I asked him tentatively if he would consider keeping my tour payment in exchange for a personal favor, when it was safer and lockdown eased. *A small pilgrimage.*

The subject of his response email: "Homage to a Beloved One."

꧁

ON MAY 26, 2020, Edoardo walks me through the cemetery gates, tilting his camera toward the trees. It is mid-afternoon in the Algarve and blazingly bright. The camera moves along a short corridor of sparkling white marble tombs, all topped with white crosses. I wait for Edoardo to head for the Jewish section, where I presume my father is laid to rest, but he continues walking forward. There is no Jewish section. Two stout cemetery custodians, with very short shadows, await us by my father's shed-sized tomb, their masks and graveyard stoicism capturing something of the inscrutable weirdness of Europe's first spell in quarantine.

Topped by a crucifix, my father's tomb is the only one with planters and Edoardo, still invested in being a good botanical guide, points this out. He moves in closer.

Where did the wish to be entombed come from? I wonder, freezing the video, trying to peer into the mausoleum window. My father Michael's wish was to become a part of the earth, returned to dust. Whenever I visit his tiny grave, it feels instantly intimate. I sit cross-legged on the grass and play with the smooth small stones we have collected and sometimes I add a new stone to the pile.

At the cemitério, the door to the white tomb is locked, so Edoardo steps back and lingers on my father's name and the dedication engraved on a plaque: *Um Optimo Amigo Para Todos Nós. Un Homen Serio Generoso. O Verdadeiro Espirito Algarvio.* "A Wonderful Friend To Us All. A Serious And Kind Man. The Definitive Algarve Spirit." I am too busy absorbing the words and wondering who wrote them to realize what has been omitted. Only later will I notice the years of his birth and his death are absent. His original name, also missing. At life's end, there is really nothing to identify him in any way. As for the cross, Edoardo later explains they are present on all the tombs "because this is a Catholic country." He tells me my father is the only non-Portuguese person in the cemetery and the custodians insist he was buried among people who mourn him *as one of their own.*

Up close, connected through Edoardo's phone camera, I see the plants in the four planters have not been watered for a very long time and are, as Edoardo later notes, "mostly wilted and suffering." He is openly sad about this and, I can tell, feels that it might sadden me. For a moment I regret declining his offer to bring fresh flowers to replace the faded and parched ones—maybe some mimosa or something hardy. He is clearly a man who wants to paint a happy scene for me.

The visit is almost over. Edoardo leaves the way he arrives, through the cemetery gates, tilting his camera toward the trees one last time. In his email, Edoardo explains the trees at the cemetery's entrance are *Cupressus sempervirens*, commonly known as Mediterranean cypress. "It is a tree species always being associated with death and planted alongside cemeteries for millennia in Europe and in the Muslim world. It is one of the few tree species whose roots grow only vertically. This characteristic makes it a perfect companion of the graves, which are, in this way, never being disrupted by any roots growing horizontally (far from the tree crown)."

Watching everything from a distance, in Edoardo's company, is comforting.

As he does a final pan of the area, gliding slowly with his phone, I notice how lush and almost unreal the landscape of Quarteira is, how blue the sky with no airlines sending out vapor trails.

I SHOWED MY SONS Edoardo's video a few days after he sent it and we lit a candle. We lit a candle for a father who was far from his ancestors, buried under another's sign of worship. We lit a candle for hidden names and hidden kin. We lit a candle for a story that would never be fully assembled; for the hope of cajoling old secrets out of a memory-challenged mother; for the lapses and distortions of my own memory.

What else? There were many people and things and ideas that needed a candle. As we watched the ones we had lit burn down, I wanted my sons to remember this grandfather as a person who opened a door for us. What or who lay beyond that opening was for them to grasp.

My father did not stop haunting me. I still felt those shapeless, swirling and swamping feelings every few weeks, in the middle of the night. I assumed this was our version of connecting, the way some people meet their parents for bowls of noodles or walks in the park.

❦

BUT THE VERY idea of an opening became more mysterious to me a year later when I received an unexpected email from Edoardo. "April 11, 2021: Hope all is good with you. Yesterday I was not far from Quarteira and I decided to stop at the cemetery and take a picture at your father's tomb. The door was locked but it was possible to see inside, so I also got a few pictures of the inside. As you'll see from the pictures, the place is regularly visited and looked after. There are new flowers and plants and all is cleaned and tidy."

I can't explain what happened. The photos caught me off guard. Suddenly I was weeping with my whole body.

I wrote back and told Edoardo I felt I had been there with him, along with the only words that came into my head. *Thank you.*

It's true I felt I was there with Edoardo. But I did not feel I was there in the cemetery. Not really. Not when I looked at the weathered flowers with their petals holding tight. And not when I peered into the tomb through the parted lace curtain. I did not know how to grieve the life I never had with this father. When my eyes browsed the intimate arrangement—the framed snapshots, the coffin topped with cloth roses, a red travel pillow and two soft toy giraffes—I felt a universe away, aware that I would always be a stranger to this once-alive person, this man around whom someone had arranged such ordinary objects of devotion, objects his known and legitimate children recognized but which I did not.

I cried, not because I was pained by this vast distance but because, within the social isolation of that moment and the required separation of our individual lives, I was moved by a feeling of incredible nearness and warmth.

I was moved by Edoardo and the soft tone of his message, by all the ways the stranger appears; in this case, a stranger who briefly held me up, held me close, joining me as the steward of a small but significant ritual.

"Thank you!" I repeated.

Whatever I was looking for, I could stop searching. I did not need to look into any more tombs.

RELATIONS

WHEN MY MOTHER STARTED FORGETTING, AND I WAS A
daughter advancing into the unknown, I realized that all the
recent ways I had been thinking about family lines, reduced by a
search for biological origins, by a genealogical story, needed to
be reopened.

"DNA" was once a term I applied casually to experiences and things
I felt were emotionally, mentally or thematically a part of me. I
would speak of encounters that had rearranged my (inner) DNA.
Or talk about how the DNA of certain song refrains I heard as a
teenager had shaped me.

After I received my test results, I began reserving the term for the
strictly hereditary. The definition of lineage instantly narrowed.
What was lost in the narrowing was an obvious fact: my identity
had always been shaped by forces far exceeding the biological. I
had been nourished and fed by limitless sources, some that were
chosen and others that were subtle and mysterious.

It was time to remember all my good ancestors, including the dis-
tinct and ineradicable love I had for my literary ones: the stories I
returned to again and again, dog-eared and underlined ideas that
merged with my own sensibility, beloved writers who taught me

ways of being in the world, ways of doing love and enacting attention. Books raised me. Strangers raised me. Harriet raised me. Max raised me. Wolves raised me. When someone asked about my origins, my first impulse was to point to my bookcase. Deep in my bones, I always understood where I came from.

A person I dated wrote a poem describing how I acted like an eager librarian during our courtship, feeding her all the volumes I had ever loved. She did not see that I was taking her home to meet my family, showing her what had composed me, at a cellular level, as a person. *These are the people*, I was saying, *who have built stores of thought and feeling that remain inside me.*

This kinship of influences is with me every day, making it impossible and absurd to write about heritage without also speaking of *writing as heritage*. Writing as a filial weight carried, in this case, like a hulking bouquet of gratitude.

Which is to say, I do not know where this book would be without: Kaveh Akbar's orchids ("gushing out from the faucets"), Saeed Jones's foxgloves ("trumpets of tongued blossoms"), Hanif Abdurraqib's peonies ("a flower with a short season. born dying."), Ross Gay's grape hyacinth, John Berger and the silver undersides of West Bank olive leaves, Ocean Vuong and his violet wildflowers, Tommy Pico's swamp milkweed, Richard Wright's lilac sprigs, Mama Phife's yellow oxalis, Camille T. Dungy's "Ten million exquisite buds," Mei-mei Berssenbrugge's roses, Lucille Clifton's durable daisies, Jericho Brown's mother's morning glories ("that spilled onto the walkway toward her porch") . . . Or the blooms of countless other poets who have insisted on the magic that connects plants to people and people to the land, no matter the circumstance of the day, even when hearts are bludgeoned or steeped in grief or rage. Like Gwendolyn Brooks and her "furious flower," the name she gave to tenacious beauty and creativity that "Lifts its face/all unashamed."

MA

WHEN MY MOTHER STARTED FORGETTING, AND I WAS HER
sentinel of a daughter, I tried to put things down.

"What are you writing about?"

Well, part of it is about you, I say.

"And?"

Plants.

"Plants and trees?"

I nodded. Yes.

"That's a good idea. How about forests?"

Sure.

"People don't like forests. Too many bugs. Plants are better."

Okay.

❧

IN THE LAST hours of packing up my mother's apartment before
she moved into the retirement residence, I discovered two flat
boxes in her guestroom closet. One contained random documents
and the other contained a large stack of ink drawings on the softest washi paper, all done by my mother before my birth, all stored
in this hidden box. I had never seen any of this work before.

"I am not a real artist," she said, when I asked about the box.

Her words did not surprise me—she had said them before—
but they ached, in a way other artist-daughters of immigrant
mothers may understand. It was an ache that said: Why me and

not her? My mother was so clearly full of talent, it was hard to grapple with all the ways she felt barred from making claims to what she knew. I understood she would brush away any lament for "what was lost," but I still wondered what she might have made. What if she had been born in another time, in another body, in another world? I folded my questions and notions into the box but it was hard to let them go. I sat with the ink drawings and wondered why she'd never shown them to me. Her confident brushwork, so supple, so joyful, so intensely alive. On each one, there were swaths of unpainted paper.

I stared into the blank areas.

In any piece of music, the rest is as important as sound. An incessant story would be unbearable. A garden planted without breaks would grow claustrophobically small.

I stared into the empty areas.

I could hear her saying: One day I will have a daughter and I will give her an unfinished story and it will be up to her to decide if it is a void or a gift.

WEATHER

WHEN MY MOTHER STARTED FORGETTING, AND I WAS HER dutiful but often impatient daughter, I saw her every other day. During my regular visits to the residence, the personal support workers sometimes had their break. We were all Asian women and many of us were caring for memory-challenged residents, but as a "family" carer as opposed to an "outsourced" or "agency" carer, I was invited to sit in certain areas that were off-limits to them. The invitation felt noxious. We were all doing the same work but some of us were called kin.

One day I arrived and found that a staff member had not shown up to facilitate the "Fit Mind" class, so I stepped in to help. It was a raw and boisterous group; a vivid bundle of feelings. With barriers lowered, people effused with joy and passion but also forgot to hide their reactions and were easily slighted. Feelings that had been dammed up for a lifetime spilled out from the skin. This all produced a sense of emotional hazard, which I did not fully appreciate until I left for a moment to gather more sudoku sheets and returned to a roaring fight between two women. "What happened?" I asked, looking to the group. A man shrugged. My mother fluttered her eyes slowly and disdainfully, as though shuttering out behavior she found a little batty and unworthy of her time. Another man pointed to one of the fighting women, who shook her head vigorously. There was no clear answer, just a troupe of unreliable narrators.

What was a fit mind? What qualities were consonant with fitness? I was later informed the "cognitively intact" residents tended to avoid Fit Mind class.

My mother floated in and out of a dream. Some days it was a good dream. Strangers would come up to me and remark on her charisma and creativity. Other days it was less good. She mouthed off, picked fights. The number of people who raised her ire increased until her grandsons were the only conversational companions she would tolerate. The management began warning me regularly that my mother had moments when she was ill-behaved, disruptive, *difficult*. It seemed to me that I was being asked to single-handedly solve "the problem" and it left me constantly on edge, combative, and strangely embarrassed. Somewhere in the residence there was a gold-standard mother—elegant and ruly—who went unnoticed and never made a fuss. I never met such a woman. My mother was certainly not this person.

"The rules. Can you remind her?" they said.

"I will remind her," I said again and again, frazzled in the face of their messages and threats. They wanted her brought under control and I wanted her not to be evicted. But it was clearly a farce. No matter how often I took notes or wished her to be blandly perfect, I knew the rules would never hold my mother. Not listening, being inconvenient: this was all vintage. She had all the time in the world yet no time at all for *the manners, the laws, the authorities, the gangs*.

"The gangs?" I said.

"The managers are a gang of crooks!"

A few days later she briefly formed her own tiny gang. It was composed of tough, glowering women who had bonded over their shared disdain for the management and a particular phony-bubbly front-desk coordinator. Most of these women were known for their "erratic sociality" and had no plans to stay on the cute or proper side of the geriatric. Cool, nervy delinquents. Gritty mutineers. *Uh-oh*, said my husband.

Pure social disinhibition is a nightmare. I have no desire to romanticize "civility," particularly when the concept has been used as a tool of domination to punish those deemed "misbehaving," "riotous" or "rude," but I have seen what it looks like when a group of thin-skinned people run with the directive: *Do not give a damn.*

When I told my friend J. about the scene at the residence, she fell quiet for a moment before saying: "I know people think that talking about the weather is shallow and small but WE NEED TO TALK ABOUT THE WEATHER, PEOPLE."

I asked my mother to try a little harder—not because it was "Good Form" or "The Right Thing," but because I suspected a little ceasefire might make her own life easier. One day I placed Post-it notes on her mirror and walls that said PEOPLE ARE NICE. BE NICE TO PEOPLE. I wasn't looking for miracles. I thought a casual daily reminder might move the default slightly away from open pugilism toward half-hearted agreeability but, no, my mother was gnashing her teeth behind me.

"Why would you do *that*?" she asked, with a blistering look of scorn. It was unclear if she meant why would you put up Post-it notes or why would you be nice.

SOME PEOPLE NEED unresolved issues to pile up and build tension because it keeps the story moving forward, because the fight gives them *life drive*, while other people spend their whole lives trying to dodge unnecessary drama. For the latter, there is a shelf at my favorite local bookshop titled "PLOTLESS FICTION." For the former, well, probably a T-shirt somewhere that reads: "Resolution=Death."

I did not want a meek, obsequious or dead mother but sometimes a day was a grueling, almighty challenge. I took down the Post-it notes, which, truthfully, were getting on my own nerves. We were no closer to a solution, but I had at least shown I was in solidarity with the cause of keeping my mother alive. I began avoiding phone calls and email messages from the residence. I found myself looking for the woman down the hall from my mother who always, without context, patted my shoulder and said, "Good job, darling."

Blessed was the art teacher who liked my mother and the way she always said "FINITO!" when she completed a painting. He did not see her as difficult or as someone to be settled or sedated. As the Teatime DJ, he encouraged my mother to dance in her slow, mesmeric way, arms like waving fronds, while he played the most beautiful Persian songs followed by smooth-voiced disco classics. He complimented her hair when she dyed it pink and told me she was, with her persistent nonconformism, "as youthful as a teenager!" When she sought attention in flamboyantly theatrical ways or tried to foment revolution with her gang members or when she moved forward on her momentum of tension-creation like a bull ready to charge, he immediately understood she did not mean to be disobedient; she meant to be artistic and alive! He stepped in when a white resident took to calling my mother *Yoko Ono, Yoko Ono, Yoko Ono*, taunting her in a singsong voice.

One day I saw the art teacher comforting another resident, who was crying because she had not been permitted to dine with the caregiver she viewed as a daughter and whom she loved with all her heart. I had watched them together, the caregiver cooing *yes, love*, as the woman tapped her foot and danced in circles like Thelonious Monk. What is family?, I thought again, as I now watched this resident's tears fall like rain. Hours later she was still bereft, although she had forgotten why.

I knew it was not uncommon for people with dementia to experience emotional hangovers. I had read that sometimes, for example, a mood from a movie might linger even when the content was immediately forgotten. In one famous study from the University of Iowa, patients with Alzheimer's experienced elevated levels of either sadness or happiness for up to thirty minutes after viewing films, despite having little or no recollection of the movies. What they felt was a thickening of feelings, an atmosphere or tone that would not lift. Strangely, the less the patients remembered about the films, the longer the tone lasted.

Learning this made me very careful in the days and weeks that followed. *You don't need to please.* But sometimes you do. I was a fluffy cloud, breezy and chipper, drifting through the residence, trying to induce positive feelings.

"Sadness," according to the study, "tended to last a little longer than happiness."

"I just want my days to be simple and peaceful," said my mother.

FORGETOIR

WHEN MY MOTHER STARTED FORGETTING, AND I WAS A daughter keeping track of the gradual progression of her illness, I thought of all the things she did not seem to forget or lose. She did not lose a sense of what was ripe, sweet and delicious. She did not lose her love of B. B. King, Bob Marley or Misora Hibari. Playing a few bars of her favorite music was like a game of "Freeze Dance"; she instantly halted what she was doing. She did not lose her knack for outrageous pronouncements, saying what came into her head in a blurting (sometimes mean, sometimes magnanimous) rush. She did not lose her "hunches" about people or her zest for embroilments. Or, for the most part, the stir and eagerness that tilted her into a new day. She did not become a hugging person or lose her aversion to "I love you" and would, always, still meet these words with a flinch or an eye roll. She did not lose the belief that her grandsons were Future Nobel Prize Laureates. Nor did she lose their names. Or her increasingly wistful memory of her "strange husband" and his timeliness. She did not lose her love of Monet, or the wild green blood running in her veins. She did not lose her turnstile moods or her tendency to start a conversation with the third or fourth thought or her tendency to finish abruptly with "that's enough." She did not lose the little girl far inside her who ate shaved ice with syrup by the inland sea in 1947. Or the melody of the song she sang in her middle school singing contest. She did not lose her interest in large, upright stones. Her head for sums. Her capacity for ordinary joy was not lost. Her surprise sadness. Her ability to mentally wrestle me to the floor.

TWELVE:

SEKKI

(small seasons)

INK

"SOME EMOTIONS GRIP US, THEN FALL AWAY," WRITES LEWIS
Hyde. But then there are "the unforgettables." For Hyde, these are
the emotions that "reseed themselves generation after generation."
He writes, "We do not control the unforgettable; it controls us."

On days when my mother is stuck in a mood and cannot remember why, we start drawing with ink. Two chairs, side by side. We
paint our "feelings without memory." Ink surges the paper.

In the surge there is no English or Japanese. No hard or soft.

Ink and page. It occurs to me that this is how I entered the world.
Through inky brushstrokes. Through the percussive procession of
typewritten words. My mother bought ink in stubby glass jars or
in stick form. My father had ribbons of it running through his
Olivetti and through the undulating waves of his pen. He built
density and weight with his words. The lesson of my mother's ink
was that one could clarify by liquefying rather than solidifying.
Let go of force. Eventually her approach became more personal:
*allow ink to swim and reveal its own character without telling ink
what ink is.*

There are many ways of talking on paper.

I make contact with a local ink-maker I know to see if I can purchase supplies for my mother. He creates handmade pigments from plants and industrial material he forages in city parks and alleyways. Buckthorn, sumac, bedsprings, rusted nails, drywall, acorn caps, bits of rock. These seemingly disparate elements are brought together in a congress that feels joyful, difficult and sometimes sexual. I have spent hours obsessing over his ink tests—radiant splotches on paper, blooming and bloating visual poems, each more colorful and leaky than the last. I can't explain their pull except to say they feel corporeal, emotional. They say how we are with each other, never tidily contained but moving through each other's swirling puddles of being, as much connected by ink as by blood; and with any luck, joined through play, experiment and liquidity.

"There is a kind of healing that can happen by yourself with ink and paper," he writes me.

One night as my mother rests in bed, she tells me out of the blue *I know you just want me to drop dead.*

Her words, and their suddenness, shock me. *No, Ma,* I say, *I love you.* I repeat the words as she bats her arms around, swatting at the air, like a drunk semaphorist. Eventually I stop saying *I love you* but her arms will not stop rampaging. Then, before I can back away, she strikes me with her fist. Hard. Hands budded. She is a boxer now, punching out any ember of tenderness, punching her own shadow.

I don't understand but I do understand. When I'm afraid and cannot accept affection, I also box the air.

～

WHEN MY MOTHER is done, her budded fists become petals that fall to the floor.

⋙

IN THE EARLY 1980s when my mother ran a small Japanese art gallery, I would travel with her to Tokyo and Kyoto on buying trips. Thirteen hours in the air and she deplaned a different person. She led me around Japan with smooth strides, confident and easy, like a knot coming loose. But her looseness also made her seem out of place, a little improper. Her mother and middle sister chided her for being "too Western." They teased her for being overbold and *darashinai* (unkempt). I noticed she smoked more in this habitat, always had a lit cigarette between two fingers, as if she were trying to calm her nerves.

One summer, when I was a teenager, an artist showed us how to grind ink in his Shinjuku studio. I sat quiet as a mouse as he placed the ink stick on a wet grinding stone, rubbing the stick until he had the color he wanted. He loaded a brush with the ink then moved it over a page. The huge, swelling strokes of glossy black mesmerized me. I watched the ink seep into the thirsty paper. Then he added water to his black brush and a beautiful whispered cloud met the white space, pooling briefly at the edges. The artist was very old and when he was done he pressed his very old wooden *hanko* into the corner. His signature in vermilion. My mother was very old and very young. The age I am now.

⋙

THE FIRST TIME I heard of the Toronto ink-maker was many years ago, when I was contacted by an urban fruit picker who asked if I could donate the harvest from our black walnut tree to her friend. The black walnuts littered our yard, crashing to the ground every September from steeper and steeper heights as the tree grew taller. I filled our mailbox with as many exploded and intact walnut hulls as it could hold. The ink-maker took the harvest back to his house and boiled the hulls on his stovetop until he had a deep black-brown liquid—the color of mahogany. I don't know how long it took. It takes a certain kind of love and patience to distill plant life to its essence.

He later sold me a series of five black inks he had made in his kitchen from foraged elements—oven-charred peach stones, blackened and crushed Manila clam shells, kerosene soot, grapevine ash, and silty black Andalusian earth. The tiny glass jars with their labels contained drifts of particulate matter. When I looked at the floating bits, I felt everything that had ever dissolved in me, everything that made me want to dissolve, all the grit and ash that swam and churned to the surface. The ink said: *Don't settle. Swirl.* It said: *Who wants a livable story when you can have a living one?*

I pushed these handmade inks on everyone I knew who might be on intimate terms with alchemy, leaky hearts, Rorschach, weeping. I warned people the inks were temporary and a bit smelly. *They fade and change.*

Fugitive was the word the ink-maker used to describe his impermanent creations when we went for a walk along the rail path at the west end of the city. We were less than a mile from my home, strolling along a corridor of scrubby flora, hedged in on both sides by empty lots and recently converted industrial buildings. He was dressed in a French workman's jacket, bits of weed and vine poking out from his pockets.

He spent much of his time finding, mixing, and discovering it was not always the brightest or most apparent things that lasted the longest. Sometimes what you searched for was "concealed, and doubtful." Sometimes a drab-seeming harvest, once distilled, would acquire a concentrated brilliance. "It doesn't always make sense to bully the material." *Be patient.*

During the walk, when our wide-ranging conversation turned to foraging, he looked at me thoughtfully and said, "More and more I think things should just be left alone. Maybe a plant doesn't need to be turned into something else. Maybe its color in the wild is its best incarnation."

~

THE DAY AFTER my mother hits me, I visit again. Her hands are folded loosely in her lap, contrite. So are mine. We are tired of boxing the air.

Her hand reaches for mine.

"Are you there?" her hand says.

I am here.

"Shall we draw?"

Yes.

EAR

IN NOVEMBER 2020, A VIDEO WENT VIRAL OF A FORMER
prima ballerina with dementia, gracefully dancing to Tchaikovsky's
Swan Lake from her wheelchair. The elderly woman, identified as
Marta Cinta González, flutters her hands and moves her arms in
elegant arcs as the music swells. Her chin lifts, her face awakens
to the role of Odette. The music, played through headphones, has
transported her back to the stage, back to a misty lake.

What moves me when I watch this video is not only the unlock-
ing power of melody but the reaction of the caregiver seated beside
her, the music therapist Pepe Olmedo. When the Swan Theme
begins, González moves her frail hand briefly then despairingly
shakes her head, slumping into her wheelchair. Without pause,
Olmedo takes her hand and kisses it so caringly that the shadow
that is passing over González's face instantly falls away. Suddenly,
he is Prince Siegfried and she is the Swan Princess, emboldened
by his tenderness.

What is the word for what the body remembers? What is the
name for the person who gives themselves, listeningly, to their
subject? What kind of tale is this?

When I watch this video, I realize I don't need to give my mother a voice. I need to build myself a different kind of ear. I need to give myself to my mother the way Pepe Olmedo gives himself to Marta Cinta González.

OPERATING MANUAL

LOVE LEAKS. LOVE DIMS AND CHANGES. LOVE STAINS. LOVE is fugitive and doesn't often last forever. Love will transform under certain atmospheric and seasonal conditions.

The point of being truly loved isn't to keep the love in one zone, it is to let it move into and activate other zones. There's a whole living world that needs ink.

She dips the brush in black ink then raises it and sprints a line down the page. This fast stroke is repeated several times until she has a tuft. A field.

MA

MA DREAMS OF PLANTS.

THE YARD

I HEAR THE SOUND OF HER BREATH AND THE SOFT SWEEP of the brush touching the paper. A corridor runs between us as we sit side by side. There is a growing space between our words. I call it *the yard*. The yard is many things. It is a place that fizzes brightly outside the side door of the house, a constant reminder that there are bigger, unpredictable forces going on around us. It's also a relationship to time, to making time. But mostly it's the shapeless and mysterious passage between us, a region that contains none of the furniture or patterns of our lives. It is the space we have come to trust the most. Sometimes the ink frees us to cross back and forth.

When the former ballet dancer Marta Cinta González lost herself as she listened to *Swan Lake*, she was dancing in the yard. She was leading her caregivers to a place beyond her immediate needs, beyond the sound of her own voice, beyond any message. She was dancing and giving them an opportunity to learn that story is not the only means of remembering our lives. Even when the mental records have been lost or destroyed, there is still the seed and space of a person.

I mention my birth father's name one day as we draw and my mother smiles and says, "Yes. That was funny," her voice trailing away. She is inking and re-inking the flowers I have brought her.

Her face is still vivid with happiness minutes after his name is mentioned, as if the act of slipping back into the past is a physical experience. His name carries forward on a strange current, a river of something unresolved, back in time, that cannot be completed. I have stopped tracking him against the clock of her forgetting. A part of me knew from the beginning I would not get answers. I would not charm her into sharing intimacies.

My mother dips her brush again.

The longer you ink something, the more unfamiliar it becomes. Through repeat study, the world of rote seeing disintegrates. The assumed form dismantles. To love something is to let it fall apart, beyond recognition and automaticity, again and again. As I lose the contour of my mother, I re-find her. I go back to see a little bit more of what I cannot see. My head spins. I shake hands with my mother's heart.

Fugitive is also a word for a mother who will not be planted as a character in a book. A mother, full of narrative, who will always resist narrative custom and conventions.

When we are done visiting for the day, I ask my mother to finish the following sentence in as many ways as she can. I begin, "Without a story . . ."

"Without a story?" she says.

Finish the sentence, Ma.

"Without a story . . ." She opens her mouth, closes it, opens it again. "Without a story, we have to find another way to settle down . . . Without a story, we are okay . . . We will still have rice. Without a story, it's up to you to keep yourself in shape. Without a story, we make it up. Without a story, we are a boat."

A boat?

"Yes! A boat. A boat going around and around, rowing through the water."

Then she laughs.

DEAR DAUGHTER

I KNOW YOU NEED TO WRITE STORIES. I KNOW I AM A STORY inside of you just like you are a story inside of me. I was never against stories. I was just against what I had been told about them—that they had to be organized and fancy. That they had to be big and you had to act big to tell them. I wanted you to see that not everything can be woven into a pattern, some dots don't have a line to connect them. I wanted you to know I put holes in your story so we would always find a place for ourselves on the page but also a clean getaway!

Dear daughter, here is a story: Before our planet was born, the building blocks of soil were waiting in the inky darkness of space.

Dear daughter, here is another: We are made up of what we've remembered but also what we've forgotten.

"See? Make holes in the story for art. Life is full of mysteries. Don't put me or you in a story coffin. Okay? I know stories matter. They do to me too ... What would be a good story? Maybe you should write about a cat! Maybe try to make this story a good one even if no one reads it? Okay?"
Okay, Ma.
"Okay. You'll remember this?"
Yes.

"And you'll remember you're not just the child of English words? Or words, period. That the words, that they aren't it?"

Hai. Wasurenai to yakusoku shimasu.

"Okay then. FINITO!"

AFTERWORD:

I REMEMBER

I REMEMBER

I REMEMBER WHEN I THOUGHT OF ASKING THE PEOPLE connected to this book to send me the names of their favorite flowers, so I could build a herbarium. I thought of asking the family of birth, of book, of accident, of choice, the family of hypotheticals who did not yet exist. I imagined the collective press of these flowers. An unlikely biome of blossoms.

I REMEMBER WHEN my mother always wanted to know if a famous person was alive or dead—*What about George Harrison? What about Aretha Franklin? What about Paul Newman, Sidney Poitier, Toshiro Mifune?*—and then, when she learned they were deceased, she always wanted me to look up exactly how, blow by blow, they died.

I REMEMBER MY mother reminding me I don't always think practically and then saying, *Even so, I will always accept you as you are.* And I thought: practical?

I remember—I must have been ten—my mother spraying me with L'Air du Temps to repel mosquitoes ("a big worry!") only to discover they liked it. (Practical.) I remember that same year tarantulas, quicksand and piranhas were also big worries.

I remember still being ten when the miniseries *Shōgun* aired on TV. The main character, Mariko, shared the same name as my mother, who both loved and hated the "kinky Oriental show." Acid rain was another big worry that year.

I REMEMBER—DECADES LATER—A doctor deeming my mother a "fall risk" and how, as we traveled down the elevator after the appointment, I thought of all the ways we fall—*down, apart, forwards, prey, short, out, ill, in love*. My sleep was tattered with her nighttime calls and wanderings and I had brought a few dying plants to her for triage. I didn't know why they were dying but she knew and sat with them in the backseat of the car already thinking of ways to get them strong again. Things had not fallen too far apart.

I remember a small bonsai I brought her a few days later. She took one look at its over-pruned leaves and whispered: *Cruel.*

I REMEMBER DELIVERING a eulogy for my father and making a slideshow for his memorial. I stood and cleared my throat and paused and then began to read. There were people unmentioned and unshown. I remember all the sparkling glasses held up in a toast, all the bubbles slowly rising.

I remember there was a time I received condolence notes from beautiful women. *Your dad called me after D. died. Your dad stole the porkpie hat off my head. Your dad sent me to film a bunch of handsome sailors.*

I REMEMBER LISTENING to my mother talk through her dreams as she napped one afternoon. I heard the words *assassin, shadow, oh no,* and, mysteriously, the word *ankles,* and I realized the language of her consciousness was not Japanese but English. English *noir.*

I remember reading in Peter Handke, "She took her secret to the grave," and thinking: *yes.*

I remember Joe Brainard, Georges Perec, Mary Ruefle and all their *I Remembers.* I remember the trancelike listing, repetition, the shifting tones and textures, as I paced the floor of my own memory. I remember thinking that sequencing is not an issue for poets who embrace random result; that memory is full of motion, image but also hopscotching approximation, error.

I remember Joe Brainard telling an interviewer (poet Tim Dlugos): "I have a terrible memory . . . I can't remember anything. But then I began to realize that beyond that point there is another level of knowledge that could be triggered off."

I remember, when I read those words, thinking: fog! Fog is the level before knowledge. Sometimes a loose, foggy mind can creep past the lock and key of perfect alertness. Through fog we may reach a previously inaccessible recess of the mind.

I remember because sometimes a new bit surfaces out of foggy nowhere, such as the day my mother very clearly remembered that my grandfather Hugh was the one who spilled the secret of her affair. Hugh spotted her arriving at Heathrow airport with my biological father in 1969 and immediately told my father, Michael. "Hugh was the leak."

✻

I REMEMBER TWO lovers on a path that snaked among the trees in Morocco, somewhere near the water.

✻

I REMEMBER WHEN I realized life is not sectional in the way books made me imagine. Life does not progress page by page, chapter by chapter, beginning-middle-end. "Consider writing that does not resolve, socially or privately, into an artifact," writes Bhanu Kapil. "What is writing that does not resolve, obey, stop/ go, descend or arrive?"

✻

I REMEMBER REPETITION is not solely a habit of the very old and memory challenged. Some of us need to live and write the same story over and over, from different angles, obsessively. Ask Duras. Ask Kafka. Ask Murakami. What is not repeated and repeated? What is not a recurring situation? Ask the tough crocuses with their tight tiny crowns that push through the winter debris and melting snow every year. Ask the greening trees, coming back with their bright tennis-ball color no matter what, to say *It's the beginning of everything. Again. Again. Again.* Ask the peony why it perseverates; the clematis why it reiterates itself. What story do you keep telling? What idea, obsession or question has decided it's not quite done with you?

I remember feeling *birth-life-death* in the garden. And then it would start all over. *A lucky person,* I thought, *may see this cycle repeat seventy to eighty times in their lifetime. If existence must be circular and recurring, let it repeat in this nice pattern.*

I REMEMBER WHEN *enduring love* had two meanings.

I REMEMBER METAPHOR is a way of making family out of seemingly unrelated things.

I REMEMBER EXCHANGING emails with a writer I admire. He asked what I was working on so I told him. He wrote back: "Even the description sounds botanical. The spirals of history: makes me think of a plant, like a fern, unfurling. Or the spirals of a plant here in the desert, getting tighter and tighter, until it's like a sleeping big bang in the center . . . Do you live among many plants?"

I remember feeling confused but also captivated by his words, this writer with whom I felt kindredness, not least for the way he offered the following "wishful definition" of belonging: "to be long, to elongate oneself, to grow into a space."

I remember sitting with the word "botanical" and deciding I was not going to showcase the ways I was becoming more plant wise. The garden is my Ministry of Rest. Its pleasures are un-masterful, often boring, un-heroic. Besides, I don't really know my stuff. Or what I know, I know only up to a point.

I remember after I wrote a book about birds, after the promo photographs by the duck pond and the literary festivals where I was asked to lead "expert" bird walks, I was still a toe-dipping dilettante. Apparently, I am a slow learner. Or a quick forgetter. Either way, I cannot speak to what lasting qualities or insights I acquired from my closeness to birds or plants.

I remember, however, brief moments when I felt the garden break through my body's armoring, my book-learning, the preset ways I carried myself with the goal of blocking unwanted emotions. Being more plant-like became something to aspire to. As Robin Wall Kimmerer says, plants are never impervious and watertight. They are always continuous with their environment. "When the world is dry, they're dry. When it's wet, they're wet . . . What if your body were so permeable that the world just rushed inside of you, filling you up?" I filed this under *Love: An Operating Manual.*

I remember when I was non-sovereign, when I was just one among many other, small, permeable beings, weathering freakishly extreme weather; susceptible to the clemency or inclemency of the elements.

❧

I REMEMBER NOTICING, more and more, who has access to gardenable space—whether acreage or fire escape—who feels welcome in public parks, who sees their plant knowledge and history represented.

I remember, even so, being intimidated by a white man, a cool "urban cultural planner," whose email to me was full of gardening and plant DO NOTS.

I remember, when faced with this plantsplainer, who knew about everything, who tried to stump me with his knowledge, all the times humor, ignorance, humility have saved me.

I REMEMBER ORDERING two hundred bulbs. *Chionodoxa forbesii.* Bright-blue flowers with a white center called Glory of the Snow because they bloom so incredibly early in spring. I chose them because they were described as being "care-free."

I REMEMBER IN my late twenties, when I was experiencing a bout of imposter syndrome, my father told me a story. One autumn, at a film launch in Montreal, he was chatting in the corner of a cocktail party when the French-speaking host abruptly pointed at him and began shouting "Fraud! Fraud!" A dozen heads turned to face my father, who immediately froze in horror. It was eventually explained that the host had been pointing to a door that had just swung open onto a fire escape, snowflakes swarming inside. What he was saying in French was "Cold! Cold!" but my non-French-speaking father, plagued by his own sense of illegitimacy—or "hack complex," as he put it—had assumed, *The jig is up.*

I remember this story about feeling fraudulent differently now, and wonder if people who feel more worthy and entitled to parent (or less like charlatans) are more open and honest with their offspring.

I REMEMBER WHEN my father could no longer read or tell stories but, out of sheer force of habit, could not stop picking up books and turning pages. He gathered momentum, doing what he had always done. Even if it was a con, the sound of pages turning was deeply comforting.

I REMEMBER THE nurse saying "end-of-love care" before correcting herself with a shake of the head. "We are here to talk about end-of-life care."

I remember I held my father's cold hand right through the night, trying to transfuse warmth. I remember trying to remember the last thing he said to me. But the memory was already gone and I could not remember.

I remember taking only a few things—two undershirts, some books, a few pieces of art—and giving the rest away.

✎

I REMEMBER ONE of my best friends texting me during her run through the cemetery where my father was buried. She wanted to know where she might find his grave. I didn't think she would ever be able to locate it because the plot was so small, but I described it as best I could, described the thyme I had planted the week before, because I needed a plant with lift and roots and not cut flowers that would wilt by morning.

An hour later she texted me:

Found it!!!
Holy shit it's beautiful here.
Oh geez. I didn't expect to feel so much. It's really lovely here.
He's at peace.
He knows he did a really good job.
He thinks Olga (1907–1978) is a bit dense.

But he loves Mr. Sato (1940–2011) because he has a great
sense of humor.

> You found him?!?!

They play cards.

> Uh oh. Crying . . .

But he thinks Mr. Sato cheats.

I'm so glad I came.

> Me too.

I had a lot to say.

Because it was hard for him too.

> You found him.

He found me.

> Yes.

He did what he thought was right.

I forgive him.

> I love you.

I knew I'd find him.

K running now.

I REMEMBER A filmmaker friend telling me we get new family in
the middle of our life so we remember our identities are always
dying and regenerating. To remind us: we can be green again.

I REMEMBER A photo of my mother taken in a garden, in the
1970s. She stands under a chestnut tree looking up at someone
leaning out the second-floor window of our house. The light is
coming through the tree in three places. Nearby: a hoe, wet with
dew, and a packet of Japanese radish seeds. She wears a gauzy,
rust-colored tank dress. She is damp from digging.

I remember the secret of my mother's gardens was they were built in successive layers and always changing. Sections might grow loose and light with time but the shorter-lived scatter plants were always mingled with quieter structural plants that lasted the entire growing season. Nothing I had ever learned taught me to see the subtlety or wisdom of her skill.

I remember *you cannot love someone you cannot see. You cannot love someone you cannot see. You cannot love someone you cannot see.* And this thought wallops me with regret because the woman in this garden photo, standing under a chestnut tree, will not be visible to me for a very long time.

❧

I REMEMBER THE prologue to *An American Childhood* where Dillard reflects on the loss of memory the narrator will experience at life's end: "When everything else has gone from my brain ... what will be left, I believe, is topology: the dreaming memory of land as it lay this way and that." Similarly, Agnès Varda says in the opening sequence to *The Beaches of Agnès*: "If we opened people up, we'd find landscapes."

❧

I REMEMBER WHEN I wanted the love I had for my mother to be legible to her. I tried to plant it with words; but what is the value of writing addressed to a mother who cannot read it? I tried to plant it with plants to say, *Look, now we will have something to walk around together.*

I remember when I realized my love was still illegible to her.

I remember when love stopped being a matter of reassembly, of fixing and proving things, of getting memories back.

I REMEMBER THE artist Francis Alÿs pushing that large block of ice through the streets of Mexico City for nine hours and, after an absurd expenditure of energy, titling his performance *Sometimes making something leads to nothing*—an idea which speaks to the efforts of Mexico City laborers to improve their living conditions, but also, more generally, to other seemingly endless quests.

I REMEMBER READING Anne Boyer—"a garden is perhaps the only human art that can be made for the pleasure of the other animals. Neither my poetry nor my prose has ever satisfied a finch or monarch, yet even the messiest patches of echinacea do"—and I remember thinking: *yes.*

I remember thinking (further): It is possible that making the garden an extension of this story is wrong. And making the story an extension of the garden is also wrong. It is possible that neither the story nor the garden wishes to be attached to the other, that they both wish to follow their own way, without my efforts to steer them together. Therefore, I can return the garden to the birds and the bugs.

I REMEMBER MY parents whispering.

I REMEMBER THERE was one day, maybe a week, when my mother seemed more compliant with the management at her residence.

She was almost submissive. And, while it made some things easier, I didn't like it.

※

I REMEMBER ONE afternoon at a concert watching her look around, over everyone's shoulder, past those seated in front of her, seemingly dissatisfied and looking for someone whose absence preoccupied her.

※

I REMEMBER HURRYING home later that day, an ice storm looming over the city, and falling into a four-hour video call with my younger brother. I remember retracing our lives, studying his earlobes, and laughing a lot. But mostly I remember how, whenever he spoke of A., he never said *my* father. He said *our.*

※

I REMEMBER DURING that snowy week stopping at a neighborhood tree with my sons, on our way to run an errand. Protruding from the trunk was a knot that resembled an old man's ear. One by one, we cupped our mouths to the opening. Careful and solemn as penitents, we confided our secrets, whispering so the sound would not spill over. Pale puffs of breath visible in the air. When we were finished, we continued, walking side by side, buoyant, on our way.

※

I REMEMBER A photo of my father and me on the beach, taken when I was around six. He is lying on a cheap blue pool mattress. I am crouched down, touching heads, telling him something seemingly important.

I REMEMBER THAT photo as I crouch by my dad's grave and tell him, *I know we can't have regular, everyday chats but I am trying to keep the channels of communication open. I will talk to you in any form. I will have talks with the ground. There is nothing to hide anymore.* Every time I visit the cemetery, I continue our conversation. A cemetery is a good place to ponder unanswerable questions. I look at the willow tree that hangs across the path over a rich man's marble grave, and I tell my father things. I tell him he is the bones of my stories, the blood of my curiosity, the streak of my stubbornness—and that his hard-working example is what gets me to my desk many days. I tell him, *See? It's okay that it was all a scam, that you were a fraud, talk about imposter syndrome, haha!* I talk to him constantly and he is very patient and barely says a peep.

I REMEMBER THINKING: if I am no longer my father's (bona fide) daughter maybe I can stop telling stories. Maybe I have been in the wrong family business all along! The wrong family!

But then I remember Yasujirō Ozu saying some people have a natural inclination to complicate life by "waving the still water." If something flows in my direction and sweeps me up, I assume it is partly mine. How can you regard a flow of events and not feel the need to shape it somehow?

I REMEMBER A therapist friend once saying: there is always a moment when the storytelling breaks down and a client's need to impress falls away and *that is always when the work really starts: when the storyteller moves out of the room.*

I remember a yogi friend saying there is a big difference between the teachers who say, *Now settle into final relaxation pose* and those who say, *Now you are a corpse. Under all your layers of story, that's what you are: just a meaty body lying on a mat.*

I remember both these friends knew I had invested my adult life in storytelling, both professionally and psychically.

⤜

I REMEMBER ALL the times my mother patted the earth with respect and gentleness. I thought she was letting nature have its way. But even the most natural-seeming garden is a re-creation, an echo of the self-seeding wild—watered, weeded, pruned, guided and edited by the storyteller. I mean gardener.

⤜

I REMEMBER THE day the head gardener showed me where a seventy-five-year-old agave plant had shattered the glass roof of the west-side conservatory. He explained that before an agave dies it has a final, sudden metamorphosis. Hundreds of flowers, in this case, blossomed at the top of the plant's thirty-eight-foot-tall spike as it burst through the building's membrane, reaching its full glory—and all the conservatory's trapped ghosts and grief ascended through the hole, finally free.

⤜

I REMEMBER READING W. G. Sebald—"what would we be without memory? We would not be capable of ordering even the simplest thoughts, the most sensitive heart would lose the ability to show affection, our existence would be a mere never-ending chain of meaningless moments"—and I remember thinking: *no.*

I REMEMBER WHEN we sat together on a bench after my mother had finally been evicted from her residence ("in accordance with Section 16 of the Agreement") and we had found a happier and more supportive place ("Where Life Thrives"). It was spring and we sat together and for an unusually long moment, she didn't fidget or stir and I could feel our breathing slowly twin and settle.

I remember: *my mother will still be my mother when her eyes stop seeing me, when her words drift entirely away, when she forgets everything.* Her hands will remember. Even when they are empty, her hands will be shaped around shears and unseen branches. The hands that smashed and tore things, that punched and smacked, that gently made gardens bloom—they will pick dead leaves from invisible plants or curl loosely around a shadowy mound of roots and soil. In the yard, she will be, in the seed of herself.

I remember we sat holding hands, not talking.

I REMEMBER. I came too late to my story.

I remember.
Until I erode, I will remember for all of us.
It'll all go. It'll all go and I will remember. I will remember by feel. By touch.
I remember. I was a daughter. You were my mother.

I remember when we finally went to the park when the cherry blossoms were in full flower, and we stood in silence underneath a tree, gazing at the hyperreal pink, the way the petals fell down on us.

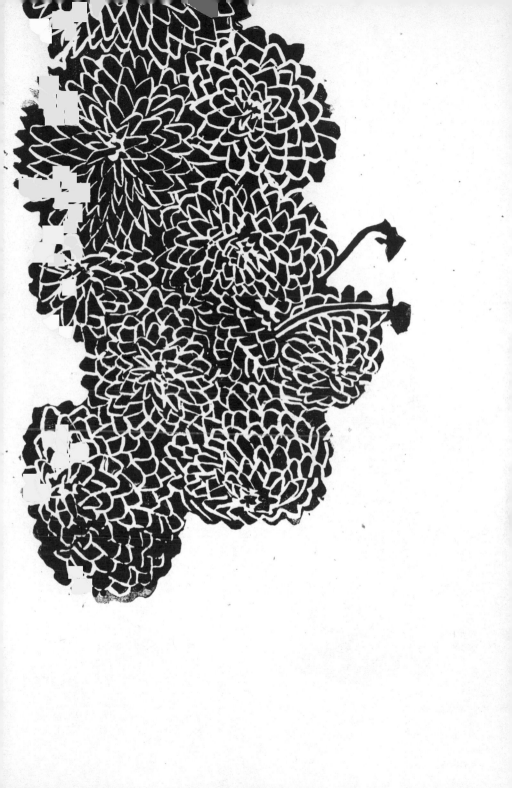

HERBARIUM

RUTH ASAWA'S BULBS

Asawa (1926–2013) sketched plants as a young child on the family farm, as a teen interned in the wooded swamplands of southeastern Arkansas during WWII, and throughout her career as an artist, making near-daily drawings of the vegetables and blooms in her garden. As a mother of six, her method was *art alongside life*. She spread her passion for growing things by promoting community gardening in San Francisco. In the sixties, before it became common practice, she led children in planting spring bulbs in their schoolyards. Her best-known works—generatively shaped, hanging wire sculptures—dance with bulbous energy, and she was often quoted as saying: "You put it in the soil, and that bulb grows every second it is attached to the Earth. I think that every minute we are attached to this Earth we should be doing something."

DIANA ATHILL'S ROSES

Athill (1917–2019) began planting in her early sixties and was instantly hooked. The experience of being "perfectly happy" while seated in a flourishing

corner or trying something new or even recovering from a garden disaster added deep pleasure to aging. At age ninety-seven, she described the adventure of planting six rosebushes she had purchased to brighten up the garden of her residential home, assisted by two ninety-four-year-old neighbors—"nearly blind" Vera and Pamela, able to kneel but not able to rise without a hand. They emerged exhausted but triumphant.

EMILY DICKINSON'S GHOST PIPE

At age fourteen, Dickinson (1830–1886) completed an herbarium that included over four hundred carefully pressed and labeled specimens. As she later wrote: "I was always attached to mud." Of all the plants, her favorite was the non-photosynthesizing ghost pipe—what she called "the preferred flower of life." Pale and translucent, the delicate woodland flower siphons nutrients from the forest's mycorrhizal networks, relying completely on the *panaro solidale* offered by other species for survival.

DEREK JARMAN'S DOG ROSE

One of the first plants Jarman (1942–1994) managed to grow when he moved to his wind- and salt-scalded cottage in Dungeness, southeast England, in the late 1980s. Staked with beachcombed driftwood, the shrub's survival encouraged further planting. As Jarman writes in *Pharmacopoeia*, a collection derived from notes he kept throughout his HIV diagnosis: "The garden had begun. I saw it as a therapy and a pharmacopoeia."

ELLSWORTH KELLY'S POPPIES

An ardent plantsperson, at one point growing corn on the roof of his Lower Manhattan studio, Kelly (1923–2015) insisted the plant subjects he chose were never anonymous specimens, but always connected to specific times and places. Recounting his drawing *Poppy II, 1984*, he described finding the flower in a ditch in California on a drive to Big Sur: "I loved it because of how I had found it. It's seeing a fragment, a flash—what one has been waiting for. And it says, 'Here I am.'" He called his plant drawings formative in his evolution as a painter, "the bridge to the way of seeing" that became the basis of his very first abstract work.

JAMAICA KINCAID'S DAFFODILS

In the novel *Lucy*, Kincaid (1949–) conveys her eponymous character's loathing of the daffodil, a "quintessentially British Wordsworthian flower," as she wrote elsewhere. For Lucy, it is a sore reminder of a colonial education that forced her to memorize a poem about a plant she had never seen outside a textbook, while ignoring the flora of her native land. Years later, I read that Kincaid, now a gardener in Vermont, had planted ten thousand daffodil bulbs in her garden, wanting to "walk out into my yard, unable to move at will because my feet are snarled in the graceful long green stems supporting bent yellow flowering heads." This agile two-mindedness feels quintessentially Kincaid. Somewhere in the midst of a history of conquest, the daffodil is also a sunny and jaunty flower.

JANET MALCOLM'S BURDOCK

Journalist and critic Malcolm (1934–2021) turned her talents for portraiture to a close photographic study of a "large rank weed," foraging for three successive summers in New England to create a beautiful book of burdock leaves. Inspired by Richard Avedon's unstinting portraits of celebrities, Malcolm wished to show "uncelebrated leaves"—tattered, veined, weathered, blighted, infested—on which "life has left its mark."

AGNES MARTIN'S FINAL FLOWER

Martin's (1912–2004) ultimate "work," made before her death in 2004, was a quick curvy drawing of what appears to be an opening blossom—very simple, literal, and uncharacteristic of her late style. At age ninety-two, Martin knew what abstraction could do but, nevertheless, picked up a biro pen and a sheet of plain paper and was moved to draw a tiny potted plant. A flower as flower. Soon after, she died and her ashes were buried under an apricot tree in Taos.

YOKO ONO'S INVISIBLE FLOWER

Evacuated to the countryside during the firebombing of Tokyo, eight-year-old Yoko (1933–) dreamt of her mother's rose garden only to be told that her wartime dwelling was too far north for any roses to survive. She kept dreaming until one day, looking out over "shining golden wheat fields," she spotted a single rose with a beautiful smell. "It was perfectly white, sitting snugly between the bushes on a distant hill."When she approached, the flower disappeared. Was it real? Why was she the only one who could see it? *An Invisible Flower* is the story of Yoko's childhood experience, a tale of conjured beauty and imagination. Written in 1952, when Yoko was only nineteen, it carries the seed of her future conceptual art style.

ALICE OSWALD'S DAISY

Oswald (1966–) grew up with a prominent garden designer mother, studied horticulture, and worked for a time as a jobbing gardener. But in her collection *Weeds and Wild Flowers* she veers from the science and typology she knows toward other forms of descriptive accuracy. There is a witchy anthropomorphism to her poems as she travels the rural English wayside encountering various flower-characters, an effort to get closer to plant *being* more than a desire to bend a daisy (or a chickweed, thrift or rambling rose) to human ways. Imagining what is sore or funny to a daisy unsettles any mechanistic view of botanical life.

STEFAN NATAN ROZENBERG'S UNIDENTIFIED FLOWER

A photo of a four-year-old boy dressed in a wool overcoat and dark beret appears in the archive of the United States Holocaust Memorial Museum. He is standing in a garden in the Lodz ghetto surrounded by flowers that rise above his knees. (Upon viewing the image, my botanically-astute friends offer differing views on the species: chrysanthemum,

Manhattan poppy, Livermere poppy, calendula.) The caption says the photo was taken circa March 1943, forty-three years after my family left Lodz. On closer look, I see a "Jewish star" has been affixed to Stefan's coat. *What happened to this boy?* I discover through LinkedIn that Stefan is still alive— the youngest child-survivor of the death camps Ravensbrück and Sachsenhausen, liberated by the Russian army on April 22, 1945. "I was six years old. I was given food and I passed out. Eight days later I was found in a pile of dead bodies." According to his LinkedIn page (November 2022), he is "retiring and enjoying life" in Florida.

OLIVER SACKS'S FERNS

An active, meeting-attending member of the American Fern Society, Sacks (1933–2015) inherited his plant passion from a mother who filled his childhood garden with ferns instead of flowers. In his book *Oaxaca Journal*, Sacks travels to a part of southern Mexico famous for having seven hundred species of ferns to better understand and indulge his pteridophilia (fern love) alongside a group of somewhat austere fellow travelers. Through this shared obsession, he experiences joy and a rare (for him) feeling of "communal affection."

LEON TROTSKY'S CACTI

In 1935, Trotsky (1879–1940) was forced to seek asylum in Mexico City after he was condemned to death in Moscow. He and his wife Natalia eventually lived in the quiet borough of Coyoacán, where

Trotsky filled his Mexican garden with cacti he hunted and gathered in the mountains. The collection became a great obsession. The exiled Russian revolutionary, writes Chloe Aridjis, was "probably unaware of what he was doing: brutal extraction, disturbance of earth, destruction of an underground network." Oblivious to desert equilibrium, Trotsky simply admired the prickly plants for their monolithic endurance. Two years after starting his cactus collection, he was assassinated with an ice ax of the sort used by mountain climbers.

THE UNNAMED WOMAN'S HOLLYHOCK IN A GARDEN AT HEART MOUNTAIN WAR RELOCATION CENTER

In a photo taken by amateur photographer Yoshio Okumoto, dated July 26, 1944, a young Japanese American woman in a pale cotton dress is seen gardening outside her barrack. The northwest corner of Wyoming is a place of extremes—bone-chilling winters and dry scorching summers—but the unnamed woman is bent over a flourishing patch, tall and exuberant stalks of hollyhock growing along the tar-paper-covered walls of her temporary home, one of 650 military-style barracks built on 46,000 acres of dusty land owned by the Bureau of Reclamation.

TENNESSEE WILLIAMS'S NIGHT-BLOOMING JASMINE

When asked by a friend why he didn't move from his suffocatingly small Manhattan apartment,

Williams (1911–1983) "pointed out a little vine of night-blooming jasmine that had worked its way up to the window." I read this in Olivia Laing's *The Trip to Echo Spring* and it has stayed with me. I picture him at his desk, a sweet smell funneled into his room by the wind.

THE WOOLFS' DAHLIAS

According to his Account Book, Leonard Woolf (1880–1969) bought dahlias from the Dobbies mail order catalog on nine occasions between 1929 and 1939, the most frequent flowers he purchased for the garden at Monk's House. Virginia Woolf (1882–1941) mentions the dahlias frequently in letters and diary entries, detailing how they light up the garden's edges, a beacon against gloom. In a September 1930 letter to Margaret Llewelyn Davies, she writes that "Leonard's garden has really been a miracle—vast white lilies, and such a blaze of dahlias that even today one feels lit up." In 1938, consumed by war anxiety and the rise of fascism in Europe, she describes being surrounded by the flowers' protective warmth, the dahlias glowing "orange against the black last night."

ACKNOWLEDGMENTS

I tried to write for you
I tried to write about you
LIANA FINCK

I LIVE, WORK AND GARDEN ON LAND KNOWN AS TORONTO/ Tkaronto, the Treaty Lands and Territory of the Mississaugas of the Credit and the traditional territory of the Anishinaabe, Wendat, Métis, and Haudenosaunee. Tkaronto is home to many Indigenous people from across Turtle Island. I offer my dedicated appreciation to all human, animal, plant hosts, to all ancestors known and unknown. I thank the land for holding me and my writing in immeasurable ways.

I WAS EDITED—so beautifully!—by Martha Kanya-Forstner [Knopf] in Canada and Kathy Belden [Scribner] in the US, who led me with warmth, rigor, and energizing editorial intelligence. Martha, you push me with the most delicate and immersive skill, always listening for the underthings. Thank you for your friendship, sensitivity, and unparalleled funny bone. Kathy, your wisdom and heartful attention have been the finest tuning forks. Thank you for your kind and musical comradeship, your exquisite ear for resonances. It was my dream that you would both edit this book and I am lucky and honored.

Thank you

TO THE LOVELY TEAM at Knopf Canada and Penguin Random House Canada, including Jennifer Griffiths for her hand lettering magic and the dreamiest designs; Melanie Little for a thoughtful and discerning copyedit; Susan Burns for consummate conducting; John Sweet and Emma Lockhart for final finessing; Ashley Dunn for helping my books find their way. With additional thanks to Christie Hanson, Linda Friedner, Kristin Cochrane, and Scott Sellers.

to the many wonderful people at Scribner: Nan Graham, Colin Harrison, Rebekah Jett, Mia O'Neill, Lauren Dooley, Stuart Smith, and Jaya Miceli for making a wish come true.

to the warm, welcoming crew at Pushkin Press, especially Laura Macaulay and Kirsten Chapman.

to Jackie Kaiser—my friend and agent—who read this manuscript first and was, as always, brilliant and attentive. Jackie, you are simply the Queen of Peerless Support. My great gratitude to Meg Wheeler, for helping this story travel, and to Michael Levine, Bridgette Kamm, Briar Heckman, and the stellar gang at Westwood Creative for ongoing assistance and advice.

A SPECIAL GRATITUDE to my cousin K. for first opening the door and to my brothers S. and D.—may we all be so lucky to find such witty and friendly siblings over the course of our lives.

Adoptees and hidden children are often asked to remain quiet to abet the secrets and needs of others. I want to thank the secret keepers and the secret breachers, some of whom at first suggested, *This is not yours to tell*, but most of whom, thank goodness, said the opposite and knew I needed to write my own life including the draft of my beginnings, contra what Lucie Elven once summarized as "the narrative-forming machine" of family. I am known to be sometimes bloody-minded and apt to mutiny against family rules, but I have tried to write responsibly and caringly in full view, rather than willful ignorance, of the possibly contentious and hurtful. I have changed the names and initials of many people in this story to protect confidentiality. In several instances, I have hopscotched in time or used narrative compression, reserving certain details, remaining faithful to the partial and disarraying nature of memory. My hope is that kindred readers can find a different axis and expression of loyalty in these pages.

Thank you

TO MY SEARCH ANGEL Maggie Stevenson and my cemetery guide Edoardo Vincenti who both showed me the kind of support and solidarity the likes of which I have rarely come across.

to Barry Stevens and Joanna Rose, for their generosity and humor in showing me how to put down the vexing weight of other people's secrets and shame.

to those (in randomized order), who have helped shape this book and given me gifts far beyond: Hiromi Goto, Brenda Joy Lem, Julie Morstad, Tara Walker, David Chariandy, Jack Breakfast,

Kelly O'Brien, Mike Hoolboom, Jillian Tamaki, Jenny Offill, Mio Adilman, Jason Logan, Michael Barker, Terence Dick, Shelagh Harcourt, Martha Baillie, Sara Angelucci, Eric Fan, Brandon Shimoda (and his "wishful definition" of belonging), John Greyson, Shelley Saywell, Stephen Andrews, Nobu Adilman, Jack Illingworth, Mireille Juchau, Sumanth Prabhaker, Katrina Goldsaito, and the inspiring students I have met over the years at the University of Guelph, the Banff Centre for the Arts and the Humber School of Writing Summer Workshop. Gassho to the many writers named in these pages—a remarkable cast who continue to undo the latches on my thinking about care and kinship.

to the Canada Council for the Arts, the Ontario Arts Council and the Toronto Arts Council for their continued support and generosity. To the Banff Centre for the Arts and the Kimpton Sainte George for space to write. To Liz Johnston, Allison LaSorda and the editors of *Brick, A Literary Journal*, for publishing "Giverny."

to those who answered all sorts of questions along the way: Ellen Henriette Suhrke, Richard Jenkins, Adam Ferrington, E.C., Curtis Evoy, Leslie Burns.

to the artists and scientists who continue to bring plants to the fore as active players: Alexis Williams and my fellow residents at Ayatana Germinate (Jo Tito, Jane Tingley, Laara Cerman, Naomi Renouf, Rocio Graham, Alyssa Ellis) and Marie-Jeanne Musiol who shared the wisdom of fragile groupings.

to the carers and family friends: Dr. Marvin Waxman, Louise Bennett, Dr. Sidney Radomski, Ruby Lacsamana, G. Chalmers Adams, Ivan Dolynsky, Brock Silversides, Bob Culbert, Oleh

Rumak, Elizabeth Klinck, Philip Pendry, Rana Jin (RN), Cara Macanuel, Dr. Rhonda Feldman, Jennifer Carr, The Reitman Centre for Alzheimer's Support, Dr. Marnie Howe, Dr. Grace Liu, Daniel Ranjbar, Carly Sztern, Kazuyo Sato, Sachiko Suzuki, Merilyn Meranez, Ofelia Whiteley, Hitomi Chikitani, and Yumi Takagi.

to the family, given, chosen and found: Sugie Shimizu, Jude Binder, Nancy Friedland, Naomi Klein, Robin Maclear, Andrew Maclear, James Maclear, D. A. Owen, S. Owen, Karen Lynn, Eliza Beth Burroughs, Rabia Agha and the Aghas, Miru McPhail, Avi Lewis, Brett Burlock, Megan Wells, Ichiyo Nagata, Sarah Levine, Jason Levine, Frank Venezia, Gideon Kendall, Julie Peppito, Richard Burroughs, Mona Stevens, Donald de Oliveira, Paula Madden, Karen and Shantih Lawrence, and Shelley Glazer. To the nieces and nephews: Coco, Oren, Ben, Sam, Little Ash, Toma, Tillie, Levi and Nate.

to Laurie and Ethel Burns, who fostered my father from the ages of 4-13; my great aunt Kenie Gallagher, who modeled iconoclasm and courage; and my obaachan, Fumiko Koide, a quiet firebrand and socialist, who taught me so much including how to be loved beyond words.

to Andrew Maclear, artist-confidante, and Robin Maclear, cosmic navigator. Somehow, it's made it all the more special knowing our relationship isn't based on genetic obligation.

to the kiosk and those to come. You all belong here.

⤙

This book was written

IN LOVING MEMORY of my father, Michael Patrick Maclear, and my other-mother, Naomi Ruth Binder Wall, whose spirits continue to remind us to unlock doors and keep ourselves ajar. *Not against family, but against confinement. Not against home, but against fortresses.*

for my mother, and her fearless, outlaw heart. An inexpressible story, I am told, will slip away no matter how you try to capture it but particularly if you try to seize it directly. Zen teachers call this "pointing at the moon" and warn against confusing the finger for the moon, or language for the thing or event it describes. Sometimes writing is all fingers but maybe that's okay if the alternative is a forgotten moon, lost in the dark. Okaasan, I love you more, the looser and more lunar we've become.

for Nancy and Naomi, my best friends but also my sisters.

for my sons—Yoshi and Mika—who bring light, laughs, dishevelment, and music into the world. I hope art and music continue to be our lineage.

for David, lastly and above all, the biggest heart I've ever known, who makes life inestimably better and funnier. Thank you for every song and every day.